Bolan tried another head strike

But this time the man was ready, jerking his face out of the way. The killer tried to twist the blade in his hand inward toward Bolan's torso, but now it was the Executioner who had the advantage of leverage. The two men struggled for a moment, grappling on their feet. Then, suddenly, Bolan gave way to the other man's pressure on the bayonet, shifting his weight to let the deadly blade pass in front of his chest. With both of the killer's arms to one side now, the Executioner worked an elbow up into the man's collarbone. Shifting his weight again, he lunged forward, driving the pointed bone down into the top of the killer's chest. A snapping sound echoed through the jungle.

The snap was quickly drowned out by the attacker's squeal of pain. Bolan changed his angle, striking again with the elbow on the sensitive broken bone. With the killer's attention diverted to his neck, the Executioner brought his right leg out wide, then swept his opponent's feet out from under him.

MACK BOLAN ®
The Executioner

DON PENDLETON'S
EXECUTIONER®
THE
HOSTILE ALLIANCE

A GOLD EAGLE BOOK FROM
WORLDWIDE®

TORONTO • NEW YORK • LONDON
AMSTERDAM • PARIS • SYDNEY • HAMBURG
STOCKHOLM • ATHENS • TOKYO • MILAN
MADRID • WARSAW • BUDAPEST • AUCKLAND

First edition June 2003
ISBN 0-373-64295-4

Special thanks and acknowledgment to
Jerry VanCook for his contribution to this work.

HOSTILE ALLIANCE

Printed in U.S.A.

Violence is just when kindness is in vain.
　　　　　　　　　　　　—Pierre Corneille,
　　　　　　　　　　　Heraclius, I, 1647

Violence is never permanent.
　　　　　　　　　　　—Giovanni Sagredo,
　　　　　"Report to the Venetian Senate," c. 1656

There are two things a person can count on:
One, evil will never go away.
Two, neither will the men who fight it.
　　　　　　　　　　　　　—Mack Bolan

To Gary Campbell

Prologue

The long length of braided leather flew softly through the air, causing the leaves and vines to stir gently in the windless jungle. To see it was to witness an age-old art, and its flight was one of beauty and serenity. But the beauty ended and horror began when it reached its full twelve-foot length.

The whip cracked like a gunshot as the tip caught Manolito Chavez high on the ribs, just under his left arm. The thinly worn cotton shirt split open as the leather passed through it as easily as a knife blade. An involuntary scream escaped his lips as he stumbled, falling into the half-dug grave.

Chavez clamped his teeth together to cut off the noise. Screaming usually brought more lashes, as if the overseers fed on the suffering of their underlings and acknowledgment of the pain served as an appetizer. And Chavez wanted no more pain. He had broken two pieces of ceramic, and the whip had bitten him a dozen times. He wasn't sure he could endure it again.

Chavez felt the wetness as new blood ran down over old

scars, soaking the ragged shirt that covered his frail torso. He glanced up out of the grave as Julio Lima jerked the whip back away from him. The overseer rolled his weapon back into a coil.

"Stand up!" Lima ordered. "And pick up your shovel." The overseer nodded toward the rusted tool at Chavez's feet. Leaning down into the grave, he picked up a large piece of the ceramic figurine that Chavez's digging had broken. The overseer set it next to the hole. "Look at it!" he demanded.

The Costa Rican stood slowly. His eyes rose just high enough to see the broken clay.

"I will leave it here. It will remind you to be more careful," Lima said. "And *this* will remind you not to make such a mistake again." The whip shot out one last time, catching Chavez in the chest and flaying open new flesh.

The man bit his lips to keep from screaming again. "Yes," he mumbled. "I am sorry."

Lima turned and walked back to where he had stood before. With a sigh of resignation Chavez wrapped his calloused hands around the shovel and began to dig again. Around him, he heard dozens of other shovels at work as dozens of other men like himself churned the earth. This was their third night at the ancient grave site—a recently discovered Diquis burial ground. So far their digging had uncovered hundreds of ceramic and golden antiquities that he knew would bring thousands of dollars on the black market. None of it, however, would go to the men doing the work. They would receive only their usual wages that were barely enough to feed their families. No, Chavez thought as he stabbed the loose earth with his shovel again, these riches that came from his ancestors would stay in the hands of his boss, Francisco Gothe.

Sweat poured from Chavez's forehead, soaking the cloth tying back his shoulder-length black hair. A few drops rolled into his eyes, burning like acid. He ignored the fire as he dug on.

Chavez knew it was a very fine line he had to walk. To dig

too slowly would bring the whips of Lima or Gothe's other main overseer, Franco Mantara. Mantara also carried a heavy wooden cane that he used for special punishments. But to dig too fast was equally risky—then one chanced breaking the artifacts, as he had already done twice that night. Either way, it was a rare man who went home in the morning without at least some new wound on his body. And sometimes men didn't go home at all.

Just to his side, in the grave next to him, Chavez heard a sudden "Don Julio!" He knew better than to stop digging, but he glanced up as his shovel continued its work. Not far away, in another of the graves, Reinaldo Vallejo held up his arm. A dark object rested on his outstretched palm. Vallejo held it— and it appeared to Chavez that he held his breath as well—as Lima walked forward.

Lima took the object and stared at it for a moment, then spit upon it and rubbed it on his pant leg. A moment later, he held it up again and a piece of gold in the shape of a jaguar shone brightly under the moon. Slowly Lima nodded. "Good," he said. He waved his hand toward a wooden bucket set beneath a tree.

Vallejo scrambled out of the grave and hurried toward the water bucket. He grabbed the dipper and drank thirstily as the other men continued to work.

Manolito Chavez dug on, letting his mind drift as he worked. It was the only way he had found—the only anesthetic for the pain—to get him through these nights. He didn't feel sorry for himself. He knew what he was, and what his situation was, and he would make the best of it. He had a wife and two daughters to feed and clothe, and there was only one way to do so on Costa Rica's Osa Peninsula: work for Francisco Gothe.

The rusty shovel struck something hard, and Chavez gasped under his breath. Kneeling in the soft jungle earth, he pried the loose dirt away with his hands. His lips formed a silent prayer that he hadn't broken yet another of the pre-

Columbian artifacts. And if I have, oh Lord, he added soundlessly, help me hide the pieces before they are found. The prayer was answered in a way he hadn't expected. All he uncovered in the dirt was an ancient rotten tree root.

The night wore on, and Chavez did his best to ignore the pain in his overworked arms and shoulders. He let his mind drift back to his early childhood in Puerto Jimenez. They had been better times, he remembered, if only through the recollections of a child. At least there had always been food and clothes. And while he and his mother hadn't been wealthy, they had never gone hungry. The 1980s had been gold boom times on the Osa Peninsula, and those who sought the yellow riches had come from all over the world. Puerto Jimenez had prospered with miners buying bottles of whiskey to pour them over their heads or smash against the walls. They had lit Cuban cigars with American hundred-dollar bills. Prostitution had flourished.

A flash of shame fell over Chavez to mix with the sweaty heat. His mother, he suspected, had been one of these women. It was something of which they had never spoken. Nor had they spoken of his father, whom Chavez had never known.

Overhead, a white-faced monkey danced through the treetops. Around him, the lulling sound of shovels digging into the earth continued. A rare breeze trickled through the dense foliage, and Chavez smelled the heavy odors of unwashed bodies. He dug on.

Suddenly a light appeared through the trees and, even though it was forbidden, Chavez and the other men looked up. Lima and Mantara didn't seem to notice. They were too busy racking back the bolts of their M-16s to chamber rounds. The sharp sounds of modern steel seemed out of place in the ancient Diquis burial ground.

The Costa Rican watched as the lights appeared, then disappeared, flickering back and forth between the trees. An automobile was making its way down the bumpy jungle road.

A few seconds later an engine neared close enough to be

heard. It sounded distant, barely audible over the clicks of insects and chirps of nocturnal birds. Then the engine grew louder and the jungle wildlife went silent. The men waited, frozen like stone statues.

Lima and Mantara aimed their rifles toward the trees.

Car doors opened and shut on the road behind the trees. Loud footsteps padded toward the grave site, the new arrivals making no attempt to conceal their approach. Finally the footsteps halted just inside the tree line. A voice called out, "Hello. Don't shoot."

Both Lima and Mantara snorted nervously, lowering their weapons. "Come forward, you bastards," Mantara said. "Quit scaring us. We weren't told you were coming tonight."

Two men, dressed in the uniforms of the local police, stepped out of the trees smiling. The one who led the way toward the graves was in his midfifties with gray hair and a belly that hung low over his scuffed black gun belt. The man who followed was younger and had the hard features of the Boruca tribe. Chavez recognized him—Carlos Vito. They had grown up together in Puerto Jimenez. Chavez's mother was also of the Boruca tribe.

Vito and the older officer strode forward confidently, laughing. "You shouldn't be so frightened of the dark," chided the gray-haired man. "Or are you afraid of the spirits you disturb?"

"It wasn't us I was frightened for," Lima said, patting his M-16. "It's not us who could get shot sneaking up on people." Perhaps it was the fact that others were now watching, but for whatever reason, Lima seemed finally to notice that the workers had stopped digging. Turning toward the graves, he snapped, "Back to work!" To emphasize his order, the whip shot out. Since he was the closest, Chavez caught it and again he felt the fire spread across his skin.

The sounds of shovels hitting earth resumed as Lima, Mantara and the two police officers continued to trade good-natured insults. Chavez glanced up once and saw Vito staring at him. The young police officer looked as if he knew he should recognize the face but didn't. Chavez was hardly surprised.

Life had changed him far more than it had Vito. He suspected he bore little resemblance to the youth who had once run the streets of Puerto Jimenez with him.

Chavez's shovel bore down through the earth, and again he felt it strike something foreign. There was a loud cracking sound, and he froze, his eyes shooting up out of the grave in time to see Mantara handing a white envelope to the older police officer. He knew what it contained, and even through the fear that now permeated his body he couldn't help but envy the two men. But he forgot about the money as both Lima and Mantara turned toward him.

"What was that sound?" Mantara demanded.

Chavez tried to remain calm. "Nothing, patron," he said. "My shovel struck a root."

"Show it to me," Mantara said.

The Costa Rican squatted in the hole, thankful that he hadn't thrown out the broken piece of root he'd found earlier. He rose again, holding up the twisted piece of mud-covered wood in his hand.

"Throw it out," Mantara ordered.

Chavez tossed it halfway to the man, careful that it didn't splatter Mantara's boots with mud.

Mantara stepped up to the root and tapped it with his rifle barrel. The sound was dull, distant. Certainly not the cracking sound that had come from the grave. The man with the rifle looked back to Chavez. "You are a liar," he said.

Chavez didn't respond.

Mantara stepped forward to the edge of the grave. "What did you break this time?" he asked. He dropped the rifle to the ground and pulled the whip from his belt.

Chavez stood helplessly as the heavy braided leather arched around to strike him across the eyes. The blow knocked him back into a sitting position in the loose dirt.

"Stand up!" Mantara ordered, and Chavez struggled back to his feet. "Hand me the pieces of whatever you broke," the overseer said through gritted teeth.

As Chavez knelt to scrape though the dirt with his hands, he saw Mantara glance back over his shoulder to make sure the police officers were watching him. It took only a few seconds to dig down to the object he had cracked with his shovel. Careful not to damage it further, he lifted a large ceramic shaman from the ground. The figurine wore an intricate headdress, earrings and had a large erect penis. But one of the arms had been broken off. Quickly, Chavez knelt again and sifted through the earth, coming up with the arm.

"Here is the rest, Don Franco," he said nervously. "Please believe me—I think it was already broken when I—"

The whip sliced across his mouth, cutting off his words.

The salty, coppery taste of blood filled his mouth as he fell backward again. He looked up to see Lima hand his rifle to the older police officer and step up next to Mantara, his whip in his hand. The digging had gone on all around the site, but now Lima put an end to it by yelling out, "Everyone! Halt and come forward!"

The sounds of men scrambling out of their holes sounded through the jungle night.

When they had all gathered around where Chavez sat in the ground, Lima smiled. "This man has broken three expensive pieces tonight," he said. "This cannot happen. I want everyone to watch closely. I want you to see what happens to such incompetents."

The whip lashed out, snapping into Chavez's cheek and tearing away a large chunk of flesh. He felt rough hands—Mantara's—reach down and jerk him from the grave. He landed on his face, and saw the blood gushing from his mouth and cheek to mix with the damp jungle earth beneath him. Again the leather struck, this time slicing into his bare back. The other whip sounded like a pistol as the tip cracked against the back of his thigh, ripping his trousers. Then something hard—Mantara's cane?—came down at the base of his skull, and he was driven into an almost pleasant semiconsciousness.

The beating continued. Cane. Whip. Cane. Whip. Then, as

his mind drifted further and further away from the pain, he could no longer tell which instrument of torture was striking him. Chavez's eyes stared down at the jungle floor, but instead of the earth he saw the streets of Puerto Jimenez.

He was there with his mother. But he was no longer a child. He was a grown man, and his wife, Florencia, and the twin girls—Julia and Lola—were with them. They were all clothed in the finest of garments and were about to sit down to a long table laden with food. Dully, distantly, as if the blows were striking someone else, he continued to feel the whip and cane. But in his mind, he sat down with his family to feast.

Then, finally, a feeling of peace he hadn't known since childhood swept over him. He smiled at his mother, his wife and his daughters, and began to eat.

And the pain was gone forever.

Costa Rica has no army, navy, air force or marines.

In theory.

In actuality, the small Central American country has a national police force with branches more than capable of defending its borders. In addition to regular police duties, officers bearing M-16 A-1 rifles, wearing camouflage fatigues, and using the best military equipment available in Central America, can be seen both within the country's interior and along the Nicaraguan and Panamanian borders. To distinguish between such police officers and soldiers is difficult, if not impossible.

All of which made Costa Rica's superintendent of national police one of the most powerful men in the country.

Mack Bolan, also known as the Executioner, and Jaime Pacheco, watched Superintendent Ricardo Toledo as he exited the restaurant of the Hotel Aurola Holiday Inn. From their vantage point, across the street just outside Morazan Park, they saw Toledo's eyes scan right, then left. The tall man with the carefully trimmed mustache dropped his cigarette on the sidewalk and ground it beneath one of the high-gloss shoes he wore with his light tan suit.

Bolan and Pacheco stood up from the park bench on which they sat. "He looks nervous," Pacheco said.

"He should be," Bolan replied as Toledo turned right and started for the parking lot. "He knows he's about to be killed."

Bolan and Pacheco paralleled the superintendent's path, finally dodging through the heavy traffic on the street just before Toledo reached the lot. They watched him reach into his pocket for his keys, again glancing in all directions as he turned between two buildings to the rows of parked cars. His vehicle was in the first row, right next to the sidewalk.

"Here?" Pacheco asked.

Bolan nodded. "Good a place as any. Wait until he starts to unlock the door. And make it look good."

Both Bolan and Pacheco wore blue jeans, baseball caps, sunglasses and light cotton sport shirts—the shirts were large but not enough to draw the attention of the other men and women moving hurriedly up and down the sidewalk. The Executioner silently thanked the fashion designers who had promoted the oversize look of the past several years. He cared nothing for style, but it certainly came in handy for concealing weapons in hot climates.

Toledo stopped in front of a late model sedan with Costa Rican government plates. Facing the car, his back to the two men, he bent slightly and stuck his key in the door.

"Now?" Pacheco whispered.

"Now," Bolan said. Then, in a louder voice, "Hey."

Toledo's shoulders jerked suddenly upward. Then, slowly, he straightened and turned.

Bolan jerked both his .44 Magnum Desert Eagle and Beretta 93-R from under his shirt. At the same time Pacheco pulled a mini-Uzi from his own belt. The Executioner squeezed the trigger in his right hand and the hand cannon roared. The 93-R's fire selector switch had been lowered to 3-round burst mode, and the weapon cut loose with a trio of

9 mm slugs a second later. Behind Toledo the windows of the sedan exploded. Bullet holes appeared in the auto body beneath the flying glass.

Jaime Pacheco triggered his miniature submachine gun into play, the mini-Uzi dancing in his hand. At almost the same time, a flurry of crimson exploded from Toledo's chest. The Costa Rican superintendent of national police jerked like a marionette on strings, slammed back against the side of the car, then slid to the ground.

Behind Bolan and Pacheco, a woman screamed. The Executioner turned to see that several people along the sidewalk had frozen in place. One old man looked as if he were about to go into convulsions.

Good, Bolan thought. He wanted plenty of witnesses to what he and Pacheco were doing. The more the better.

A third man, however, was not just watching the assassination. Dressed in dark gray cargo shorts, athletic shoes and an I Love San José T-shirt, he was excitedly recording the events with a video camera.

Bolan kept the smile off his face as he turned toward the cameraman. Most hit men avoided witnesses, and a videotape of an execution would be considered the worst of all possible evidence to leave behind. But in this case, the Executioner had to consider it an unexpected and added dividend. Still, it had to look good. He had a part to play, and he intended to play it well.

Aiming just to the side of the cameraman's head, Bolan squeezed off three rounds from the Desert Eagle. He had removed the sound suppressor he usually carried on the Beretta, and now another volley of 9 mm hollowpoints rounds detonated right behind their .44 Magnum counterparts. All of the rounds struck the building at the tourist's side, showering both man and video camera with flying dust and chips of concrete.

Suddenly the fact that this was real and he could die sank into the cameraman's brain. He screamed far louder than the woman had a moment before, then ducked back around the corner.

By the time Bolan had turned back to the car Pacheco was kneeling next to Toledo. The superintendent's shirt, tie, sports coat and slacks were all soaked a deep, dark, reddish-black. His eyes were still open but he had the thousand-yard stare that bespoke death.

Tires squealed behind them on the street as a black Nissan Maxima skidded to a halt. The back door facing them opened. Bolan and Pacheco lifted Toledo and carried him toward the car.

"Murder!" an elderly Hispanic woman wearing a shawl around her shoulders screamed. The rest of the people along the street still stood motionless, their mouths agape.

Bolan and Pacheco threw Toledo into the back of the Nissan. Pacheco slid in after him, and the Executioner jumped into the front next to the driver. A moment later, the tires screeched again as they drove off. But not before Bolan saw the tourist with the video camera step back out of a doorway and begin taping once more.

Pacheco had seen the cameraman, too. "Lucky," he said. "Maybe we'll even make the evening news." He took a deep breath. "I can see the newspaper headlines in the morning— Top Cop Slain on the Streets of San José." Behind them, the wail of police sirens began to sound.

The man behind the wheel of the Nissan was older than the other men in the car. But he exuded the vitality of a man half his age as he guided the vehicle through traffic, expertly turning corners and changing lanes. When they were a half mile from the scene of the shooting, he slowed to a normal speed. "We're all set up at the airport," he said, his voice betraying an unusual accent that sounded part French, part Israeli.

Bolan nodded.

Next to Pacheco in the back seat, another voice spoke. "Is it safe for me to sit up now?" Toledo asked.

Bolan turned and nodded. "I think so. Nice acting job, by the way."

Ricardo Toledo's face was almost as bloodless as if he'd

really been killed. "Unlike my friend here," he said, indicating Pacheco with a nod, "I have never done any acting. But knowing a bad performance could cause death seems to bring out unknown talents in a man."

Bolan turned back to face the front as they drove on toward the airport. He pulled down the visor, and in the mirror attached to the back he saw Pacheco helping Toledo out of his wet clothes. Beneath the superintendent's shirt, taped to his chest, he could see the exploded blood bombs. They had been timed to go off with the blank rounds in Pacheco's mini-Uzi. Bolan's pistols had carried live rounds to make holes in the car and add to the reality of the fake hit.

But there was another reason the Executioner had suggested Pacheco's weapon be loaded with blanks. Toledo had told him privately that while Jaime Pacheco was the best undercover officer Costa Rica had to offer, and as brave as men came, he was a notoriously mediocre with a gun.

So Toledo had welcomed Bolan's suggestion of using blanks.

By the time they reached the airport, Toledo had changed into another suit. He still had blotches of red on his hands and a small spot on his face. But that would make no difference. They were heading for the private terminal where he would encounter no one but other personnel from the ultracovert Stony Man Farm, and the wig, hat and sunglasses he was now donning would disguise him during the brief walk from the car to the plane.

"I don't know how to thank you," Toledo said as they turned down the access road toward the tarmac. He extended his hand over the seat.

Bolan took it. "No thanks necessary, sir. I just hope we can get this over quickly and you and your family can come home."

Toledo nodded. He turned to Pacheco. "My life...many lives...perhaps the very life of Costa Rica, is in your hands, my young friend."

Pacheco nodded slowly. "I won't let you down."

The Nissan came to a halt twenty feet from a Learjet 55C. Through the windshield, Bolan could see Jack Grimaldi in the cockpit. Several other Stony Man blacksuits—dressed like business executives in suits and ties but wearing a variety of weaponry beneath this "urban camouflage"—stood outside the doorway. Toledo's wife, two sons and baby daughter were already onboard.

The Executioner turned to the man behind the wheel and shook his hand. "Thanks, Katz."

"Don't mention it," Yakov Katzenelenbogen said. The former leader of Stony Man Farm's Phoenix Force grinned. "I love to lend a hand whenever it's needed."

"You can back me up any day," Bolan said.

One of the men outside the Learjet had come over and opened the back door for Toledo. The superintendent was halfway out when he turned back to Bolan. "So the story will be that after my assassination my family went into hiding?" he asked.

"Affirmative," the Executioner said, nodding. "That's what the public will hear."

Toledo looked as if he were about to speak again, but he didn't. Instead he glanced once more at Bolan, then Pacheco, nodded and got out. He followed Katz to the plane.

Bolan slid over behind the wheel of the Nissan as Pacheco left the back seat for the front. The Executioner waved through the window to Grimaldi, who waved back.

"What now?" Pacheco said as the soldier pulled away and started back in the direction they'd come.

"We've got work to do," Bolan stated.

Costa Rica was by far the most modern of the Central American nations. Certain sections of San José, in fact, were hardly distinguishable between their counterparts in U.S. cities with large Hispanic populations. The Centro Commercial El Pueblo in San José's Barrio Tournon was one such example. Within El Pueblo was Restaurante Lukas, an open-air eating establishment, where waiters and waitresses served the local cuisine as a guitarist coaxed Latino strains from his acoustic guitar.

Bolan had arrived in Costa Rica just in time to take part in Toledo's phony assassination, and had not yet had time to get to know Jaime Pacheco. All Bolan knew was that the man had received extra training in undercover work at Stony Man Farm, and recently Pacheco had worked his way into Francisco Gothe's confidence. Bolan had been told that the young man could be trusted, that he excelled at undercover work and that he wasn't a particularly good shot with a gun. His background had been in the theater before he turned to police work, and he'd even obtained a B.A. degree in both drama and criminal justice. A strange combination, but one that had come in handy considering his law-enforcement specialty.

Pacheco was also, according to Toledo, something of an amateur psychologist and a master of body language and facial expressions—another plus in undercover work. It not only enabled him to read criminals, he could use the same body language to "convert the Pope to Islam" according to Toledo. All but the part about the shooting was impressive.

Bolan wanted to know more about the man. If he was going to risk his life with Jaime Pacheco, he needed to know exactly who he was dealing with. And if they were going to destroy the operations of the man who had put out the contract on Toledo—an illegal artifacts dealers known as Francisco Gothe—they needed to come up with a battle plan.

The Executioner had chosen the upscale outdoor Restaurante Lukas for the strategy session for one simple reason. It had a high profile and, although the restaurant itself was legitimate, it was frequented by many of San José's underworld. There was a better than even chance that someone within that underworld would see the two of them together and wonder who they were. In the world of crime, information was valuable. It could be bought and sold, or traded for favors just like any other commodity. And while he hadn't yet worked out the details of how he planned to go after Gothe, Bolan had a general idea. Making sure he was linked to Pacheco in Gothe's mind was an essential part of it.

Pacheco had recently worked his way into Gothe's confidence. The illegal artifacts dealer had hired him as one of his chief enforcers. And, ironically, Pacheco's first assignment had been to kill his real boss, Ricardo Toledo.

Bolan and Pacheco followed the maître d' to a table by the sidewalk and took their seats. The man in the black tuxedo bowed low, then disappeared. A second later, a waiter stood in his place. "What may I bring you gentlemen to drink?" he asked.

"Campari soda," Pacheco said.

Bolan ordered a beer and the waiter followed the maître d' out of sight. The Executioner kept his voice low, just above a whisper. "I was winding up another job when I got the call," he said. "Let me make sure I've got the general idea of what's going on. You stop me and correct me anywhere I'm wrong."

Pacheco nodded. Bolan started to speak, but the waiter returned with their drinks. He waited until there were no listening ears again, then continued. "Francisco Gothe is pretty much the godfather of southern Costa Rica. His main enterprise is the procurement and smuggling of pre-Columbian antiquities and he may, or may not, be involved in other criminal activity."

Pacheco took a sip of his Campari. "Right," he said. "Whether he's running drugs and guns too, I don't know yet. But there are rumors about him and a guy who owns a lot of the ships he smuggles his artifacts on."

"But the main operation, at least the one you're hired into," Bolan said, "consists of artifacts. Gothe's men find ancient tribal burial grounds, probably from the Boruca, Bribri and Cabecar tribes—"

"That's very good," Pacheco interrupted, an impressed expression on his face. "I'm part Cabecar myself, by the way."

"And Gothe uses local natives to dig up the graves. They mainly find ceramic and gold artifacts. Fetishes and the like."

Pacheco had lifted his drink to his lips, but he paused to answer before sipping again. "He not only uses the local tribes to dig up their own ancestors, he *uses them up*," he said.

"Treats them like dogs. Worse than dogs. It's slavery at its worst." He took another sip. "The poor bastards arc beaten unmercifully if they don't work fast enough, and beaten even worse if they break something. Just last night they whipped a man named Chavez to death." His face now turned hard. "I'm part Cabecar, and these are my people. Hell, nobody deserved to be whipped like a dog." He stared into the Executioner's eyes with fire in his own. "Not to mention the fact that the antiquities Gothe steals belong to my country. They should be in museums, not hidden away in the dens of a bunch of spoiled American and European collectors." He had looked down at the table as his anger rose, but now his eyes shot up. "No offense to you, of course."

"I'm American," he said. "But not an antique collector." He quickly looked Pacheco over. The young man was in his late twenties but had a prematurely balding hairline that was unusual for Borucans or Hispanics. He still wore the jeans he'd had on when they'd "killed" Toledo earlier in the afternoon but, like Bolan, had changed from the baggy sport shirt to an equally loose-fitting T-shirt. Both men had also gotten rid of the tourist-looking baseball cap and sunglasses. The police were scouring the city for both the superintendent's body and the hit men, and the last thing they needed was to be recognized and detained. Bolan still carried the Beretta and Desert Eagle, but Pacheco had traded his blank-loaded mini-Uzi for the Glock 21, which was his usual carry piece.

"You've worked your way into Gothe's world," the soldier finally said. "What's your status?" He lifted his beer mug and took a sip.

"I'm pretty much on equal ground with his top two men," Pacheco said. "Franco Mantara and Julio Lima. Which doesn't make either one of them very happy. But Gothe says he's got some big deals coming up, and he felt like he needed another man near the top."

The waiter returned and took their orders. The conversation went on.

"Okay," Bolan stated. "Like I said, there wasn't time to brief me before I got here, so I've got some catching up to do. You're blacksuit-trained, right?" In addition to fielding the world's top counterterrorist teams, Stony Man Farm provided top-flight instruction to select police officers and military personnel the world over. The select few chosen—called blacksuits because of the all-black night operations battle garb they trained in—were flown to the Farm blindfolded, trained, then blindfolded and returned to their countries of origin without ever knowing exactly where they'd been or who their instructors were. However, they each left the Farm with a very special phone number—dubbed the "hot line"—they could call if they ever needed to. And that's exactly what Pacheco had done.

"Yes," Pacheco said. "I don't expect you to remember me, but I remember you. You were introduced as Mike Belasko although none of us believed it was your real name. Is it?"

The Executioner shrugged. "It's real enough for our purposes."

Pacheco grinned. "Yeah, okay. Whatever."

"Tell me about the Toledo hit," Bolan said.

The man across from him squinted his eyes, and his receding hairline dropped slightly. "Gothe tried a dozen times to get Toledo on his payroll. But the man couldn't be bought. So Gothe finally decided to have him killed, and his assassination was sort of an initiation for me." Pacheco paused to take a deep breath. "It was my baptism of fire, my proving ground. What better way to find out if he'd accidentally hired an undercover cop, right? Anyway, he gave me two days to pull it off and told me not to come back if I didn't. I went to Toledo, of course. We decided something drastic had to be done. Too much time and effort had gone into my gaining Gothe's confidence to throw it all away."

"But why not handle it yourselves?" Bolan asked. "You have special units. Plenty of good men who could have pulled off this fake hit."

"Yes," Pacheco agreed. "Many could have pulled it off. But could they be trusted? Maybe yes, maybe no. We didn't know.

Gothe's wealth is great, and enough money can turn almost any man away from the true path, especially in the Third World."

"Costa Rica is hardly Sudan," the Executioner pointed out.

"No. It's one of the more affluent Third World countries, but that doesn't mean that no one goes hungry, or that there's no corruption within the police. There is. Especially within what we think of as the lower branches—what you'd call locals—which are severely underfunded. And Costa Rican officers are underpaid by tradition. That leads to bribery. Add to that the fact that many senior officers are not career cops but political appointees. You see the problem?"

"Yes," Bolan said. "Several of them."

"And there's one other thing I try never to forget when it comes to trusting other cops, something vital when you work undercover."

Bolan suspected he knew what it was but he asked anyway. "What's that?"

"Some men always want more no matter how much they already have," Pacheco said.

The Executioner nodded. He couldn't disagree. There was even a name for it. Greed.

The waiter returned bearing two steaming plates of mixed tacos, fried pork, chicken and chopped vegetables known as *picadillos,* and grilled corvina. "May I get you anything else?" he asked.

Both men shook their heads.

As soon as the man was gone again, Pacheco said, "I was in Toledo's office, and we were at a loss as to what to do. That's when I remembered my training and the hot line."

Bolan and Pacheco began to eat.

"Tell me something," Bolan said.

"What?" asked the man across from him.

"Once you'd called us in, a very obvious and simple answer to this whole problem should have become apparent, but doesn't appear to have."

Pacheco frowned as he started to take a bite of corvina. "What's that?"

"I could just fly down to the Osa Peninsula and kill Francisco Gothe."

There was a moment of silence, during which the Executioner's words seemed to hang in the air.

Pacheco glanced around nervously as if someone might have overheard. Bolan didn't bother. He had already checked to make sure no one was listening. Otherwise the words would have never left his mouth.

"I thought of that, of course," Pacheco said. "And although such action is highly illegal in Costa Rica—as it is in your country as well—I am not against it from a moral standpoint. As I said, Gothe is directly responsible for the deaths of many locals as well as others who have gotten in his way." He finally took the bite off the end of his fork, chewed and swallowed. "But there is a practical reason why he can't be killed outright. At least not yet."

Bolan waited for the man to continue.

"The man I spoke of earlier," Pacheco said. "The man who owns the shipping company?"

"The guy you think might be involved with Gothe and running guns and dope?" the soldier asked.

Pacheco nodded. He bit into a piece of chicken. "Yes. If we kill Gothe we'll never find out who he is."

"You don't have any idea?"

Pacheco shook his head and swallowed the chicken. "No. But if we play this right we should be able to find out. Gothe's getting ready to retire. He's getting old, and he wants out. He told me that himself. What he didn't tell me is where he plans to go to retire, although there's another rumor that he bought his own island somewhere."

"I see the problem," Bolan said. "We've got to play along long enough to find out who the other guy is. But we can't get caught napping and let Gothe slip away, either."

"Right," Pacheco agreed.

The soldier continued to eat. Pacheco's thinking was sound, and what they had to accomplish was clear. They had to get close enough to Gothe to find out more about his retirement plan and who he was involved with. Bolan wanted Gothe—wanted him for the deaths of his helplessly impoverished slave labor, and for the other crimes he had committed. But Bolan didn't want to stop there. Not if Gothe could lead him to another offender.

When they had both finished eating and shaken their heads at the waiter's offer of dessert, Bolan said, "Tell me two things, Pacheco. First, exactly what do Lima and Mantara—and you—do for Gothe? What's your job description?"

Pacheco wiped his mouth with a napkin. "Mantara and Lima are Gothe's top men. They're more or less the overseer's overseers, if that makes sense. When a particularly large burial ground is located, they go out to the site themselves. Most of the time they just send their underlings, usually locals who're willing to beat their own people for more money." He paused and took the final drink of his Campari.

"What else?" Bolan asked.

"They're the final wall of insulation between Gothe and the law," Pacheco said. "They do the payoffs to the police and politicians. And they do the special assignments that come up."

"Hits?"

"Yes, hits. Like I said, the Toledo thing was to see if I could keep pace with them. Hold my own. It was a test. Gothe wanted to make sure I wasn't what I am—a cop."

"Go on."

"When there's an extra-large shipment of antiquities going out, either Lima or Mantara accompanies it. Sometimes they both go, but that's pretty rare."

"Where do the antiquities go, and who takes them?" Bolan asked.

"Some shipping company out of Nicaragua handles it," Pacheco said. "I don't know exactly which one yet. Like I said, I was barely hired on when he sent me off to kill Toledo and, well, here we are. I have picked up on the fact that most of the shipments go to the U.S. and Europe. Although the Japanese seem especially crazy about these ceramic figurines. And Mantara just got back from South Africa where some buyer had bought close to a million in gold artifacts."

"That's what you're supposed to be doing from now on?" the soldier asked. "Same thing Lima and Mantara do?"

Pacheco shrugged. "As far as I know. Like I said, I was just hired on when I got sent away. It hasn't all been ironed out yet. But I've presented myself as an energetic young up and coming bad guy who isn't afraid to take chances to get ahead. And Gothe liked me." He lifted his glass, saw that it was empty and set it back down again. "He treats me differently than Lima and Mantara. He's hinted that he wants to make a few more big scores, then retire and turn things over to me."

The Executioner drained the remainder of his beer and set down the glass as the waiter returned with the check. He set it on the table in a small rectangular plastic frame and moved away again.

"He's told you that already?" the Executioner said, frowning.

"Yeah," Pacheco replied. "Which doesn't particularly make sense unless you look below the surface. I mean, he's still testing me by sending me to kill Toledo, but at the same time he's offering to turn the reins over to me? But if you look at it another way, it makes all the sense in the world."

Bolan nodded. "He's lying. He sees a good man he can get some good work out of if he hangs a carrot in front of you."

"Right." Pacheco grinned. "In other words, he's simply lying."

Bolan pulled out a roll of bills and dropped enough to cover the meal and tip on top of the check. "Okay," he said. "Here's another question. Who do you know in the press who you can trust?"

Pacheco appeared slightly taken back by the question. "The press?"

"Yes. Who can you trust in the press?"

"That's like asking where I could find an honest lawyer," Pacheco said. "I'd say Jeronimo Gomez could be trusted. At least to a point. He's obnoxious but credible. We could trust him even more if we promised him an exclusive story somewhere down the line."

Bolan stood up. "Promise him," he said. "We'll deliver." He moved around the table and left the restaurant for the sidewalk. Behind him, he heard Pacheco hurrying to catch up.

"Where are we going?" the Costa Rican cop asked.

"First, we're going to call Gomez and arrange a meeting," Bolan said.

"And then?"

"Then we're going to create an opening so I can apply for a job."

"A job?" Pacheco said, raising an eyebrow. "What kind of a job?"

The Executioner smiled as they walked on. "I think I should try my hand with Francisco Gothe, too," he said.

JERONIMO GOMEZ, Pacheco informed Bolan, had once been the main man in San José. He'd first made a name for himself as a cub reporter for the *Tico Times*, South America's largest English newspaper. During his rookie year, he'd cracked a front page story about a Sandinista connection within the Costa Rican government that had led to a full investigation and the quick removal of several key political figures. From there, he'd moved on to host a popular radio talk show, and within another year he'd landed his own television news program with ratings through the roof. Scandal of any and all kinds had been what rocketed him to the top, and what kept him there for three seasons. Then, like so many other belligerent newscasters who specialized in setting up and then humiliating their guests, his appeal had worn thin.

The undercover specialist advised Bolan as they got out of the cab down the street from the Soda de Sol that Gomez's drinking hadn't helped much, either. Now, the man was back at his old job with the *Times*. And according to Pacheco, he'd become an almost permanent fixture at the Soda.

Bolan and Pacheco walked down the sidewalk across the street from Parque Central to the café where Gomez had agreed to meet them. *Sodas*, the soldier knew from past experience, resembled snack bars, and were scattered all over the city. They served San José's working class, doling out simple food at fair prices. Bolan let Pacheco lead the way inside and saw that a long bar ran across the back of the room. An overhang ran the length of the bar, and a television had been bolted to its center. Screams and shrieks of excitement blasted from the set as a young couple won a new car on some game show. Behind the bar, in addition to the usual assortment of bottles, were stacks of packaged sandwiches, cookies, chips and other junk food. A shiny stainless-steel grill stood to one side, and a man wearing a white apron was busy flipping hamburger patties.

Spotting Gomez was no problem—the down-on-his-luck reporter was the only other patron in the *soda*. He sat with his back against the far wall at a round three-chaired table across from the bar. Gomez saw them, too, and waved them over.

The soldier took stock of the man quickly, adding what he saw to what Pacheco had told him. Gomez looked as if he'd just stepped out of a cheap B-grade movie where he was playing the part of a reporter. In his midfifties, he wore a dusty navy blue snap-brim hat and cheap suit. The lapel was unbuttoned, and Bolan could see where the inside coat pocket had torn away and been repaired with a stapler. A plate full of rice and beans sat in front of him, growing cold, apparently untouched. The three beer bottles on the table next to it, however, had seen all the attention.

Gomez had the bulbous nose of a heavy drinker, angry blue and red veins threatening to burst at any second. A strong odor of alcoholic beverages—more than beer—drifted across the table as they sat down.

Bolan wasn't crazy about the seating arrangement, as both he and Pacheco had their backs to the street. But Gomez looked firmly entrenched, as if he sat where he was all the time and might even have a nameplate at the seat proclaiming it his. It wasn't worth the effort to make him change.

Pacheco took the other chair at the table and stuck out his hand. "Long time, no see," he said in English. Bolan had expected Spanish, but considering the fact that Gomez worked for the English-printed newspaper, his grasp of the language had to be good.

"What have you got?" Jeronimo Gomez asked without preamble.

"Right now," Pacheco said. "Nothing. We need a favor."

"So go find somebody who does favors," Gomez said, his voice slightly slurred. "It ain't me." He lifted one of the empty beer bottles and shouted in Spanish, "Oswaldo! In *this* lifetime, please!"

A disgusted groan came from the grill area behind the bar. Pacheco turned to look at Bolan.

The soldier said, "We'll have a story for you. A big story. Within a week. But in order to get it, we need your help."

Several seconds went by during which Gomez's watery eyes stared into the Executioner's. Then the man said, "CIA?"

It was a question Bolan was often asked under similar conditions. He shook his head as the game show on the television behind him ended and the evening news began.

The conversation came to a halt as the man in the apron appeared at Bolan's side with a beer bottle in each hand. "I have brought you two, Jeronimo," the man said, "My shift ends in five minutes, and as I'm sure you're aware, Juan is not as patient as I am."

Gomez grinned from ear to ear and lifted one of the bottles from the table, chugging half of it. He burped without shame, then looked back at Bolan and said, "Well, you aren't down here to scuba dive or fish. Not when you're hanging around him." He shrugged toward Pacheco. "What kind of story are we talking?"

Pacheco cleared his throat. "Like the man said, a big one."

The reporter's eyes seemed to clear. "This have something to do with Toledo's murder today?" he asked.

Bolan nodded.

"Thought so," Gomez said. "I've seen the tape."

The soldier knew he had to be referring to the tape the tourist had taken. The man had either sold it to the news media or had it confiscated by the police. But it wouldn't do to let Gomez know too much about what was going on, so he said, "What tape?"

"*What tape,* the man says." Gomez snorted. "I just told you I'd seen it, and you're in it. You're in it trying to shoot the guy who was making it." His liquid eyes cleared even further. "Or at least trying to look like you're trying to shoot the guy making it." He paused, then pointed a shaky hand over Bolan's head at the television. "But we can get into all that later. See for yourself."

The Executioner turned in his seat to see an attractive Hispanic woman behind a news desk, quickly setting up the tape that was about to be played. A second later, the video began to roll.

The tourist hadn't picked up the shooting until after Toledo had already hit the ground. The footage showed Bolan and Pacheco's backs only, and the baseball caps hid most of their hair. Then Bolan suddenly turned and fired toward the camera. There was a flash of his face behind the sunglasses, but it was too fast for the eye to pick up and identify before the tape began jumping crazily as the cameraman dived for cover.

Bolan couldn't have asked for more. The police would lift stills from the footage and zero in on his face. The public would not see that picture for at least another day. In the meantime, he wasn't in danger of being spotted in San José, and by the time the photos began circulating he'd be out of town. Gomez, of course, had recognized him from the brief flash of face, but he doubted that even the experienced newsman would have made the connection had they not been talking about the subject already. And the fact that Gomez had hinted that he might not have really been trying to shoot the cameraman didn't bother the soldier either. That a man would help kill the superintendent of police, then hang out with a cop, was bound to raise suspicions.

In short, Gomez had more information than anybody else except Bolan and Pacheco. All it proved was that while the alcohol might have affected his brain, it hadn't killed it.

Turning back to Gomez, the soldier said, "What we want you to do is play up the fact that the man you just saw—the man who shot at the camera—is American."

"How do I know he's American?" Gomez asked. "My credibility is on the line."

"I'm telling you he's American," Bolan said. "You have my word on it."

"Okay, you sound American and you look American, but for all I know you could be Canadian or Australian or Russian for that matter. Why is it so important that you're American?"

"It just is," Bolan said.

"And I'm supposed to take the word of a stranger on this?" he asked. "I'm supposed to believe you when you tell me you'll have a story worth my time and effort in a week?"

"Yes," Bolan answered simply.

Gomez's eyes had begun to water again as the alcohol hit his system. The rheumy orbs stared at Bolan with a different kind of clarity that only the best cops, soldiers and news hawks developed. "Okay," he said. "I will, because I think you're telling me the truth. But answer me one thing first."

The Executioner waited.

"You *are* the man in the video, right?"

"I am."

"I don't know exactly who you are, but I get a feeling about you. I think you're honest, and I think if you'd wanted to hit that idiot with the camcorder he'd be dead." He paused a moment and his eyes flickered down to the bottle sticking out of his open jacket. Thinking better of yet another drink—at least for the moment—he added, "You didn't really kill Toledo, did you." It came out more statement than question.

The Executioner stared deep into the man's eyes. "No," he said. "All the rounds in the Uzi were blanks. I had live ammo to make holes in the car. We did the blood with special effects. You're welcome to all that as an exclusive—but keep it to yourself for the time being."

It was enough to convince the reporter than Bolan was on the level, and that there would indeed eventually be a story in it all. It was also cause for celebration and another drink, and the bottle came out of his jacket pocket.

The barman was out of sight behind him and Pacheco, and Bolan heard the man say, "Good night, Juan" and guessed that the new shift was replacing the old.

"So we can count on you?" Bolan asked Gomez.

"For now, all I'll do is stress the fact that one of the gunmen was an American," he said. "I'll chalk it up to an unnamed reliable source, which is only partially pushing the truth."

"And you'll keep the fact that Toledo's still alive to yourself until we tell you otherwise?"

"No," Gomez said, shaking his head. "I'll keep it to myself for one week. That was the deal. A week."

The soldier nodded. It was fair enough. And he should be finished with the mission within a week easily.

Another man wearing a white apron suddenly appeared at Bolan's side. "May I get you gentlemen any—" he began, then stopped suddenly when his eyes fell on Jaime Pacheco. There was a moment of awkward silence while the two men stared at each other, then the bartender turned to look at Bolan. His eyes bored into Bolan, as if he might be trying to memorize the soldier's features for a pop quiz the next day. Clearing his throat nervously, he finally finished the sentence. "May I get you gentlemen anything?"

Bolan and Pacheco shook their heads. Gomez didn't miss the chance to have another beer delivered.

When the man had gone, Bolan looked at Pacheco. There was no need to verbalize the question.

"Juan Escabar," Pacheco said. "I busted him several years ago when I was still in uniform."

"For what?"

"Coke. At least that was the initial case. But when we got in to serve the search warrant, we found stack after stack of child pornography." Pacheco's face hardened into granite. "They made me file that, too."

"Made you?" Gomez asked incredulously. "You didn't want to?"

"No," Pacheco said. "I wanted to kill him. Especially after we pursued the lead and found out he'd molested a whole string of little girls."

"He didn't make any bones about studying me," Bolan said. "He still in the drug business?"

Pacheco shrugged. "Do they ever really get out once they're in?"

"How well is he connected?"

"I don't know. This is the first time I've seen or heard of him in years."

Bolan turned to face the bar. Escabar was uncapping the top of a beer bottle. He brought it back and set it in front of Gomez, studiously avoiding both Bolan's and Pacheco's eyes. Walking back behind the bar, he disappeared through a door at the rear of the building.

"He knows you, he knows you're working undercover, and he's making a call to tell somebody about me," the soldier said. "Giving them my description." He stood. "If we don't stop him, the fact that you're now a cop working undercover—with me—will be all over Costa Rica in ten minutes."

Bolan walked swiftly behind the bar with Pacheco at his heels. Through the door, he could hear the almost archaic sound of an ancient rotary phone. As soon as he'd passed through the opening, he saw the man in the white apron standing in front of a pay phone, the receiver wedged between his shoulder and ear as the other hand dialed.

In his other hand was a revolver.

Juan Escabar looked up as the Executioner approached. He fired.

BOLAN HIT THE FLOOR a split second ahead of the bullet, feeling, more than hearing, it pass above his head. He rolled up on his left side, his right hand snaking beneath the bottom of his T-shirt to find the grips of the Desert Eagle stuffed into his belt holster. Pacheco had been only a step or two behind him. Bolan had heard no grunt, groan, or any other sound that would indicate that the bullet, which had missed him, had struck the Costa Rican undercover officer.

Bolan had little time to wonder. As he glanced up, Escabar aimed the revolver again. The Executioner rolled once more.

The revolver exploded again, and the second piece of rocketing copper and lead singed along Bolan's back, burning his skin and ripping his shirt. He made a 180-degree revolution on the ground, coming back to a halt on his belly again. Bringing up the Desert Eagle's barrel in this prone position, his trigger finger automatically began to squeeze even before his target came into view. But before the Desert Eagle could explode, he saw that Escabar was no longer there.

A door next to the pay phone was swinging back to slam against the wall.

Bolan glanced over his shoulder to see that Pacheco had been forced to the ground as well. The cop had drawn his Glock from beneath his shirt, and now held it down in the ready position. "Let's go!" the Executioner ordered and bolted for the open door.

The door led to an alley. Twilight had fallen while they had been in the *soda,* and now only the last rays of day lit the narrow corridor. The odor of trash assaulted the soldier's nostrils as he saw a blurry shadow move at the end of the alley.

Then there came a flash of red and yellow light, followed

shortly by a whipping noise that passed an inch from Bolan's right cheek. A split second later, the loud boom of yet another round rocked the narrow alleyway. The Executioner stretched out his arm, his eyes focusing on the center of Escabar's chest. But as his finger moved back on the trigger, a young couple appeared on the sidewalk at the end of the alley. Holding hands, they froze in place, directly behind the man with the revolver.

Again, Bolan was forced to halt the trigger squeeze in mid-stroke. The powerful .44 Magnum round would pass straight through Escabar and into the two lovers.

The shadow darted around the corner, out of sight on the street.

The woman caught her composure enough to scream as Bolan executed a three-point turn at the end of the alley, pivoting onto the sidewalk to continue the chase. As he turned, he raised the Desert Eagle yet again, aiming down the block to where Escabar's back could be seen. More men and women, out for a stroll in the cooler evening air of downtown San José, lined the sidewalk. No way Bolan could take the chance of hitting one of them.

Such concern for innocent bystanders didn't stop Escabar, and he turned long enough to trigger two more rounds before cutting right again at the end of the block. The rounds forced the Executioner to flatten against the side of the building. Both projectiles struck the bricks above his head.

By the time he had recovered, Escabar was gone again, taking the sidewalk back in front of the Soda de Sol. They had circled half the block by now, and people along the streets had heard the gunfire and seen the running men. Where was Escabar headed? Bolan wondered as he took off again. Behind him, he could hear Pacheco's running feet. "Why's he running from us?" Bolan shouted over his shoulder.

The voice that answered was slightly out of breath. "He's done...something," Pacheco puffed. "Something we don't know about...but he thinks we do."

Bolan reached the corner and stopped, peering cautiously around the bricks. Just as he'd suspected, Escabar stood in front of the Soda del Sol, the revolver aimed toward him.

Two more slugs boomed out in the night, followed by the gasps and screams of people on the sidewalk. The Executioner ducked back, then dropped to one knee, edging around the corner once more in time to see Escabar duck back into the *soda*. Standing back up, he moved cautiously along the side of the storefronts, the Desert Eagle leading the way. "Get out of here!" he whispered to the frightened people he passed.

He slowed as he neared the *soda*. He hadn't been able to make out the exact make and model of the small revolver in Escabar's hands, which meant he couldn't be certain how many rounds it held. If it had been a Smith & Wesson of that size, the cylinder held five. Some of the smaller model Colts were stuffed with six. And if the weapon in Escabar's fist happened to be one of the newer Taurus wheel guns, it could even be a seven-shooter. All of which meant the ex-con could have as few as one, or as many as three rounds left.

Suddenly the Executioner knew why the child molester had decided to return to the *soda*.

He had more firepower hidden behind the bar. He was on his way to reload. Or rearm.

Bolan turned to Pacheco. "Go back to the rear door. Cover the alley."

Pacheco nodded and took off.

The bottom half of the plate-glass windows in front of the Soda del Sol had been painted with advertisements, blocking his view into the small café. Bolan dropped below them as he passed, letting the same ads keep Escabar from seeing him. His head rose briefly, scouring the dining area and ascertaining that it was empty. Even Gomez, who Bolan had been afraid might have stuck around to get a story, had decided that discretion was the better part of valor and vacated the premises.

Good. No innocents to get in the way.

The Executioner took a deep breath. He had sent Pacheco

back to block the rear exit. Even if Escabar had cut straight through the *soda* and back out the rear door, there had been plenty of time for the undercover man to get back to the alley and see him. Could Pacheco stop the man on his own? Bolan remembered what Toledo has said about the undercover man's shooting abilities.

The question was moot, however. Escabar hadn't left the *soda* yet. Bolan listened carefully as he made his way to the front door. No more gunfire came from either inside the building or the alleyway behind. And no matter how bad Pacheco might be with a gun, he knew the man well enough by now to know he'd at least try.

Bolan rose to his full height as he stopped just to the side of the doorway. He cleared his throat. "Throw down the gun and come out with your hands up, Escabar," he called into the open doorway.

The answer took a long time coming. But when it did, the ex-con's voice sounded like a frightened woman. "No!" he screamed. "No! I won't go back to prison!"

The Executioner nodded to himself. Pacheco hadn't finished telling him all about Escabar but the man sounded like a typical child molester—a house full of kiddie porn, and probably a dozen unknown victims for every one that had come to light. Bolan knew how child molesters were treated in American prisons, and he doubted it was much different in Costa Rica. The cons had their own pecking order, and those with "short eyes" were at the bottom. They received a form of justice from their fellow inmates—often fathers of little boys and girls themselves—that was far more "just" than any justice system could ever mete out.

But Bolan tried again. "Maybe we can work it so you don't have to go back," he yelled around the corner. "All I want is to make sure you keep your mouth closed about seeing us." He had little hope his words would work.

And they didn't. "No!" Escabar shrieked. "You lie!" The man was crying now. "I will tell no one! Just let me go!"

"I'm afraid I can't do that, Juan," the soldier said. He stuck his head briefly around the corner, then jerked it back again as another round whipped past his face. The roar was followed by several metallic clicks. The weapon was empty.

Bolan didn't know if the man planned to reload or snatch up another hidden weapon. Either way, this was the time to move. He wouldn't get a better chance.

The Executioner came around the corner low, the big Desert Eagle raised in front of him. He saw Juan Escabar's head and shoulders above the bar. The man was reaching for something beneath the barrier. Escabar saw Bolan, too, and ducked just as the Executioner pulled the trigger.

A .44 Magnum steel-jacketed hollowpoint slug exploded from the Eagle's barrel, sounding like an atomic bomb compared to the revolver's rounds. The bullet was on its way to Escabar's face before he ducked. It struck the man in the left shoulder and nearly tore off his arm. Escabar squealed like a pig as he spun crazily back to strike the wall behind the bar. But he held on to the sawed-off 12-gauge shotgun he'd retrieved from below the counter.

Now, the ex-con either panicked or acted out of reflex. Both hammers of the double-barreled shotgun fell simultaneously, and a huge hole appeared in the ceiling behind the bar. The recoil jerked the stubby weapon out of Escabar's hands and it clattered to the floor.

Suddenly Pacheco appeared at the door to the back storage room. His Glock was gripped in both hands and aimed at Escabar. "Freeze!" the undercover cop yelled in a loud authoritative voice. His words were unnecessary. All of the fight had left Juan Escabar and he wasn't going anywhere.

Except maybe to jail.

On the street outside, Bolan heard the wail of police sirens. They would be there any moment, and the police could take Escabar into custody. Would that solve their problem about Escabar identifying Pacheco as a cop and word getting back to Gothe?

"Hey, Jaime," Bolan said. "Costa Rican prisoners have access to phones?"

Pacheco gave him a quizzical look as he kept his Glock trained on Escabar. "Yes," he said. "Why?"

"How long did this guy get in the penitentiary after you busted him?" Bolan asked.

"I don't know," Pacheco said. "But it couldn't have been over four years, maximum. That was when I busted him. Four years ago."

"Less than four years for both the drug and child molestation cases?"

Pacheco nodded.

"How many little girls did he molest?"

Pacheco frowned at the question. "He was convicted on seven," he said. "There were more."

The Executioner shook his head in disgust. He knew they'd have to get word to the other prisoners in the holding cells where Escabar would be taken. If one of them didn't take him out, Bolan might have to do the job himself.

2

To Jaime Pacheco, the most overwhelming aspect of the jungle had always been the colors. People unfamiliar with the rain forests always thought of them as green. Pacheco, however, had grown up in the jungles of Costa Rica's Osa Peninsula, and knew they exhibited every hue known to humankind. Maybe even a few that had never found their way to a color chart.

Pacheco twisted the grip of the Ossa 250 motorcycle and made the wheels spin on the loose dirt. He navigated the bike around a breakneck curve in the jungle road, smiling contentedly to himself as he passed begonias, anthurium, and the red-spotted blood of Christ plants. A thrill of excitement raced through his soul, a sense that only came over him when he mixed the beauty of the jungle with the danger of a speeding motorcycle. It was a strange mixture of feelings—potential death combined with the aesthetic perfection of his surroundings. Like dying in Heaven.

Pacheco dodged a large chunk of concrete—fallen off a pickup—and rode on. Overhead in the trees, a family of monkeys protested his presence as he rode under them, calling out in anger as if he'd invaded their property. And in a way, Pacheco supposed, he had. A movement deeper in the foliage caught his eye, but the animal that had made it was gone before he could see it. An ocelot? Tapir? Perhaps even a jaguar awakened by the Ossa's engine? He didn't know if it had been one of those animals. But he knew they were there, hidden from the human invaders who refused to go away.

The road narrowed, and Pacheco could see where a passing pickup had recently broken vines on both sides of the narrow pathway. Several perfectly round granite spheres lay just off the road—*bolas,* they were called. They could be found all over the peninsula, and scientists dated them back as far as A.D. 400. But their purpose, and how such ancient people had carved them to such faultless spheres, was lost to history. The *bolas* made him think of the natives of this southern region of Costa Rica, so different from their northern brothers in tradition and culture. The ancient indigenous Diquis peoples had even had ties to South America, to the great empire of the Inca and other tribes. Did the purpose of the mysterious *bolas,* and the golden ornaments Gothe robbed from the grave sites, have their roots to the south? Perhaps. He knew that when the first Europeans arrived they found goldsmiths already hammering out these ornaments as well as using a now-lost wax technique to form amulets and talismans significant to their animistic religions. Every night, Gothe's slaves dug out tiny eagles, scorpions, crocodiles and jaguars.

The road led out of the jungle and began to follow along the waves of the Golfo Dulce. Pacheco revved the engine even higher and raced along the black sand beach—the end product of ancient volcanic eruption. At several points along the beach, far from the water, he could see areas fenced in by chicken wire. The sight brought yet another smile to his face.

It was laying season for the sea turtles, and every night the females came ashore to plant their eggs in the sand. These eggs would eventually hatch, and the baby turtles would begin to struggle their way instinctively back to the sea. But predators meant that less than one turtle in a hundred would complete the journey on its own. So the natives dug up the eggs each morning and replanted them within the protection of the cages. Sticks poked up out of the sand to mark the spots where each egg lay, and at least one of the human caretakers was always on duty to scare away birds, dogs and other hungry animals as they escorted the newborns to the water.

Jaime Pacheco rode on, spotting a school of bottleneck dolphins cavorting in the blue waters just beyond the tide. He took a side road near Carate, then followed it deeper into the jungle. A few miles later, he passed a sign pointing toward Corcorado National Park. A deserted ranger station led into the area. He passed by, riding another two miles before coming to a flooded stream where he was forced to stop. Pacheco's eyebrows lowered in concentration as he weighed his chance of jumping the water versus lifting the heavy motorcycle and wading across. Finally he chuckled to himself. "Nothing ventured, nothing gained," he said out loud behind the visor on his helmet, then turned and retraced his path for twenty yards. With a quick twist of the grips he took off again, gaining as much speed as he could in the muddy ground. He angled toward a bump in the road just before the stream, then pulled upward on the handlebars with all his might as he hit it.

The Ossa sailed up into the air, over the water and came down on the other side.

A half mile later, Pacheco turned onto another gravel drive. Gone now was the smile behind the visor. Behind it was the grim face of a young man determined to make a difference both to his people and his country.

Pacheco had just been though the closest thing to heaven he had ever seen on earth. But he was about to enter hell.

THE STORY HAD BEEN AROUND so long that no one even thought to question it.

Francisco Gothe was the son of a former Nazi colonel who had escaped postwar Germany and fled to South America. Soon, he had met the lovely young daughter of a Peruvian government official—no one seemed to know exactly what kind of an official he had been. They fell in love and were married. By the time their son, Francisco, was born a year later Franz Gothe had been firmly set up by his new father-in-law in the arms-smuggling business.

Francisco Gothe was now over sixty. As he walked behind the wet bar in his den, he studied the bottles lined up on the wall along the shelf, finally deciding on the green bottle of Pernod. He poured three fingers of the yellowish-green substance into a highball glass, then added water from the tap in the sink. The two fluids seemed to explode together rather than mix, and the result was a cloudy gray that looked very much like liquid smoke.

Gothe walked around the end of the bar and stopped in front of a bookshelf in the corner of the room. Tastefully displayed on the shelves were some of the best pieces of gold and ceramic he had uncovered over the years. Huge golden birds, many bearing human-shaped heads. Solid gold scorpions the size of his fist. Shamans. Jaguars. Crocodiles. And sculptured clay figurines that Gothe suspected represented some long-forgotten pagan. All were exquisitely crafted. Museum quality, Gothe thought, and that made him laugh. These pieces, at least, would never see the inside of a museum.

Gothe continued to study his treasures as he sipped his Pernod. The ancient craftsmen of the Osa Peninsula had made him rich. They would make him even richer before it was all over. And it would all be over. Soon.

Gothe sighed. He was tired. He had worked hard all his life. It was time to take his money and run.

The man people knew as half German and half Peruvian walked to the bar and took a seat on a stool. He snorted, took another sip from his glass and shook his head in amazement. Former Nazi father? Politically connected mother? If he wasn't careful, he'd start believing it himself. He didn't know how the story had gotten started, but he liked it. It had been good for business, and so he had never denied it. Rather than correct the rumors he had, in fact, fueled them on, adding his own mysterious details over the years. Like the part about his family owning Peruvian oil land, Or about his wife who had died when they were young, or the tale of how he had gotten lost in the Amazon when he was five years old.

Gothe chuckled softly. That was his favorite story, and made him suspect he could have become a successful fiction writer had he chosen that path in life. The story went that he had gotten lost from his father's party while they were delivering weapons to the Boro tribe, and wandered aimlessly through the jungle until he finally stumbled onto a forgotten city of untold riches. More frightened of the ghostly atmosphere of the deserted city, he had fled quickly back into the jungle. He had then been rescued by the same Boro tribesman who had purchased his father's guns.

Gothe liked being coaxed into telling the tale by Costa Rica's more affluent citizens and government officials, and was careful to tell it the same way every time. He always ended the story by closing his eyes, slowly shaking his head, and sadly saying, "Even at the age of five, I knew to keep the story of the city of gold to myself. But what I didn't know, at so tender an age, was that by the time I was old enough to return, I would have forgotten the location." This usually called for a another round of drinks, and was followed by another story or two about his unsuccessful searches for the lost city as a younger man.

Gothe took another drink from his glass, tasting the licorice bite of the Pernod. He had always had the ability to sound as sincere as a saint when he lied, and at the same time amuse himself at how stupid his listeners were to believe him.

The man on the bar stool took another sip from the glass, then set it down on a coaster in front of him. The truth was, he had never been to Peru. His father had been an Austrian sailor and his mother a waitress in a Havana café. His father had shipped out never knowing he'd conceived a son, and never returned to the island. His mother had died when he was young, and he'd been shipped off to Miami to grow up with her sister and brother-in-law.

Good thing, too, Gothe knew. He had been in the U.S. less than a month when Fidel Castro came to power.

Far in the distance outside the house, Gothe heard a motorcycle. Pacheco? Possibly. He lifted the remote control on the bar next to the phone and hit the Power button. The television in the corner of the room clicked on. Grabbing the phone with the other hand, he pressed it against his ear and tapped in several numbers. A moment later he said, "Mantara. Come into the den. Bring Lima with you." Then he hung up.

Gothe stood up from the stool and moved to the large picture window facing the road. He could still hear the motorcycle. Closer now. Yes, it was on the road leading into the house so it had to be Pacheco. The new man was returning to give his report about the Toledo hit. Gothe chuckled and mixed another Pernod. As if a report were necessary. The entire country, and half the world, had seen the videotape that had played on every newscast on every channel in Costa Rica since the incident. Gothe himself had taped it from one of the programs, and it was in the video machine now.

A small figure appeared in the distance, then disappeared again as the road dipped out of sight. The motorcycle became visible once more a moment later, then continued to disappear each time the road declined or curved, only to show again, each time a little larger. It was Pacheco, indeed.

Gothe returned to the stool. A few moments later, Mantara and Lima came into the den from the hallway. He waved at a couch, and the two men sat down.

Gothe held his glass to his lips and studied them out of the corner of his eye. Both Lima and Mantara had done well for him. They were loyal, trustworthy and they didn't hesitate to kill when he commanded. But God hadn't blessed either of them with an abundance of brain power, and they both liked the killing just a little too much. That was fine as long as Gothe kept tabs on them. But it would hardly do after he was gone.

The older man glanced toward the window again. He needed someone with intelligence to run things when he was gone. He hoped he had found that man in Jaime Pacheco. He sipped at the new drink. Pacheco was bright, appeared to be well-educated and had just proved that he could be trusted to do what was necessary. He could carry out orders, even killing, as well or better than the other men.

He was smart. But was he *too smart* for Gothe's future plans? That was a dangerous possibility, too.

The roar of the motorcycle peaked outside, then suddenly died. Far away, at the front of the house, Gothe heard the door-bell ring. The high-heeled shoes of his live-in housemaid Maria clicked across the tile of the foyer. He heard the door open. A few moments later, Pacheco was standing in the doorway.

Gothe raised his glass and smiled. "What would you like?" he asked. Still watching out of the corner of his eye, he saw both Lima and Mantara frown. He hadn't asked them if they wanted a drink, and he hadn't asked them on purpose. It didn't do to let your employees get too comfortable in your presence. Besides, they deserved no reward. They hadn't just killed the Costa Rican superintendent of police.

Pacheco smiled back. "A beer, please, sir," he said.

Gothe nodded, more to himself than to Pacheco as he walked back around the bar and pulled a beer from the re-frigerator. The boy had manners as well as brains. And re-spect. He liked that, too. As long as it wasn't just a show for his benefit.

Time would tell, the older man thought as he grabbed the remote control from the top of the bar and came around the corner. He had set a few traps to ensure Pacheco wasn't re-ally an undercover cop. Now he would set a few to test his loyalty.

Gothe handed Pacheco his beer, motioned the young man to one of the padded armchairs across from the couch, then dropped into the other chair himself. When they were seated, he jabbed the remote toward the television. The tape began to play, and he saw Ricardo Toledo die for perhaps the twentieth time. As the man slid down the side of the car, Gothe hit the Pause button and stopped the tape. "It seems somewhat silly now, considering all this—" he nodded toward the television "—but did you bring the proof I requested?"

"Yes, sir," Pacheco said. He reached into his hip pocket, pulled out a small leather case and tossed it through the air. Gothe caught it, then opened it to see a Costa Rican National Police badge, and the face of Toledo on the identification card.

"Very good," Gothe said.

"Thank you, sir," Pacheco replied, grinning.

Gothe started the tape again. When the footage came to the part where the big American turned to fire at the camera, he hit the Pause button. "You didn't tell me that you planned to engage outside help."

Pacheco shrugged. "It was a last second decision." He pointed toward the screen. "I have known that man for some time. But I didn't know he was in San José. When I bumped into him, he needed work. And I had just come from scoping out the place I wanted to do the hit, and the thought of hiring a backup had crossed my mind." He took a long pull from his beer can. "Stumbling across this old friend seemed to be providence." He held up the beer can for emphasis before adding, "On a job as important and delicate as this one, I figured I couldn't be too careful."

On the couch, Lima snickered. "It was a simple job," he said, his voice betraying his jealousy and anger. "Find a man and shoot him." He made a gun out of his hand, extending the index finger, then dropping his thumb as if it were the hammer. "Anyone could have done it. *Alone.*"

Mantara nodded.

"Yes," Pacheco said. "It was a simple job. But the man himself...he was not so simple, eh?" He grinned at both men good-naturedly

Gothe had to hide his own smile at the way the young man handled himself. He wouldn't let the older men intimidate or anger him. They were beneath him. Good, very good. "Exactly who was this man?" he asked. "All the papers say that a reliable source has divulged he is American."

Pacheco turned to face him. "Yes. As I said, I have worked with him before. In Colombia. I knew he could be trusted. He had proved to be a man of honor many times, even once saving my life. And as I also said, he was down on his luck and needed work. He came cheap."

Gothe laughed. "Yes," he said. "Cheap for you, perhaps. How much did he cost me?"

Pacheco shrugged again. "I paid him reasonably for what he did. You may deduct it from my own payment if it doesn't please you."

Gothe shook his head. "I will reimburse you for it. It was a wise decision, considering Toledo's position. As you said, one cannot be too careful."

"There is an additional advantage to using him," Pacheco added.

"Ah? What is that?"

"It is *his* face on the videotape, is it not? It is *he* who the police are looking for." Pacheco paused for another drink of beer. "Did you read the piece in the *Tico Times* this morning? The one by Jeronimo Gomez?"

"I did," Gothe said. "He seems to be the first who was convinced the man was American. Only one thing concerns me. Where has this man gone now?"

"He is in hiding, of course."

"In Costa Rica?"

"I don't know."

Gothe frowned for a moment. He didn't like loose ends. Before he could speak again, Pacheco continued.

"I thought it best if neither of us knew where the other was going," he said. "If that was a mistake, I apologize, sir."

Gothe leaned forward and finished what remained of his Pernod and water. "My only concern is what he might say should he be caught," he said.

"He will say nothing," Pacheco said. "As I told you, I know him well, and he is as tough as they come. Besides, there is little he could tell the police should they find him. Even if he spilled his guts all he could say is that he and I killed the superintendent. He knows nothing about you, or why there was a contract on Toledo." Pacheco smiled in genuine good humor. "And he doesn't even know my real name."

Gothe couldn't keep the smile off his face either. The kid *was* smart. Smart enough not to trust even the trustworthy. "Do you know his name?" he asked.

"Mike Belasko," said the young man sitting across from Gothe.

"And that is his real name?"

Pacheco shrugged once more, again showing the total confidence in himself, his abilities and his skills that Francisco Gothe liked. "Maybe," he said. "But I doubt it."

HE HAD CHOSEN the Santuario de Agua resort hotel just outside La Palma for specific reasons. First, it was one of the many resorts owned by Gothe that served as both as a legitimate cover operation for his criminal enterprises and a way to launder the money they made. Second, it was a place frequented by both locals and tourists, and had exactly the kind of atmosphere Bolan was looking for. A few older retirees and families were guests of the resort, having come for the sun and sea. But the hotel catered primarily to single men and women, lonely people who were looking more for recreation with each other instead of that provided by the beach and water. Which meant one more unattached male wouldn't draw undue attention.

Unless, of course, there was something different about that male. And there *was* something different about the man stretched out across the lounge recliner on the beach. Not different enough to make people stop and point but different enough to make him memorable in these surroundings.

Bolan was just different enough to stand out to the exact degree that he wanted to. He would be noticed, but unless there was a reason for him to be remembered later, he would be forgotten by all the people who saw him as soon as he was out of their sight again.

Bolan rose slightly, straightened his sunglasses and looked down the beach to his left. A volleyball game had just started near the water, and a half-dozen twenty-something couples whooped with glee each time the ball rose over the net. Several young children played in the sand or on the jungle gyms, merry-go-rounds and other toys within a fenced-in, easily observed playground not far away. The soldier caught himself smiling at the kids. They were the future, and he hoped they would grow up to be as innocent as they were now. They were the reason he was there doing what he was doing. They were the reason for his very existence, he realized. The reason he fought the good fight against drug dealers, terrorists, robbers and killers.

Children. They were too young to have been corrupted. The innocent ones were why he risked his life every day. And why he was sometimes forced to take other lives, lives of men who had once been children themselves but who had lost not only their innocence but also their morality as their years were added. Men who had grown up to be animals rather than men.

Bolan shook a thin layer of windblown sand off his sunglasses and replaced them across his eyes. A pleasant ocean breeze was blowing in from the water, and he felt it cool his skin. He enjoyed these respites from his War Everlasting—they were too few and far between. His life was a hodgepodge of air flights, gun fights, strategic planning sessions and clandestine activities all running together in a continuous string until they were no longer single operations but only one huge mission.

Bolan lay back down on the recliner and closed his eyes. He didn't regret the life he had chosen. The fact was, he hadn't chosen it at all—it had chosen him. He had been given three gifts: talent, courage and a sense of right and wrong. He had taken the talent and, with hard work, developed it into skill. The courage of iron with which he'd been born had been forged into steel. He had forced himself to the edge so many times that it no longer seemed like courage when he stepped into battle, just second nature. And his innate sense of right and wrong had become even more clear and well-defined as he fought the evils of this world.

The soldier turned and glanced at the hotel. To his right, he saw a huge near-Olympic-size swimming pool. Beyond it was a smaller children's wading pool where the voices of more children could be heard giggling as they splashed one another. Far in the distance, on the other side of the road, was a small natural lake fed by a subterranean river. A soccer field and picnic area were set to one side of the lake, tennis courts on the other. He hadn't seen it, but the desk clerk who had checked him in a few hours earlier had assured him that the resort also boasted a waterfall hidden in the nearby jungle.

Bolan forced himself to turn back to the sea and lay back down. He was a man of action, and waiting for that action— although a necessary component of every operation—was always the hardest part. He had to remind himself now that choosing to do *nothing* for a purpose was doing *something*. And right now, he was doing exactly what he should be. He was looking like a man who was trying *a little too hard* to blend in with his surroundings.

The plan was simple enough. Since he was the man who had helped Jaime Pacheco kill Ricardo Toledo—the man whose profile from the videotape was now being shown all over Central and South America—it was only natural that he would go into hiding. And what better place than a resort hotel far from San José? What better place than the hotel where dozens of men like him came to meet unattached women?

But there was a difference between him and the other men. A difference not noticeable enough to make people stop and stare but one he hoped was sufficient enough to ensure that word of his presence got back to Francisco Gothe. Bolan took off the sunglasses again and glanced at his body. He wore only a swimsuit, and the muscles in his arms, chest and legs were hard—far different than most of the other men who paraded up and down the beach looking for women. But what stood out even more were the scars of past battles that decorated his skin like a history of the soldier's life: old bullet wounds, a blade that had passed close to an artery. The scars were so numerous he couldn't even remember the origin of many.

Bolan stood and walked down to the incoming tide, letting it curl gently around his ankles. In his peripheral vision, he saw a young man in his late teens walking by. The kid was staring at him, his face slightly confused. The boy could tell there was something different about the man he now saw wading in the ocean, but he wasn't sure what it was. It went beyond the scar tissue, Bolan knew. It was the different persona he projected from the life he had led, and continued to lead.

A school of several small fish swam quickly in to check out his ankles, then darted away again. The resort staff undoubtedly had orders to report suspicious characters who stayed at any of Gothe's resorts. Was he doing enough to draw their attention? And how much was too much? At what point would he stand out so much that the antiquity smuggler would suspect a setup?

Bolan studied a conch shell just beneath the surface of the water. There was no way to be certain how much attention was too much or too little. No distinct line to be careful not to cross. He would have to play it by ear. His gut instinct had begun telling him it was time to create at least some minor scene.

The soldier turned away from the ocean and walked back to his lounge chair. Again, he felt eyes upon him and glanced down the beach to see two young women in bikinis looking his way. They smiled, and he smiled back. But rather than pursue what was an obvious come-on, he gathered up his towel and walked back to the hotel.

Okay, he had been seen at the beach. Now it was time to make himself visible around the other areas of the resort, and hope that at least one of Gothe's employees was sharp enough to become suspicious. And he'd have to pray that suspicion led to a phone call to the smuggler.

Bolan entered the lobby and took the elevator to the second floor, using his key card to open the electronic lock on the door. He left the Spyderco Chinook folding knife hooked to his swimsuit as he slid out of it and tossed both on the bed. Beneath the suit, he had worn a small North American Arms .32 caliber automatic pistol in a Thunderwear holster—basically a pouch that rode just out of sight below the waistline. Dropping the little pistol on the bed as well, he entered the bathroom and stepped into the shower to wash off the sand.

Ten minutes later, he slipped into a pair of khaki cargo shorts and a white T-shirt. The Chinook was transferred to the shorts as he knelt to check under the bed.

The two pistols were right where he'd left them. The Beretta 93-R and Desert Eagle were his standard arms, and he had grown so accustomed to the Eagle on his hip and the 93-R in a shoulder rig under his left arm that he felt half-dressed without them. But he was playing a role right now, and they didn't quite fit in. He was Mike Belasko, wandering mercenary who had known Jaime Pacheco in Colombia and recently helped him assassinate the superintendent of the Costa Rican police. He was a man on the run, in hiding, and such a man wouldn't risk being caught with a firearm. At least not if he had any sense. Cops the world over took it personally when one of their own was killed, and the Costa Rican boys in blue would like nothing better than an excuse to kill their superintendent's assassin rather than arrest him.

A savvy merc would know this, and he would leave the guns at home. But that hardly meant a man of action would go unarmed completely. And knives were a different game. Particularly in a blade culture such as Central America.

The soldier replaced the guns and crawled a few feet along the side of the bed. He reached under the box springs and pulled out a large plastic equipment case. Flipping open the latches, he reached inside.

The Survival Sheath Systems double-shoulder rig was currently in use by U.S. Army Rangers at Fort Benning. The Green Beret version was designed to carry a large knife on one side and a fighting-utility tomahawk on the other. The one Bolan now took out of the equipment case, however, was a custom-made two-knife system designed especially for situations such as the one in which he now found himself. Under his left arm, where the Beretta usually rode, would hang a bowie knife with a twelve-inch blade. Designed by Laci Szabo, it was aptly named "Szabowie." On the other side, available for left-hand use and to counterbalance the Szabowie's weight, was a Keating Crossada. The Crossada was also twelve inches from guard to point but featured a double-edged spear-point blade.

Bolan had used both knives many times in the past. And together, they were the next best thing to firearms. At close range, they were equally deadly.

The soldier slid his arms into the rig. The grips of the big knives hung just below his waist. He covered them with the long tail of a Hawaiian shirt but left it unbuttoned for quick access to the blades. The shirt not only hid the big knives, it strengthened his American-tourist-in-Costa-Rica image.

A few minutes later Bolan left the hotel, strolling along the sidewalk toward a building adjacent to the office. He opened the door, stepped inside and was blasted in the face by refrigerated air. The hotel bar was dark, but as his eyes adjusted, he saw it was made up of two different rooms. Booths lined the walls of the room he had entered, with tables covering all but a small dance floor. The bar, and behind it a door that probably led to the kitchen and on into the restaurant, were against the wall to his left. As his pupils continued to adjust, he saw several couples in the dark booths. All looked American, or at least Anglo of some type. It was still midafternoon, and bar business was slow while the guests pursued other activities around the resort.

Bolan took a seat at the bar. There was another door on the opposite wall, and through it came drunken laughter and the sounds of a jukebox belting out Latino pop music. The voices he heard were all speaking Spanish.

A man wearing a white chef's jacket and very bad toupee came out through the kitchen door to stand behind the bar. "What may I bring you, señor?" he asked.

"Beer," Bolan answered.

"Dos Equis, Tecate, or—"

Bolan cut him off. "Tecate is fine."

The waiter went to work and a moment later a frosted mug, with a salted rim and a twist of lime hanging off the side, stood in front of Bolan. He lifted it and took a sip, then turned to face the room.

While he doubted there was serious segregation going on in the bar, it appeared that the tourists favored the room he was in while the locals stuck to the other side of the wall where the music was playing. People did that on their own sometimes, chose to stick with the people and things with which they were familiar rather than risk learning something new. The soldier slowly drank his beer, watching the couples in the booths. There were also two unattached females at one of the tables, and a lonely, hungry-looking male at the other end of the bar. The man had the scars of adolescent acne covering his face and wore a loose pink polo shirt. Bolan watched him observing the women, gradually working up his nerve. Finally he lifted the drink before him and walked over to the table with the gait of a man on his way to the gallows. He said something Bolan couldn't hear, and both women shook their heads.

His head, or at least his ego, having been neatly chopped off, the man returned to his seat at the end of the bar.

Bolan finished his beer and ordered another. So far, none of the staff seemed to be giving him a second glance. That was getting him nowhere. If the plan he and Pacheco had cooked up was to have a chance of succeeding, he needed word of his presence to get back to Gothe.

When the fresh Tecate arrived, Bolan picked it up and strolled through the door into the next room. He was surprised to see that there were perhaps two dozen people—mostly men with only a spattering of women—on the "native side" of the lounge.

In a movie, they would have all stopped speaking when the gringo walked in. That didn't happen. But they all looked up. None of the locals appeared too happy to see him.

Bolan wove his way through the tables, passing a half-drunken man who sat at a table with a startlingly beautiful young woman. The drunk kept trying to slobber something in her ear, and she kept pushing his face back with a bored look on her own. She glanced up at Bolan as he passed, the boredom suddenly vanishing.

Finding an empty booth in the corner, the soldier sat with his back to the wall and set his beer on the table. At the next booth was an elderly man who was two sips from passing out completely. His head rocked back and forth, his eyes slits. The booth just beyond his was empty, but at the next one were four men who might have been on their way to the set of some Mexican *bandido* movie. Long, drooping mustaches, unshaved faces and dirty clothes were the prominent aspects of their appearance. The two who faced Bolan stared at him with cold eyes.

Bolan pretended he hadn't seen them. The last thing he was looking for right now was a fight with the local tough guys.

Or was it?

The thought suddenly struck him like a sledgehammer between the eyes. It appeared that he was playing things too low-key if he wanted word of his presence to get back to Gothe. What better way to draw attention than a good, old-fashioned bar fight? He had no intention of hurting innocents, but the men at the booth trying to stare him down looked anything but innocent. Tourists might be in a bar during the middle of the afternoon, but when locals were there at the same time it meant they had no jobs. And there was no shortage of work in Costa Rica. The country had one of the strongest economies in Latin America. The men in the bar were there by choice. They had enough money to drink, and that meant an illegal income of some kind.

A few bumps and bruises wouldn't hurt them at all.

The Executioner took a drink of his beer and looked out over the room. It was then that he saw the woman staring at him. The drunk was still sitting at her table but had given up trying to whisper in her ear. He now lay across the table with his head on his folded arms.

When the woman saw that she had caught Bolan's eye, she smiled seductively, then blew him a kiss.

Bolan stifled a laugh. There were lots of ways to start a bar fight, but this was a true classic. He smiled back encouragingly.

The woman wasted no time rising from her seat and making her way toward his booth. The drunk looked up suddenly, surprised, trying to remember where he was, what was happening, and probably even *who* he was. His glazed eyes tried to follow the woman, finally coming into semifocus as she slid into the booth next to Bolan and placed a hand on the soldier's thigh.

"Hello," the woman said.

"Hello," Bolan answered back. He studied her quickly. She was younger than he'd thought as he passed the table earlier. And prettier. There was little of the hard, worldly look that prostitutes picked up after a few years of selling their bodies. And she was clean, smelling of both soap and a light perfume. Huge golden hoop earrings hung from her ears, and she had the high cheekbones of a native Costa Rican. Her complexion, however, was even lighter than the Executioner's weather-tanned skin.

"My name is Rocio," she said.

"I'm Mike."

"Mike and Rocio. They sound good together, no?" Rocio

batted her eyes at him, and her smile became even more se-
ductive. "Are you looking for a companion, Mike?" she asked.

"Maybe so," the soldier said. He had kept one eye on the
table and now saw the drunk staggering to his feet. The man
began weaving toward the corner of the room, too inebriated
to even show much anger. He was working on tradition rather
than rage. Somewhere, sloshing around in the alcohol-soaked
brain, he remembered that he was a man, and that custom re-
quired he not allow another man to take a woman from him.
But his heart wasn't in it.

Bolan frowned as the man fell against a chair, dropped to
one knee, then struggled back to his feet. This was not what
he was looking for. He wanted word of his presence to get
back to Gothe, but not at the expense of some pathetic drunk.
He'd have to find another way to draw attention.

Turning to Rocio, he said, "I think your boyfriend wants
you back."

"No," she said. "Ricky is not my boyfriend. He is a drunk-
ard. I prefer you."

By now the drunk was almost to their booth. Rocio was between him and Bolan and, even in the state he was in, Ricky
was capable of hurting her. Bolan half lifted the woman out
of her seat and onto her feet, standing up himself. Rocio let
out a small squeak of protest but stopped when he deposited
her on the other side of the table. He smiled. "Just for now,"
he whispered as the drunken man neared. "Until we settle
this." He sat back down across from her.

Rocio's eyes flared with excitement as Ricky continued to
wobble their way. Two men were about to fight over her, and
the thought seemed to arouse her.

The man she had called Ricky finally made it to the table
and reached down, steadying himself with both hands. He
mumbled something incoherent. Bolan couldn't even be sure
it was Spanish.

"Go on," the soldier said. "Or sit with us and I'll buy you
a drink."

Ricky mumbled again. Then, with no more speed than a sloth, his arm went back behind him. Again, as if it were in slow-motion replay, the man's fist came toward Bolan.

Bolan caught the man's wrist and held it. "Go back to your table, Ricky," he said. He dropped the man's wrist.

Ricky swung again, this time so wildly that he did a full 360-degree spin, lost his balance and went sailing into the closest table. He fell between two men who had been sitting there, splashing beer across both.

The two men threw him off the table, then stood and turned toward the Executioner.

At the same time, the four men at the booth just down from him rose to their feet.

Bolan stood. This was more like what he had hoped for. A fistfight wouldn't hurt anyone unnecessarily and would create enough of a scene to get back to the owner.

Except a fistfight didn't seem to be what the others had in mind. As the two men at the table and the four from the booth started toward him, the Executioner saw the gleam of cold steel in their hands.

THE RULES OF THE GAME had changed, and changed suddenly.

Bolan stood his ground, his arms at his sides ready to draw his hidden weapons. Perhaps it was his size compared to the smaller men. More likely it was the fact that, in spite of being outnumbered six to one and apparently unarmed, he radiated no fear. In any case, something caused the men to suddenly halt in their progression toward the corner booth.

One man, with a beer belly hanging over his belt and sweat staining his faded blue work shirt, stepped forward. He smelled of body odor and beer, and in his hand he held a wickedly pointed dagger. "Do you think you can take us all, gringo?" he asked.

"Yes," Bolan said in return. "In fact, I'm pretty sure of it."

The answer took the other man aback. "Do you know who I am?" he demanded.

"Just a fat man with a knife is all I see."

The evil grin that had covered the man's face faded slowly into a snarl. "Tell him who I am," he shouted over his shoulder.

A tall, reedlike sycophantic follower of the obvious leader stepped forward. "He is Manuel Antonio Montoya," the thin man said in a practiced voice. "He is the fiercest fighter on the Osa Peninsula."

The Executioner couldn't keep a smile off his face at the obviously rehearsed lines. They were little different than those often used by playground bullies. "Good thing I'm not from the Osa Peninsula," Bolan said. "If I was, I guess I wouldn't stand a chance."

Montoya growled, a low, throaty, animal-like sound. "Now do you think you stand a chance, gringo?" he demanded.

"What I think," Bolan said, "is that if you and the rest of your little playmates don't put your toys away, I'm going to lose my temper."

Angry blood was rushing to the face of the man with the dagger. From the other men came sounds of astonishment. Montoya was obviously not used to being talked to like that. "Empty your pockets, gringo," he said through gritted teeth. "I don't want your blood on money that is about to become mine."

The Executioner smiled again. "What do you do for a living, Manuel?"

The question seemed so out of place that it caught Montoya off guard again. The thin man next to him answered. "He kills people."

Bolan couldn't be sure if that was the truth or just more barroom bluff. He glanced down at Rocio, who was looking up at him nervously. She nodded. The excitement was gone from her eyes. Her game had escalated past the point of fun, and she was afraid she was about to lose what had looked like a good meal ticket. Turning, she said, "Manuel, please—"

"Shut up!" Montoya screamed at her. "Or when I am finished with this gringo, I will cut out your tongue!" He turned his attention back to the Executioner. "I will give you one more chance to empty your pockets," he said. "You must decide which you want to keep, your money or your *cojones*."

"Please..." Rocio pleaded, looking up at the Executioner. "He has done this to men before—cut off their *cojones*. People say he collects them."

Bolan ignored the woman. Still looking at Montoya, he shook his head. "I think I'll keep both," he said. Crossing his arms suddenly in front of him, he drew the Szabowie in his right hand, the Crossada in his left.

A collective gasp went up around the room when the men saw the size of the blades. Their visual impact alone caused the two men who had been seated at the table to drop their own knives and back away.

A moment of indecision fell over Montoya's face. Bolan had no doubt now that what Rocio said was true. The man was a killer and a sadist. But like most bullies, he was also a coward. The soldier could see it in his eyes.

Montoya turned to one of his men, almost as tall and broad-shouldered as Bolan. The man held a large Mexican bowie in his hand. "Jorge," Montoya ordered, "end this. He isn't worth my time."

An evil gleam filled Jorge's eyes as he stepped forward, crouching.

Bolan didn't move.

Jorge began to move in a half circle, first to his right, then to his left. He smiled in pleasure, showing two uneven rows of teeth as well as a large hole where his front two had been knocked out. He held the bowie knife low in his right hand, across his body. It flicked out tauntingly several times, but still the Executioner remained motionless.

"Aye, Manuel," Jorge said. "Perhaps I will cut off his *cojones* myself and feed them to my dog."

The comment brought laughter from the other men. But it was not all in mirth. Several of the chuckles sounded more nervous than gleeful.

Finally Jorge took a quick step in with his right foot and brought the big knife across in a slashing movement. Bolan met it with the flat of the Szabowie, and the clang of steel against steel rang throughout the bar. The Executioner sidestepped and then parried downward with the Crossada as Jorge recovered and came in with a low underhand sweep. This time, when the weapons collided, Bolan slid the Crossada slightly forward, catching the blade in the "devil's horn" guard and Spanish notch. He twisted the huge dagger, and the cheap steel of Jorge's blade snapped in two, leaving what had been a ten-inch blade a ragged-pointed six.

The humiliation of his defeat enraged Jorge, and he lost all control. With the roar of an angry lion he moved forward, cutting wildly with the shortened blade. Bolan retreated two steps under the assault, then suddenly dropped low. Bringing both of his big knives across his body toward the center, he caught Jorge at the wrist with the Szabowie and at the elbow with the Crossada. For a moment, the Mexican bowie seemed frozen in place. Then Jorge screamed at the top of his lungs as two wide, deep slices appeared—one across the back of his wrist, the other at the elbow joint. There was a brief second before the blood began to shoot out, and during that time Bolan glimpsed white bone through both gaps.

The geysers of crimson brought another scream to Jorge's lips. The knife in his hand fell to the floor with a loud clank as he leaped back in horror. His left hand came across to grab his mutilated right, then stopped in midair as if what remained of the limb was too profane to even touch. His eyes opened wide as he stared at the Executioner in disbelief.

Bolan met his stare. "I'd suggest direct pressure and a quick trip to the nearest doctor," he said.

Jorge wasn't the only horrified man in the room. The other men around him began moving back, their blades in front of them more out of habit than hope. A few seconds of silence passed, then one man sheathed his knife, turned and bolted for the door. It didn't take long for the others to follow. In seconds, only Bolan, Rocio and Montoya remained in the room.

Montoya dropped to his knees, his dagger falling before him. "Please," he blubbered out. "I didn't know you...I didn't know...."

"You didn't know I wasn't easy prey?" Bolan asked in disgust. "Is that what you're trying to say, Montoya?"

"I...didn't mean to...I didn't—"

Bolan lifted the Crossada high over his head and Montoya's eyes followed it. "Good God, no!" he screamed.

The Executioner brought down the heavy spear-point blade, twisting the edge at the last second. The flat of the blade struck Montoya between the eyes, knocking him cold.

Bolan walked to the bar, grabbed a bar rag and wiped down both blades before resheathing them under his shirt. He had done what he had come to do. He now had little doubt that word of this incident would go straight to Gothe.

And he had taken the fight out of quite a few low-level predators at the same time.

As he left the bar, the soldier heard footsteps behind him. He looked over his shoulder to see Rocio following, her face a combination of shock, fear and interest.

Bolan turned back and continued toward the building where his room was located. By the time he'd reached the door to the stairway, the footsteps behind him had drawn up to his side.

3

Francisco Gothe held the phone tighter to his ear and felt the skin tighten above both eyes. "Tell me more," he said into the instrument.

"That is all there is to tell, Don Francisco," Benito said on the other end of the line. "It was over almost as quickly as it had begun. But I assure you the big man was American. And while I don't know who he is, there was something vaguely familiar about him."

Gothe nodded to himself. Although he said nothing to the effect, he knew exactly why the big American looked familiar to the bartender at his hotel. The gringo should look familiar—his profile had been on every newscast since Toledo had been killed. It hadn't really registered in Benito's brain, but he had seen the big man on television—first shooting Toledo, and then shooting at the very man who held the video camera.

"Thank you, Benito," Gothe said into the phone. "You will find a little surprise in your next paycheck."

"Thank you, Don Francisco," the bartender said in an excited voice. "But it is not necessary. You are a great man to work for. And it's part of my job."

Gothe shook his head at the man's unashamed flattery. Old age was making him more irritable than he had once been, and he had far less patience with such phony adulation. Or perhaps it was the transparency of the statement that irritated him—such an obvious attempt to influence the bonus check. He decided to teach Benito a lesson. "All right, if you insist," he said. "I shall send only your regular salary. But please accept my most gracious thank-you for your good work."

There was a long pause at the end of the line. Then, in a weak voice, Benito said, "You are welcome, Don Francisco...of course I can always use a little extra money...as you mentioned. If you believe I deserve it."

"Then I will send it," Gothe said. "And Benito?"

"Yes, Don Francisco?"

"Next time, a simple thank-you will be sufficient."

"Yes, sir."

Gothe heard the man hang up quickly before he lost his bonus again. He replaced the receiver in the cradle and swiveled away from the bar to face the den, frowning. He couldn't be one hundred percent certain, but the man who had been involved in the disturbance at the hotel sounded like the American Pacheco had used on the Toledo hit. If that was the case, they had trouble.

The antiquities smuggler sighed. The stupid gringo should have been out of the country by now. Why had he stayed? Perhaps he feared tightening of security at the borders. But if that was the case, and he had chosen to remain in Costa Rica until the heat died down, he should be keeping a much lower profile. Getting involved in a bar fight could bring the attention of the police, and not *all* of them were on Gothe's payroll. Besides, when it came to a murder as highly publicized and as personal as Toledo's death, all bets were off. Even some of his own cops might decide to cross the line.

Gothe turned back and faced the mirror behind the bar. His face looked long and drawn. Yes, he was forced to admit, he was getting older. And he was tired. Tired of worrying. The fun had gone out of his work. The adrenaline pump that used to come during such times of crisis was gone. Now, he felt only stress.

He stared at the wrinkled face in the mirror. "You have enough money," he told it. "Or at least you will soon. It's time you retired."

Gothe dropped his gaze from the mirror, focusing his eyes on the bottles behind the bar as he thought. What was the worst-case scenario? If the man at the resort really was this American, and if the police took notice of him, and if they identified him as one of Toledo's killers, what could happen? First, that was a very large number of *ifs*. But what if the long shot came through and the *maybes* turned into certainties?

Drumming his fingers on the bar top, Gothe felt his frown deepen. Pacheco had assured him his friend didn't know enough to lead the police back to him. But what if the information he told them was added to some other evidence they had collected and the sum of the parts pointed to Gothe?

It could spell disaster. And this was no time in his life to be careless. Loose ends couldn't be allowed to dangle.

Reaching to his side, Gothe lifted the phone off the bar again and tapped in the number to the overseers' dormitory. Mantara answered on the second ring.

"I must see you at once," Gothe said. "Bring Lima and Pacheco with you." He hung up without waiting for an answer.

The smuggler's thoughts returned to the problem as he waited for the men to arrive. It was stretching things to think that all the *ifs* he had considered earlier might happen. An even longer stretch to think that the police had other evidence. But the American knew about Jaime Pacheco, and that was bad enough. Gothe had big plans for Pacheco, and they didn't include the young man standing trial for killing the superintendent of police.

A knock came at the door and Gothe called out, "Come in." Mantara led the way into the den. He was followed by Lima and finally Pacheco. The smuggler waved them toward the same couch and chairs where they had all sat the day before. Gothe stayed on his stool.

As soon as the men were seated, Gothe swiveled to face Pacheco. "I have just received some very disturbing news."

Pacheco frowned. "Sir?" he said. "How can I help?"

Once again, Gothe congratulated himself for choosing this young man. His first impulse was to help. Perhaps this desire came from self-interest rather than loyalty, but at least he didn't immediately begin to squirm nervously in his seat the way Lima and Mantara were now doing. That told Gothe that Pacheco had nothing to hide from him. It also made him wonder what the other two men had been up to. Well, whatever it was could be of little consequence. Neither of them was smart enough to get into too much trouble as long as he kept an eye on them.

"A big American was involved in a barroom fight at one of my resorts," Gothe told Pacheco. "He sounds very much like your friend—Belasko. What was his first name?"

"Mike."

"Yes, Mike. It sounds made up."

"It probably is," Pacheco said. "As I told you before, it is the man I know, not the name."

Gothe shrugged. "Please describe him. We saw only a quick glimpse of his profile on the tape."

"He is a big man," Pacheco stated. "Muscular. Dark hair, dark features, and he has the hard face of a man who has lived a hard life."

"That is very much the way the bartender described him," Gothe said. "He also said he saw this man on the beach. Would Belasko have any distinguishing marks he would have noticed?"

Gothe noted that there was a slight hesitation now in Pacheco's response. Good. Again, it proved how smart the young man was. He had already figured out where all this was leading and his loyalties were torn. The test of loyalty—true loyalty—was about to come.

When the slight pause was over, Pacheco answered, "He has been wounded many times. The scars are quite evident."

Gothe smiled inwardly but didn't let it show on his face. "If it is your friend," he said, "he didn't check into the resort under the name Mike Belasko."

"No," Pacheco said. "He wouldn't do that after the Toledo hit. Do you know what name he used?"

Now, it was Gothe's turn to hesitate. Earlier, he had asked Pacheco to describe the American rather than describe the man himself and then have Pacheco confirm it. He had done so on purpose, to keep Pacheco from denying whatever description was given to protect his friend. But now he decided to try another strategy. He intended to pursue this matter regardless of what Pacheco said now, so it would be even another test of loyalty. "He is registered under the name Michael Blanski," he said.

A sad look came over Pacheco's face. He shook his head back and forth. "Yes," he said. "It's a name he used sometimes in Colombia." He paused again, then almost in a whisper, said, "It is him."

Gothe actually felt sorry for his new protégé. "It is difficult sometimes in this business of ours," he said. "Sometimes we must make decisions. Decisions that are not pleasant. But you have made the correct one." Pacheco was looking down at the floor, and Gothe waited a moment before going on. "You know what must be done, then?"

Slowly Pacheco looked up. "I fought many battles with this man," he said. "But yes, I know what must be done."

"And you are willing to do it?"

A quick flash of fear came across Pacheco's eyes. Then he turned to face Lima and Mantara on the couch. "I would prefer that this assignment be carried out by one of them," he said.

"Of course you would," Gothe said, his voice suddenly going hard. "But what if I were to order that you take care of this problem yourself? As a test of loyalty?"

This time there was no hesitation. Jaime Pacheco looked him squarely in the eye and said, "I will put two bullets in his head, then cut his throat to make sure he is dead," he said. "But only if you order it. The man has been my friend."

The answer surprised even Gothe. He found himself nodding, then smiling. He thought back to the way Pacheco had answered the questions earlier. The young man hadn't wanted to give up his friend. Who would? But he had done so anyway. "You have already passed all necessary tests of loyalty," Gothe said and saw the relief come into Pacheco's eyes.

He turned to the couch. "Mantara will take care of this problem."

Mantara's lips curled in an evil grin. "Gladly," he said, turning the smile of triumph toward Pacheco. "And I won't have to hire outside help to get the job done."

Pacheco avoided his eyes.

"Then get on with it," Gothe said, waving a hand toward the door. "You and Lima are dismissed. By this time tomorrow I want Belasko, or whatever his real name is, to be as dead as Ricardo Toledo."

The two men stood.

A sudden idea hit Gothe and he said, "Wait." Moving around from the front of the bar to the back, he found the leather badge case with Toledo's identification on one of the lower shelves. "I had planned to keep this as a souvenir," he said. "But I think it better that you leave it where it will be found with Belasko's body." He tossed the case across the room, and Mantara caught it. Without another word, the two men left the den.

Gothe stayed behind the bar but waved Pacheco forward, indicating that the younger man should take a seat. "What will you have?" he asked.

Pacheco's eyes trailed along the bottles lined up in front of the mirror. "Campari," he said when his eyes had finally stopped. "With soda, please."

Quickly Gothe poured two glasses half full of Campari and

added a touch of soda from a pressurized tap. He set them on the bar, then came around and took the stool next to Pacheco. "We must talk," he said. "I have plans for you. Big plans."

The smile on Pacheco's face hadn't gone away. And now, it grew even wider. "I suspected as much," he said. "There are rumors that you plan to retire. I don't blame you. You have worked hard, and you deserve a life of ease with no worries."

Gothe lifted his glass to his lips and tasted the bitter, berry-flavored liquor. "They are more than just rumors," he said. "They are truth." He looked at Pacheco. "You wouldn't try to talk me out of it? You wouldn't say, 'But Don Francisco, you are still a young and vital man! You have many good years left ahead of you!' You wouldn't say such things?"

Pacheco laughed out loud. "Would you believe me if I did?"

Gothe joined in the laughter. "No. It's what Mantara or Lima would say."

"If they could think of it."

Gothe lifted his glass slightly in salute. "Yes," he said. "Point taken. Intent understood and agreed with." He set the glass on the bar again. "Which is why I will need someone else to take over this operation. Someone I can trust, and someone whose shoulder I don't have to look over constantly to ensure that he doesn't run the business into the ground, get caught by the authorities, or steal me blind."

"If you were forced to do that," Pacheco said, "you would do well just to stay here yourself."

"My thoughts exactly," Gothe said. "Tell me, what are your thoughts on the matter?"

Pacheco closed his eyes in thought for a moment, then opened them again. "Neither Lima or Mantara would double-cross you," he said. "Not because they are honest but because they would be afraid to do so. But neither man has a mind for business, and yes, I could see them behind bars, with warrants out for you wherever you were—within a month."

Gothe shook his head and chuckled. "Yes, I am afraid you

are right. They are too smart to steal from me but not smart enough to run the business. What I need is a man who is both trustworthy and clever."

Pacheco took a drink from his glass. "Someone to continue things while you are lying somewhere on the beach with a bevy of teenaged girls?"

Gothe laughed again. "Perhaps not an entire *bevy*," he said. "As you pointed out, I am older now." His tone suddenly grew serious. "I will allow Mantara and Lima to stay on for the time being. And for our purposes, I think it best that they believe they will be the ones who take over the operations upon my retirement."

"A wise decision," Pacheco said, and Gothe could tell the younger man had picked up on the word *our* rather than *my* when he'd spoken of purposes. He looked directly at Pacheco. "The man I actually leave in charge will have to decide what to do with Mantara and Lima after I'm gone."

Pacheco's eyes danced mischievously. "I suspect that man already knows how to handle them," he said. He lifted his glass. "So why don't we drink to it, Don Francisco. For I think we both know exactly who that man should be."

THE EXECUTIONER WASN'T thrilled about having Rocio around. But he wasn't sure quite how to get rid of her, either. He'd slept on the sofa in his suite, while she took the bed. She was terrified that Montoya would find her and beat her.

Bolan heard a soft snore and glanced toward the lounge chair next to his. The attractive young Costa Rican woman lay in the sun, her eyes closed behind sunglasses that had fallen down over her nose to reveal her eyelids.

Bolan had positioned them that morning on another section of the beach—an area reserved for adults only. He had picked the location because it afforded an excellent view of the office area. It was close to the jungle but not so close that anyone was likely to sneak up on them unnoticed. Rocio had taken advantage of the adults-only area to work on an overall tan. She had worn only the flimsiest of bikinis to the beach, and the top had been discarded as soon as they hit the sand.

Bolan frowned as his eyes scanned from the resort office across the sand to the jungle, then turned back toward the sea. The woman had followed him back to his room after the incident with Manuel Montoya and his cronies, refusing to leave his side for fear that Montoya would take his anger out on her when he regained consciousness. The soldier knew that her fears were more than just fantasy. She had been involved in the fight, if only remotely, and a coward like Montoya was indeed likely to turn his frustrations on her if he saw her. Such behavior was a trademark of such men. So Bolan had allowed the young woman to spend the night in his room. Besides, it would have looked strange if he'd refused the offer. He was supposed to be different enough from the other single men at the resort to draw Gothe's attention. But he wasn't supposed to be *that* different.

Rocio opened her eyes and caught him scanning the area again. But the young woman misinterpreted his objective. "I don't think Manuel will come back while you are here," she said.

Bolan decided it best to play along. It was the perfect cover for the fact that his eyes continually searched the grounds. "Can't be too careful."

"No, you can't," Rocio agreed. "But Manuel has seen your prowess. He would never face you one-on-one. He is mean, he is dirty and he is a killer. But he isn't stupid."

When the soldier didn't answer, she changed the subject. "Tell me about yourself," she said.

Bolan shrugged. "Not much to tell."

"That, I don't believe," Rocio purred. "There is a mystery to you. There are many stories you could tell."

The soldier changed the subject. "What were you doing in that dive with those drunks yesterday?" he said. "It doesn't fit you."

Rocio shrugged, and her breasts bounced up and down. "I

usually work the other side," she said. "The tourists. With the money. Yesterday, business was dead so I went next door for a drink." She laughed. "Did you know the same drink costs twice as much on the tourist side of the wall?"

Bolan laughed with her. "No, but I'm not surprised."

"Now," Rocio said, "do not ask the question you are wondering."

"What's that?"

"If *I* cost more on one side than the other."

Bolan shrugged. "That wasn't what I was thinking."

"Well, I will tell you anyway. I don't work the other side. They have no money. And they are all like Montoya. The worst men the Osa Peninsula has to offer."

"This is none of my business," Bolan said.

Rocio's face grew serious. "You don't hate me?"

"Hate you?" Bolan asked, genuinely surprised. "Why would I hate you?"

"Sometimes men hate me," Rocio said, "because of what I am. Oh, they will pay me money to sleep with me, but they hate me nonetheless. They hate me because I remind them that they need me. And that makes them hate themselves as well as me."

Her words sent the soldier's mind back over the years, to the beginning of his one-man war against injustice. He thought of his father, hopelessly indebted to Mafia loan sharks, and that same crime family forcing his sister into prostitution to pay the debt. When his father finally learned of it, he had lost his mind. He'd killed Bolan's sister, then his mother, then himself.

The Executioner, in turn, had killed the loan sharks who had begun the chain of terror. But, as the whole story had unfolded to him, he had learned much about human nature. He had learned that circumstances sometimes forced people to do things they had never dreamed they would do. His sister had prostituted herself to save their father. She wouldn't have done so for any other reason.

Bolan had known many other prostitutes since that time.

They all had a story. They all had a reason. And they were all human beings.

"I don't hate you," Bolan said again. "And I don't judge you, Rocio."

The woman smiled.

They dropped into silence for a few minutes. Bolan turned back to the sea. He liked the young woman and hoped she might be one of the few who somehow found her way out of the business she was in. Maybe that would happen before the whole seedy atmosphere hardened her to the world, and she lost the spark that he found so appealing. He wished there was some way he could help her. She was smart and capable of a much more productive life than she was leading now.

Rocio finally broke the silence, rolling over onto her side to face him. "You asked me a question and I answered. Now I want to ask you one. Why do you carry those big knives?"

"For men like Montoya," Bolan said simply.

"That wasn't the first fight you have ever been in."

"No," Bolan conceded.

"You could easily have killed them all."

"Yes," Bolan said. "But how easy it would have been I have no way of knowing."

"So, why didn't you?" Rocio asked.

Bolan shrugged. "There was no need to."

Rocio licked her lips provocatively. "Yes," she said. "I think there are many stories you could tell. But you won't."

Bolan's eyes made a quick sweep of his surroundings again. "You are good."

The Executioner didn't know exactly what to say so he said nothing.

"You are a good man. You have a good heart." In his peripheral vision, Bolan saw a lone tear begin to trail down her face. "I am not used to men who are so good." She rolled back on the lounger and closed her eyes again.

Bolan continued to scan the area every few seconds, moving only his eyes rather than his head. He kept particular watch on the cars coming and going from the office area. Most were patrons of the resort, either checking in or checking out. But every so often, lone men came, stayed a few minutes, then left again. He had no idea what their business was, and right now he didn't care. He did his best to keep track of them as they moved. But it was impossible—there were too many, and his view was only partial.

The soldier had far more serious problems to deal with at the moment. Like trying to stay alive when the man, or men, sent by Gothe came to kill him. And Rocio had added to his problems. He knew Gothe would waste no time eliminating any source who might lead authorities back to Pacheco, and perhaps even him.

Someone would come to try to kill him. Soon.

So Bolan's original plan had been to spend the day on the beach—far away from the innocent tourists who might get caught in a cross fire if something went down in the hotel. But what to do with Rocio? If he abandoned her completely, she was likely to run into Montoya again. But if she stayed with him, Gothe's man might decide to kill her, too. The only solution he had been able to come up with was to allow her to remain at his side until he saw the first signs of an attack. Then he would have to get rid of the young woman, and hope she saw nothing of Montoya until things had cooled down. At that point, the local ruffian would definitely be the lesser of the two dangers.

Bolan stared out at the deep-blue sea in front of them. He literally felt caught between it and the devil in relation to Rocio.

He settled back in the lounge recliner and let a hand drop over the side. Beneath the towel, and on top of his shirt, he felt the hard steel of the Beretta 93-R. He'd had the devil of a time getting it, and the Desert Eagle, out of the room and down to the beach without Rocio seeing it. She hadn't batted an eye, however, when he'd wrapped the Szabowie and Crossada in another towel. Those weapons, she had already seen. And blades she was used to. But the soldier worried that the sight of a machine pistol like the Beretta or the huge size of the .44 Magnum would send her scampering to the police to report a terrorist.

The sound of another car entering the driveway to the office caught his attention and Bolan looked that way. A black-and-white police car parked just outside the lobby, and two uniformed men got out and entered the resort. Bolan doubted it had anything to do with him, or the problem with Montoya and his men the day before. First, both officers were strolling along as if they hadn't a care in the world—one of them was even whistling. Second, men like Manuel Montoya didn't report incidents such as that to the police. The police undoubtedly knew him, and had he told them what happened they would have laughed in his face, considering his humiliation and Jorge's injuries as long overdue street justice.

Bolan heard a soft noise to his other side and turned to glance into the jungle. A small mixed breed dog was rooting after a lizard or some other unseen prey. He turned back to the office in time to see the two cops leave again. Both men were carrying white envelopes. It didn't surprise him to learn that the resort was one of Gothe's payoff spots for local police.

Bolan watched the cops get back in their car. He wondered briefly who Gothe would send. It would have to be Lima, Mantara or Pacheco himself. If it was Pacheco, they had problems. They would have to go up to Bolan's room and come up with a backup plan. Fast.

The police car drove away. Bolan could only hope that Pacheco's skills of subtle persuasion were as good as Toledo had said they were. Somehow, the Costa Rican undercover expert had to maneuver things so that he was not the one sent to execute the Executioner.

Bolan and Rocio lay silently for another hour, with Rocio dozing off and on and Bolan continuing to keep watch on the parking lot, beach and jungle. In addition to the two pistols and big knives, he had the North American Arms auto pistol in his Thunderwear and the Spyderco Chinook clipped to his suit. He was ready.

But he was still worried about Rocio. He had grown to like the young woman. He didn't think whoever Gothe sent would try anything there on the beach. There were too many witnesses around, and it would be far safer to just wait until he returned to his room and surprise him there. But there was always the chance that he was wrong, and that wouldn't be the way it would go down. The killer might decide to take him out from the jungle with a rifle. And there was always the chance that Rocio would get in the way and catch a bullet meant for him.

Bolan was considering this problem when something suddenly registered in his brain. It took a moment for him to define what it was, and during that moment he turned toward the jungle, expecting to see the dog again.

But he didn't. He saw nothing.

Then, just as suddenly as it had invaded his thought, he realized what it was. A strange scent was drifting through the air on the breeze. A scent that shouldn't be where it was.

Aftershave lotion. And it was coming from the jungle.

Bolan rose to his feet, quickly wrapped the weapons up in the towels and woke Rocio. "Time to get up," he said, taking her by the hand.

The beautiful young woman opened her eyes. "I was dreaming," she said. "About you."

Bolan glanced quickly toward the jungle again, making it look like a natural movement. "Come on," he said, tugging her to her feet. "We've got to go. Now."

Bolan wrapped an arm around her waist and began guiding her away from the beach toward the building. He needed her not only away from the jungle but away from himself. He wasn't worried any more that a sniper's bullet would come out of the trees—if that was going to happen, it would have happened already. No, whoever had approached the resort through the foliage simply wanted to get a better look at him. The killer was going to wait on the hit itself. Probably go to the room as Bolan had guessed.

Stopping suddenly, Bolan turned to Rocio. "Where's the nearest store?" he asked.

"There is a small one here at the resort," she said. "A much better one a mile down the road. Why—"

Bolan reached into the pocket of his suit and pulled out a roll of bills, stuffing them into her hand. "Go get us some wine," he said. "Get some cheese and bread, too, and—"

"What kind of wine do you—"

"I don't care," Bolan said quickly. "Whatever you like. And get anything else you like. Take your time. I want to take a shower and then a nap."

Rocio looked puzzled and even slightly hurt. "But I thought—"

Bolan didn't have time to spare her feelings. "Go on," he said, pushing her gently away.

Rocio took several steps and then turned back to face him. Her expression was that of an unhappy little girl. "You...*do* want me to come back, don't you?" she asked quietly.

The soldier hated to hurt her, but what was about to happen at the resort stood the chance of hurting her far worse. "No," he said. "Don't come back. You're on your own."

He turned away and started for the hotel before he was forced to look at her face.

FRANCO MANTARA HAD BEEN thirteen years old when he killed his first man. The bandit had crept into his mother's house in the middle of the night, pocketed the small amount of money hidden in the fruit jar under the sink and been carrying out their food when Mantara had awakened. When the man saw him, he kicked the boy in the groin. The kick had hurt, but it hadn't stopped Mantara. He had grabbed the closest weapon—a frying pan—and beaten the man to death.

His mother had found her son on his hands and knees in the kitchen, vomiting on the floor. She had taken Mantara to the police, who ruled the death justifiable. They had gone directly from the police station to the church, where a priest heard the young man's confession and told him the same thing—the killing hadn't been a sin in God's eyes. He had only been defending the life God had given him.

Mantara had killed many other men since then, and few could be called justified except by the wildest stretch of imagination. But he always found a way because something had happened to him the first time he had drawn blood. He had liked it. And now, it was no trick at all to find a good reason to kill a man.

His reason this day was that it was his job.

Mantara walked along the hallway as confidently as if he owned the resort himself, a round tray bearing a silver champagne bucket in his hands. In the side pocket of his white room-service jacket was the extra key card he had obtained from the desk clerk. Hidden beneath the light linen jacket, thrust into his belt at his side, was a 9 mm Kahr Arms ultra-compact pistol. But he had no plans to use the semiautomatic weapon—not unless he absolutely had to. It was far too noisy. If all went well, he would simply knock on the door, greet the American with a smile and tell him his champagne had been iced down and was ready—then ask where should he set it down. Mantara was counting on the uniform to give him the half-second delay he would need to slide the fourteen-inch Spanish bayonet hidden beneath the tray into the man's heart.

Quick, neat. And a minimum of blood. He could then simply push the tray, champagne, bucket and body back into the room, close the door and disappear.

But Franco Mantara hadn't survived the life he had led over the years by counting on things always going as planned. Which was why he had also armed himself with the gun and the extra key to the room. Just in case.

Gothe's man stopped in front of the room and glanced up at the peephole beneath the number. He drew a deep breath. He wasn't really nervous. The extra oxygen was needed by the adrenaline that was suddenly pumping through his veins. It was the same excitement he had felt when he'd killed that first man so many years ago, but it no longer made him sick.

Now, he was more likely to have a tingling in his groin when it was over. Not an erection, and Mantara refused to allow himself to think that the feeling was evenly remotely connected to sex, even though he always visited a prostitute named Regina as soon as possible after killing a man. It was just his way of celebrating.

Mantara knocked softly on the door and waited. He got no response from inside the room. He knocked again, louder this time, but again there was nothing. After the third time, he shifted the weight of the tray to his right hand, making sure to keep the bayonet handle in place. With his left, he fished the key card out of his jacket and inserted it into the lock. A green light appeared as he heard a click.

Cautiously, fully prepared to hand out lavish apologies and claim he had planned to leave the champagne on the table should the room be occupied, Mantara entered the room. The maids hadn't been there yet, and the bed was unmade. He checked the bathroom and found it as empty as the bedroom, then walked to the sliding glass door that led to a common balcony around the building. It was locked from the inside.

Turning back toward the door, a flash of red on the crumpled sheets caught his eye. He moved closer, at first thinking it was blood. Had the American been wounded in the encounter the day before? If so, the bartender hadn't reported it. As he neared the bed, Mantara saw that the red was not blood at all. Lipstick. He grinned to himself.

So, the gringo had found himself a woman. Good for him. Mantara hoped it had been good. For it would be the last he ever had.

Still carrying the tray, Mantara exited the room, walked to the elevator and returned to the lobby. He carried the tray back behind the front desk and disappeared into the rear offices. Leone Jimenez, the manager of the Santuario de Agua, still sat nervously behind his desk where Mantara had left him a few moments ago. He had never met the man before but had taken an immediate dislike to him. The fact was, Mantara knew, he instinctively disliked all of the employees Gothe retained in positions within his legitimate businesses. They all knew who, and what, was behind the front operations, and they all cooperated as Jiminez was doing now when legitimate and illegitimate overlapped. But some, like Jiminez, resented the intrusions and maintained an aloof attitude when he or Lima came around. Such hypocrisy infuriated Mantara. Did they think they would even exist without men such as himself?

Mantara set the tray on the table and closed the office door. He began undressing.

"Did everything go well?" Jiminez asked. "Whatever business you had, I mean?"

Mantara turned to face the man as he slid back into the navy blue walking shorts and pin-striped shirt he had worn to the hotel. He glared at the frightened manager behind the desk and said, "You have nothing to clean up, if that is what you are asking." He paused, buttoning his shirt, then added, "Ask me no more questions. Understand?"

"Yes." The little man drummed his fingers apprehensively on the desktop. Mantara noted that Jiminez had avoided looking at the gun when he'd removed it. And the empty bayonet sheath that he carried in his waistband. Now, he rested both on the desk next to the tray while he changed clothes. Jiminez averted his eyes again as Gothe's lieutenant stuck the gun into his shorts and pulled the bayonet from beneath the tray. To make the little manager even more uncomfortable, he slowly shaved a few hairs off his forearm with the long blade. Then, grunting with satisfaction, he wiped the bayonet on the edge of the desk, sheathed it and hid it under his shirt opposite the pistol.

"Do you know where he is?" Mantara asked Jiminez.

"Who?" the manager asked.

The answer irritated Mantara even further. "You know who I'm talking about. Don't play games with me. I can kill two men as easily as one."

Jiminez's mouth dropped open. "Mr. Gothe will—"

"Not care," Mantara interrupted. "Mr. Gothe will not care one bit. Don't make me repeat myself."

"No. I haven't seen the man you seek since he checked in."

Mantara didn't know whether to believe him or not. But it would be far easier to locate the American himself than continue prying answers out of this idiot, he thought. Without another word, he turned and walked out of the office.

Strolling casually, like any other of the lone men trolling for female companionship, Mantara scouted out the soccer fields, tennis courts and swimming pools. He considered going down to the beach and walking along the shore, but decided against it. At the other amusements, people were busy doing things, preoccupied with their own pursuits. On the beach, most people did nothing but sit in the sun. Which meant they paid more attention to others who passed by. He would resort to that tactic if he eventually had to, but there were better strategies he could try first.

Walking through the parking lot, Mantara passed the car he had parked at the rear, out of sight from the beach and most of the other attractions around the resort. He moved onto the road, walking along as if he were just another middle-aged man who had decided he needed some exercise. But a half mile down from the hotel he stopped, looked both ways to make sure there was no one watching, then suddenly darted into the jungle.

He made his way quickly at first, knowing he was too far away from the beach to be heard. But he slowed as his instincts told him he was nearing the resort again, careful to avoid the twigs and leaves which, even when damp, might give off some telltale noise if stepped on. Finally he saw a glimmer of black sand through the vegetation and dropped to his knees.

Mantara moved forward even more quietly now, almost to the edge of the jungle. He stopped suddenly when he realized he had finally had a stroke of luck after a half day of dead ends. Through the foliage, not thirty yards from where he hid, he saw two lounge chairs. A big, muscular, dark-haired and heavily scarred gringo lay on one of the lounges. On the other was a woman of Hispanic descent, although her skin was light. She had removed her top, and Mantara stared at her breasts for a moment.

Now he knew where the lipstick on the sheets had come from. Was there a way to take out the American and then have a little fun with the woman before returning to Gothe? He wouldn't have to pay for Regina if he did. Maybe he could....

Mantara forced himself to snap out of the almost hypnotic state into which he'd fallen. No, he told himself. Forget that. Concentrate on killing the big gringo. He reminded himself that things were changing around Gothe. His employer had brought in the new kid. Gothe said it was because he would be expanding his operations before retiring and needed more help. But both he and Lima wondered if one or both of them hadn't displeased the wealthy antiquities smuggler. It was possible that he planned to replace one of them with "the golden boy" as they called Pacheco behind his back.

Mantara continued to watch through the trees. Suddenly he saw the big gringo stand and pull the woman to her feet. They started to walk back in the direction of the building. Had the American heard him approach? No, that was impossible. He hadn't made a sound. The big man just wanted more of the woman.

Before he knew what he was doing, Mantara had drawn the 9 mm Kahr from his waistband. Should he shoot the man now and get it over with? No. There were few other people on the beach, but there were enough to get a good description of him as he made his way back to the car.

Mantara watched the American and the woman walk back up the beach, then stop. Were they going back to the room for more sex? If so, he could return to a slight modification of his original plan. He could listen at the door, wait until they were well into their lovemaking, then use the key card to enter the

room silently. With any luck the gringo would be on top, and
he could plunge the bayonet between his shoulder blades before the man even sensed his presence.

Of course, he would have to kill the woman, too. But
maybe first...

No! It would be too risky. He would kill the man, then kill
the woman, then he would go visit Regina.

Mantara waited, watching. There was no need to retrace
his steps through the jungle. He could wait until they entered
the building, then simply follow once they couldn't see. But
again, they did the unexpected.

Suddenly they stopped in the middle of the sand. The big
gringo reached into his pocket and pulled out a roll of money,
handed her some, then waved her away. From where he
crouched, Mantara could see the woman's face, and it didn't
look happy. He watched her stand there looking as if she
might cry as the American turned his back on her and headed
alone toward his room.

The man in the jungle found himself nodding. So that was
the case. She was only a prostitute. And the gringo was finished with her. Sadly the woman turned and walked off in another direction, the American disappearing into the building.

Mantara frowned, trying to decide on his next move. The
man was likely to go into the room and take a shower. Maybe
even a nap. Should he go back and get the room-service tray
again, or try to creep in while the man dozed?

But the big gringo surprised him again by suddenly reap-
pearing outside the building. Mantara watched him scour the
area—he supposed the man was making sure the woman was
gone—then walk toward the cantina. What had happened was
now obvious. The big man had told his whore some excuse
just to get rid of her. Perhaps he had tired of her and was ready
for a new woman who he hoped to find in the bar.

Mantara had almost decided to go to the room, let himself
in and wait in hiding when the big guy appeared once again.
He held a six-pack of beer in each hand as he walked back

toward the same lounge recliners he and the woman had occupied earlier.

Franco Mantara smiled ear to ear, what he would do finally taking shape in his mind. There was no need to go anywhere. He would stay right where he was in the jungle and let the big gringo come to him. The American was about to settle in for an afternoon of solitary beer drinking.

Mantara would wait for the perfect opportunity.

The beautiful thing about it all was that he could even wait until the American had consumed most of the beer and was tipsy, his judgment clouded and his reflexes dulled.

Franco Mantara dropped from his crouch to a sitting position, shifting slightly so he could still see the lounge chairs. He drew the bayonet.

The biggest problem he had now was not giving himself away by laughing at how easy it was all going to be.

4

Bolan entered the bar, careful not to be seen by anyone through the connecting door to the other side. He doubted that Manuel Montoya or his minions had returned after what had happened the day before, but he couldn't be sure. And he had no time to waste on such low-level dregs of Costa Rican society right now.

The bartender recognized him immediately, the bad toupee shifting slightly on his head as it jerked up in surprise. The soldier stared into his eyes and suddenly knew that this was the man who had called Gothe. The astonishment on his face had to come from seeing Bolan still alive.

"Tecate," Bolan told the man. "Two six-packs. To go."

The bartender nodded and moved slowly toward a refrigerator.

"I'm in a hurry," the soldier said in a stern voice.

The bartender had seen the knife fight the day before. He doubled his pace, digging down frantically into the cooler and coming up with the beer.

Bolan left the bar, keeping his eyes pointed toward the lounge chairs down the beach. It was the natural thing to do if he was returning to the spot he and Rocio had occupied earlier, and it covered the fact that he was really scanning the jungle beyond. His mind worked furiously as his bare feet waded through the sand. Whoever Gothe had sent was fairly good. Not a complete pro but at least a gifted amateur. The man had made no noise to alert Bolan of his approach. The only clue had been the whiff of cheap aftershave that had come from the jungle. But that wasn't really what had caused his sudden realization that the man was in the jungle. The out-of-place scent was only the catalyst.

The Executioner shifted the six-packs slightly as he neared the chairs. What had actually tipped him off couldn't be put into words. It was an instinct that had been developed by near-constant action, countless battles and more life-or-death situations than he could remember. Some called it a sixth sense, while others swore extrasensory perception was involved. Bolan didn't discount a certain amount of ESP in the world around him, but he was far too grounded not to accept that explanation with open arms. As he reached the lounge chairs, he supposed if he had to put it into one word he'd just call it experience.

Bolan sat back down on the recliner, setting the beer in the sand next to him. He pulled a bottle out of one of the cartons, twisted off the cap and took a sip. A tiny footprint in the sand next to the other lounger reminded him of the woman who had been there with him earlier, and again he was sorry he'd been forced to hurt Rocio's feelings. But it was either that or take the chance of getting her killed, and he didn't want that on his conscience.

Bolan leaned back into a half-sitting, half-lying position. He had left the Beretta, Desert Eagle and his big knives in the room just now. While carrying them out wrapped in a blanket had fooled Rocio earlier, the man in the jungle would be looking for such clues. And if his plan went well, they would be of no use to him anyway. He still carried the North American Arms pistol and the Chinook, and he would rely on them. They would be enough.

Bolan's *mind* would be the real weapon during the rest of the afternoon.

The soldier stared out at the sea, watching the trees in his peripheral vision. As quickly as he had sensed the presence of the man in the nearby jungle, he had also realized how the man would try to kill him.

He knew how the killer would come because it was how he would do it if their roles were reversed.

Bolan took a long pull from the bottle, feeling eyes on him. He had to play this right if his plan was to work, and that meant drinking—or at least looking like he was drinking. But at the same time, he could hardly afford to get drunk. Whether Gothe had sent Lima or Mantara made no difference. Both were experienced killers, and he was setting himself up as bait, hanging way out on the limb to draw them in. The only advantage he had was that he wouldn't be drunk when the killer thought he was, and he couldn't afford to trade that small edge off for the sake of appearance.

Somehow, he had to fake it. And he had to do it in full view of the killer.

The soldier slowly let one arm drop off the side of the recliner away from the jungle. Out of the killer's sight, he slowly began to drag it back and forth across the sand. The man in the jungle would see movement, but Bolan was careful to make sure it looked like nothing more than the dawdling of a bored man drinking beer in the sun. What he was really doing was digging a hole.

Bolan finished the beer and held the empty bottle in the air, turning the neck down and letting the last drops fall out of the bottle and down into his mouth. He hoped the man in the jungle was watching—the sight would subtly reinforce the fact that he had consumed the entire bottle. The human mind being what it was, the killer should then subconsciously jump to the conclusion that he would also drink all of the next beer. And the next. And the next.

Bolan shifted the bottle to his left hand, away from the jungle, and dropped it onto the sand next to the hole. From where he hid in the jungle the killer should be able to see it beneath the lounger. It would act as yet more psychological persuasion that Bolan was drinking beer.

Twisting the top off another bottle, the soldier held it to his lips and took a swig. But this time, he did so with his left hand, bringing the bottle back down to his side. He waited a moment, then leaned forward slightly to put his body between the bottle and the jungle. And as he did, he dumped the rest of the beer into the hole.

Bolan sat back again, holding the empty bottle to his lips as if drinking once more. He repeated the motion every few seconds, sometimes pantomiming a sip, other times a gulp. Then he dropped the bottle next to the other empty and reached back into the carton.

The afternoon wore on, with Bolan taking no more than one sip from each bottle, then pouring it into the hole where the sand quickly soaked it up. He continued to hold the empties to his mouth a suitable number of times before moving on to the next bottle.

He was nearing the end of the second six-pack when he decided it was time. When he'd finished the next to last beer, he rose unsteadily to his feet. Weaving slightly, he started toward the jungle pretending he needed to urinate. The soldier hummed to himself, doing his best to look drunk as he made his way clumsily through the branches and vines. The smell of aftershave was stronger now. The man had moved closer.

Bolan suspected Gothe's man planned to use a silent weapon like a knife or club. If he'd planned to shoot him, or had a sound suppressor, he could have already done so a thousand times while Bolan lay on the lounger chair drinking beer.

Only battle-trained ears could have picked up the subtle

noises that now moved from his right side around toward his back. Bolan continued to stand there, like a dedicated beer drinker who wanted to empty his bladder. The movement behind him halted, and he heard a soft inhalation of air. A deep breath. Exactly the kind of sound men made just before beginning an important task. The sound was soft, low, muffled. No drunk would have noticed it.

Bolan grabbed the North American Arms pistol. He ducked, twisting to his side, and felt a cold, flat object pass across his belly. Glancing down, he saw the blade of a long thin bayonet.

Reacting out of instinct, the Executioner let the blade pass his body, groping for the hand he knew had to hold it. He felt skin, hair and bumpy knuckles, and he curled his fingers around those that gripped the knife, clamping down with a grip of iron. Such a defense had to be precise; to grab too far out meant that he'd cut his own fingers off on the blade. But to grab too far up on the wrist gave the experienced knife fighter the opportunity to arch his hand around and cut the grabber's wrist. The hand was the only place safe to hold.

A surprised sound came from the man who was still half hidden in the thick jungle foliage. Bolan brought the pistol around, intending to raise it to head level and fire.

But the man was too close. The Executioner's gun hand came up and around, then suddenly stopped as his forearm struck the man's side. Bolan realized his wrist had been halted in the attacker's armpit. The other man, his face partially visible now through the leaves and vines, let out a snarl and clamped his arm down over Bolan's gun hand, trapping it and the tiny pistol.

Maintaining a firm grip on the killer's knife hand, Bolan tried to wrest the pistol out from under the man's arm but was unsuccessful. He threw all his weight forward, knocking his attacker off balance and driving him backward. But the man with the blade not only kept the small pistol pinned under his arm, he reached up and grabbed Bolan's hair with his free hand. Both men tumbled deeper into the jungle.

The Executioner's strategy was simple as he regained his equilibrium. His feet churned in short choppy steps, like a football lineman engaged in an agility drill. The other man pulled down on his hair. Bolan fought back with his neck—but only long enough to let the killer feel the pressure. Then, suddenly, as he continued to drive the man back though the trees, he released that pressure and drove his head forward.

The crown of Bolan's head struck the other man hard on the bridge of the nose. Blood spurted forth from the ruptured capillaries, splattering both fighters. The attacker—was it Lima or Mantara?—bellowed. But he still didn't let go with either hand.

The Executioner tugged again on his gun hand, trying to free the pistol. But the other man was strong, and at the angle at which they fought the leverage was all his.

The two men finally struck the trunk of a tree, and the assassin let out an "Ooomph" as the air was driven from his lungs. But instead of letting go, his grip on both the gun and Bolan's hair seemed to get stronger. He rebounded off the tree like a professional wrestler coming off the ropes, and now it was the Executioner's turn to be driven back a step.

The two men came to a standstill well inside the tree line and out of sight from the beach. Bolan kept his grip on the hand holding the bayonet. Gothe's man continued to bear down with his shoulder, keeping Bolan's other hand—and the pistol—trapped under his armpit. At the same time, he tugged again on the Executioner's hair.

Bolan tried another head strike, but this time the man was ready, jerking his face out of the way. The killer tried to twist the blade in his hand toward Bolan's torso, but now it was the Executioner who had the advantage of leverage. The two men struggled for a moment, grappling on their feet. Then suddenly Bolan gave way to the other man's pressure on the bayonet, shifting his weight to let the deadly blade pass in front of his chest. With both the killer's arms to one side now, the Executioner worked an elbow into the man's collarbone. Shifting his weight again, he lunged forward, driving the pointed bone down into the top of the killer's chest. A snapping sound echoed through the jungle.

The snap was quickly drowned out by the attacker's squeal of pain. Bolan changed his angle, striking again with the elbow on the sensitive broken bone. With the killer's attention diverted to his neck, Bolan brought his right leg out wide, then swept his opponent's feet out from under him. Both men went down, Bolan on top.

But the fight hadn't been knocked out of Gothe's henchman, and he continued to hold on to both the gun and the Executioner's hair. In the wrestler's mount position, Bolan could look down and see the man's face. It was contorted in both agony and hatred, blood spattering the skin from the injured nose while more crimson fluid continued to pump from the nostrils. The Executioner pulled with all his might on the gun, trying to work it out from under the man's arm. But he was trying to pry the weapon through an opening far too small. He couldn't get his hand out unless he dropped what was in it.

The bayonet came in dangerously close to his ribs, then was diverted away again as the men continued to arm wrestle for its control. The Executioner was thankful for the fact that the bayonet was so long. The point was past his body, and he needed to worry only about the edges. Had it been a shorter blade, the killer might well have found some way to drive it into him by now.

Leaning forward, Bolan fought the other man, strength for strength. Slowly he was able to bring his head down until they were staring each other eye to eye. Gothe's underling spit at him, hitting him in the forehead. Bolan hardly noticed as he bore farther, finally getting his forehead onto the attacker's bleeding nose once more.

At first, the contact made little difference because the nose was already broken and the pain was severe. But gradually, as he continued to overcome the strength in his opponent's arms, the Executioner put more and more weight on the broken bone and cartilage. He felt the splinters beneath his forehead break further, and suddenly the man with the bayonet screamed at the top of his lungs.

And when he did, he relaxed the shoulder pinning the pistol under his arm.

The Executioner yanked hard. The attacker realized his mistake a second later, bringing his arm down tight against his side once more. They were back where they'd started. Almost. The slight lessening of pressure had allowed the Executioner to get the barrel of the tiny .32-caliber weapon inside the other man's armpit.

He fired.

The explosion couldn't really be called an explosion. The small round wasn't loud to begin with, and was muffled by the attacker's underarm. The soldier wasn't sure exactly where the bullet had gone, but blood suddenly shot from the top of the attacker's shoulder and the man screamed once more—and released his hold on the pistol.

Bolan pulled the gun the rest of the way out, shoved it into the man's throat and pulled the trigger. But the slide failed to cycle. The gun was jammed.

With no time to clear the jammed weapon the Executioner dropped it to the side and drove his fist into the broken and mutilated nose. This time, when the attacker tried to scream, all that came out was a bubbling froth of blood. Bolan reached across his body to where the assassin had the bayonet secured. He didn't even have to take the weapon away from the man. With both hands now, he simply turned the killer's own wrist inward and drove the blade downward through the heart.

Bolan felt the tip come out the man's back and burrow into the soft jungle earth. He fished quickly through the undergrowth and found the gun. Working the slide manually, he ejected the spent brass and chambered a fresh round. Quickly he shook the man down and found a Kahr pistol. Ricardo Toledo's badge case was in one of the killer's pockets—ready to be planted on the Executioner, Bolan assumed. But the would-be assassin had carried no billfold of his own or any means of identification.

Bolan still didn't know if the man was Lima or Mantara.

Holding the Kahr in one hand and the NAA pistol in the other, he stood. The descriptions Pacheco had given him had been vague and would have fit either man. But whoever was lying dead on the jungle floor still had his own fingers wrapped around the grip of the bayonet protruding from his chest.

BOLAN LEFT THE DEAD MAN where he was. The fight had taken them deep enough into the jungle and well off the path any of the tourists were likely to take should they decide to go on a hike.

Making his way through the jungle toward the ocean, Bolan stopped just inside the tree line. He looked out along the black sand, scanning both ways to make sure there was no one in the water along the beach. Satisfied that there were no prying eyes, he lay the Chinook and the NAA pistol on the ground, stuck the Kahr into the Thunderwear holster and walked down to the water.

The soldier waded in waist deep, then reached down through the water for a handful of pebbly sand. Using the gritty substance in lieu of soap, he scrubbed the blood from his body. Once the telltale signs of violence were gone, he swam farther away from shore.

Bolan's mind raced as his arms stroked the water. He had hoped to find some identification on the killer, and perhaps even a phone number for Gothe. It would be necessary for what he planned next. He already had Gothe's phone number, of course. But when he called in a few minutes, the antiquities smuggler would wonder how he'd obtained it. And the soldier couldn't tell him that his source was Pacheco. One of the old cardinal rules of undercover work was to have a story and a reason to be there. In this case, his story needed a way he could have gotten the number that didn't lead back to Jaime Pacheco.

A quarter mile from shore, Bolan reached into his suit, pulled out the Kahr and let it sink to the bottom of the sea. He swam back in, still working on the logistics of the problem at hand. By the time he reached the beach again, he had the answer.

The soldier returned to the tree line, found the NAA pistol and dropped it back into the hidden holster. After picking up the knife, he followed the shoreline back to the resort, then cut past the lounge chairs and his pile of empty beer bottles. Returning to his room, he took a quick shower, then dressed in khaki slacks, a T-shirt and lightweight jacket. He wasn't sure exactly what kind of man he was about to encounter during the next phase of the mission, so the Desert Eagle went into his hip holster beneath the jacket. But he was still playing a part and, unless it became a matter of life or death, he didn't plan to use the big hand cannon or even let it be seen. There was a good chance he'd need to use intimidation as a device to obtain what he wanted. But one, or both, of the big knives would serve him just as well in that role without endangering his cover. The Crossada and Szabowie might even coax information out of the man he was about to speak to even better than a gun. The story of what had happened in the bar with Jorge the day before would still be fresh in the minds of the resort staff.

Five minutes later, the soldier walked into the hotel lobby. The desk clerk looked up as Bolan pushed through the half swing door that separated the office area from the public. "Sir, I can't let you—" he started to say.

Bolan ignored the man, passing on through a door in the wall just behind the desk and turning down a hallway. The first door he came to had a nameplate outside: Leone Jimenez. And beneath that: Manager.

The door was closed; Bolan opened it.

A small man wearing thick horn-rimmed glasses looked up from a pile of receipts on his desk. When he saw Bolan's face, his mouth fell open.

"Surprised to see me?" the Executioner asked as he entered the office and closed the door behind him. When the little man didn't answer, he took a seat in one of the chairs in front of the desk. Looking the frightened manager in the eyes, he smiled. "Or just surprised to see me *alive?*"

"Señor," Jiminez said. "I don't know what—"

"Shut up and listen," Bolan said, his voice growing hard. "You're going to do me a favor."

"I am the manager of the Santuario de Agua," came the trembling voice. "Surely one of our staff could better assist you if—"

Bolan leaned in and crossed his arms on the desk between them. "Didn't I just tell you to listen instead of talk?"

Jiminez fell silent.

"You're going to make a phone call for me," the soldier said. "I don't want one of your staff doing it. I want you to do it. Do you understand?"

The little man remained frozen.

"You can speak now." Bolan said.

But all Jiminez was willing to risk was a nod of his head.

"Pick up the phone," the soldier ordered, nodding toward the instrument to the side of the invoices.

Jiminez lifted the receiver. "Who do you wish me to call?" he asked in the same squeaky voice.

"Francisco Gothe."

Jiminez's dark brown face went gray. "I don't know any Fran—"

Bolan was losing patience with the little man. "Yes, you do. He owns this place. Now call him."

The resort manager knew he had already lost that argument. So he tried another. "Please. Señor Gothe can be a very vindictive man."

"Call him," Bolan growled.

"But he will—"

The Executioner sprang to his feet like a cat. The Szabowie—one of the same knives he knew Jiminez would have heard about from the incident the day before—came out from under his jacket. The almost needle-tipped point came up in a fast arc, stopping just under Jiminez's chin. The tip disappeared into the loose, quivering skin just above the knot in the man's tie. "Would you rather he be vindictive with you later?" Bolan asked. "Or would you prefer I be vindictive with you now?"

Trembling fingers tapped numbers into the phone while the Szabowie stayed in place. It took three tries, but Jiminez finally got the right keys punched.

A few second later, he said, "Yes. This is Jiminez at the Agua, calling for Señor Gothe." There was a brief pause, then Jiminez said, "Yes, very important."

Bolan took the knife away from the little man's throat and motioned for him to sit back in his chair. He took the receiver from Jiminez's shaking fingers and pressed it against his ear as he waited. They sat like that for nearly ten minutes while whoever had answered went to get Gothe. Finally a voice that sounded as if it belonged to an older man came on the line.

"Jiminez?" it said.

"Wrong," Bolan told him. "Blanski. At least that's the name I checked in under here. I get the feeling you may know me better as Belasko."

There was a long pause, then Gothe said, "Ah, yes, Señor Belasko. I didn't expect to hear from you today."

"I'd imagine you didn't," said Bolan. "Today, or any other day for that matter."

Another pause came, shorter this time. Finally Gothe said, "What may I do for you, Señor Belasko?"

Bolan kept one eye on Jiminez as he spoke. "First of all, you can call off your dogs. Since you're talking to me, I'm sure you're smart enough to figure out that one of them has already gone to that great kennel in the sky."

"I see," Gothe said.

"Do you?" the Executioner asked. "I hope so. Because the way I see it we have only two possible ways to play this game. You can take my advice and drop this matter altogether, or you can keep sending men after me. You do that and you're going to lose all your best men."

Silence reigned once more over the phone lines. But again it was Gothe who finally broke it. "You are wrong, Belasko," he said.

Bolan's voice was sarcastic. "Really?" he said. "And how's that?"

"There is a third way to play this...game, as you call it."

"And what's that?"

"You can come to work for me. I could use a man of your skills." A low chuckle came over the line. "And as you said, the fact that I'm talking to you instead of the man I sent after you tells me I have a vacancy that needs filling." The low laugh came again. "Are you interested?"

This time, Bolan created the silence. He didn't want to appear too anxious. "Maybe," he finally said.

"Our mutual friend, Pacheco, has already told me you were in need of work when he found you in San José."

"Don't get the idea that I'm living in a cardboard box in some alley," Bolan said. "I'm not." He paused a moment to let it sink in, then said, "But I might be willing to discuss your offer with you."

"Good," Gothe said. "Return to your room. I'll call you in ten minutes and have Jimenez transfer the call there."

"Agreed," Bolan said and hung up the phone.

The Executioner glared one more time at Jiminez as he shoved the Szabowie back under his coat. Then he turned quickly away before the manager could see the grin spreading across his face.

So far, everything was going according to plan.

THE MANSION WAS BUILT along the lines of a medieval European castle and looked out of place in the middle of the jungle near the Corcorado National Park. But it was impressive to say the least. Built of rough stone that had to have come from a distant quarry, the three-story dwelling looked to be close to ten thousand square feet in size. Bolan had taken the turn off the main road, been waved through by the guards at the gate and driven the Nissan along the gravel drive until the house had suddenly appeared up in the distance.

The soldier wore lightweight cargo pants and a white tank top, which hung outside his belt. The Aloha shirt he'd worn went over the tank top. This time, however, he not only had on shoulder harness with the big knives, he also carried the Desert Eagle and Beretta, hidden by the tank top.

Bolan knew he was walking into the lion's den, and all he could be sure of was that it would be full of predators. Other than that he didn't know what to expect. And he was in the process of changing his undercover image slightly. He was making the transition from "assassin on the run" to a mercenary who might, or might not, be about to sign on with a very influential man.

For perhaps the thousandth time since landing in Costa Rica, Bolan sighed inwardly. He had a great deal of respect for men like Jaime Pacheco who could play roles such as they did, over and over, every day. And for the most part he didn't mind working undercover himself. But there was also a part of role camouflage that went against his grain. He was, first and foremost, a soldier. And given the choice, he preferred an up-front approach any day.

The Executioner knew that in the war against evil, he didn't always get to choose the way he wanted to go after it. He did what he had to do. And in the end, he would kill that evil however he could.

The Nissan he was driving was the same one that had delivered Toledo to the airport two days before, and now Bolan parked it in the circular drive in front of the jungle castle. Several men—dressed in rags that looked even worse in the presence of such splendor—were at work around the grounds. One man cut the grass with a riding mower the size of a small tractor while others used machetes to trim the exotic plants and bushes decorating the grounds. Others, although not in uniform but dressed better than the yard men, were obviously security. Like the men who had guarded the entrance to the driveway, they all wore pistols on their belts and carried rifles or shotguns as they patrolled the perimeter of the house.

The Executioner got out and closed the car door behind him. A winding rock staircase led up from the drive to the front porch, and he took it. As he approached, his trained eyes didn't miss the small surveillance camera mounted on the roof as well as the one on the guard shack at the entrance to the estate.

Bolan pushed the button to ring the doorbell, glancing up at the surveillance camera above his head. Besides the one at the gate, others had been scattered periodically along the gravel drive. The place might have a sixteenth century look about it, but it was equipped with twenty-first century technology. It was obvious that Francisco Gothe liked security. But he liked it low-key, relaxed and at least partially hidden. The bottom line, however, was that Gothe could present himself to the world as a legitimate entrepreneur who owned resort hotels and other real estate.

The doorbell played some Latino tune with musical bells as the soldier waited. A minute had gone by before the door opened and a beautiful young woman in a French maid's uniform swung it back. She smiled as she ushered him in. But the smile was forced, and in the eyes behind it Bolan saw an emotion he had seen thousands of times in the past. It was not just nervousness.

What he saw in the woman's eyes was absolute fear.

The maid led Bolan from the foyer into an elaborately decorated living room with antique mirrors, carefully carved Italian furniture and a baby grand piano. He followed the swaying hips in the short black skirt and fishnet stockings from the living room into a sunroom larger than some greenhouses. From there they took a side door down a short hall. The woman stopped at another door.

"Señor Gothe," she called out. "Your guest is here."

"Thank you, Maria," a voice from somewhere inside the room replied. "Please show him in."

Maria stepped back, curtsied and waved Bolan around her toward the door. The smile was still on her face. So was the fear.

Bolan took two steps down into a large denlike room. The walls were made of teak, as was the wet bar at the far end of the room. A floor-to-ceiling stone fireplace stood along one wall—more for show than practicality he had to guess, considering the Costa Rican climate. Across from the fireplace two couches and several heavily padded easy chairs had been formed into a conversation area. One man, Hispanic, sat alone on the couch. Pacheco occupied one of the chairs, and the third man who looked to be in his early sixties sat in the third. Like the maid but more sincerely, both Gothe and Pacheco were smiling. The man on the couch, either Lima or Mantara, as Bolan still didn't know who he'd killed in the jungle, was not smiling.

All three men stood as the Executioner entered the room. Pacheco moved across the room with outstretched arms. "Welcome, Mike!" he shouted. "We have been waiting for you!"

Bolan let the undercover expert get within arm's reach, then sent a right cross crashing into his jaw. The blow hadn't been hard enough to break bone or knock Pacheco unconscious, but it was hard enough to send him sprawling to the floor.

"Jeez—" Pacheco said as he rose to a sitting position. His hand rose to his face, and he rubbed his jaw.

Bolan stepped forward, leaned down to grab Pacheco's arm and jerked him back to his feet. "That's for not warning me I was about to be killed." In the corner of his eye he could see the surprise and concern on Gothe's face. It was exactly what he wanted. But Bolan was still playing a role, and a man who had been set up to be killed by someone he counted as a friend *should* be angry. Besides, even though Gothe knew that they had worked together in the past, it wouldn't serve to further their purposes if the antiquities smuggler thought they were *too* tight. It would just make him suspicious, wondering if they were plotting against him. No, better that he believe they would turn on each other if it benefited them personally.

Pacheco continued to rub his jaw as he looked at Bolan. "I'm sorry," he said. "You're an old friend. But business is business."

The soldier continued to watch Gothe in his peripheral vision as he let out a chuckle. "We'll call it even," he said. "I might have done the same thing in your place." He glanced around the room to indicate that Pacheco seemed to have stumbled on to a sweet employment deal.

Now the cop forced another smile. "I'm glad to see you still have the strong right hand." He turned to Gothe. "His left isn't so bad either. But I'm hoping he will not feel obligated to demonstrate it on me, too." Now, all of the men except the man on the couch laughed good-naturedly.

Gothe stepped forward, extending his hand. "We are businessmen," he said. "And as our mutual friend has said, 'business is business.' But we are all in business *together* now." He shook Bolan's hand and continued. "But where are my manners? I am Francisco Gothe, your potential new employer." He turned toward the couch. "This is Julio Lima."

Bolan stuck his hand out toward Lima. The man took it, slowly and reluctantly.

"And who was the man I left with a bayonet in his chest in the jungle?" the soldier asked Gothe.

"His name was Mantara," the antiquities smuggler said, shrugging. "That was unfortunate, of course." He glanced toward Lima. "But we must move on."

His eyes narrowed slightly as he continued to look at the man from the couch. "I know Mantara was your friend, Julio," he said. "But please, promise me now that there will be no problems between you two." He indicated Bolan with a nod of his head.

Bolan saw Lima wince at the words. The man was obviously angry and upset, and the Executioner suspected there was more to it than just losing his friend. If Mantara was so dispensable these days, Lima had to figure he was, too.

The man standing in front of the couch turned to face Bolan. "His name was Franco Mantara," he said in a noncommittal voice. "And, yes, he was my friend. But life must go on."

Twisting back slightly toward Gothe, he said, "There will be no problems."

The Executioner wasn't so sure. And he'd look like a complete moron in front of Gothe if he accepted the words so easily at face value. So, staring into Lima's eyes, he said, "Are you sure about that?"

The words caught Lima off guard, and now his true feelings were exposed on his face. "I have said there would be no trouble over Mantara," he suddenly growled, taking a step toward the Executioner. "But if you would like to make other problems—"

"Hey!" Gothe said, quickly stepping between them. "Gentlemen, please! Mantara is gone. It's unfortunate, and I will take the blame myself. But as you yourself said, Julio, life must go on." The grave robber attempted a good-natured chuckle to ease the tension. "Now, are you two going to get along, or must I keep you both after school and stand you in separate corners?"

Bolan turned to Lima. "Business is business," he quoted. "I'm willing to let it drop if you will."

It took a little while, but Lima finally nodded. "There is nothing we can do now to bring Franco back."

"Very good," Gothe said, "because we must all get along if we are to grow rich together."

The soldier cast an eye around the room. "Looks to me like you're doing pretty well already."

Gothe laughed as he leaned down to pick up a small silver bell off an end table. "You will grow rich," he said. "I will grow richer." He rang the bell, then set it back in place and motioned toward the couches and chairs. "Shall we all sit? Maria will be in shortly to take orders for drinks. But I highly recommend that you try a very special beer I have brewed myself." He held his fingers to his lips and kissed them. "It is a hobby of mine, and a batch just became ready yesterday."

No sooner had he finished than Maria appeared in the doorway. Gothe looked from Bolan to Pacheco expectantly, and they both nodded. It was obvious that he didn't ask what Lima wanted. The man on the couch would have what his boss wanted him to have.

"Four of my special brew, please, Maria," Gothe said, and the maid disappeared again.

"We have much to discuss, Señor Belasko? Blanski? Which do you prefer?"

"Belasko is fine," Bolan said.

"We have much to discuss then, Señor Belasko. But we will wait until Maria has brought the beer. In the meantime, tell me, how did you enjoy your stay at my resort?"

"It was a nice place when no one was trying to stab or shoot me," he said.

Gothe looked down modestly and shook his head. "Yes, so I heard," he said. "For the first incident, I'm not responsible except perhaps indirectly for allowing people of that ilk to drink in my bar." Looking up, he shook his head again. "Those scum. I have asked Jiminez to rid the place of them several times. Perhaps I will have to be more forceful with him."

Bolan didn't see any need to answer.

"But I apologize anyway. Such incidents are not good for the hotel's reputation." He paused, then said, "For your second problem—Mantara—yes, I am afraid I am directly responsible and I ask that you accept my apology. But it has all worked out for the best, no? You are here, you are alive, and perhaps I can have a better man working for me now than I had before." He glanced toward Lima, added, "No disrespect meant," then opened a humidor on the same table where the bell rested. Looking up at Bolan he said, "Cigar?"

The soldier shook his head. "Don't smoke them."

Gothe nodded approvingly. "Nor does our friend Jaime, or myself," he said. "I simply keep them for guests." He closed the humidor's lid. "May I ask a favor of you while we wait, Señor Belasko?"

"Call me Mike. And yes, ask the favor."

Gothe leaned forward slightly. "My bartender could not express how impressed he was with your weapons," he said. "May I see them?"

The Executioner smiled. Reaching under his jacket, he drew the Szabowie, flipped it around in his hand and extended the handle to Gothe.

The antiquities smuggler's eyes grew wide at the size and design of the elaborate bowie knife. He examined it lovingly for a few seconds. "And the other one?" he asked. "My man said you used two?"

Bolan drew the Crossada with his left hand, turned it around and said, "You're welcome to see it, too, Señor Gothe. But it's hard to look at both at the same time. No one can do justice to either when they try. So..." He kept the Crossada out of Gothe's reach and held out his hand for the Szabowie.

"Ah," he said. "A wise man as well as talented. You are right, of course. You should never leave yourself unarmed. Or hand over all your weapons for the examination of someone you've just met." He handed the Szabowie back and Bolan gave him the Crossada.

When he was finished examining the big dagger, he handed it back as well. "You are a good judge of steel," he said. "Are you as good a judge of—" He stopped talking as Maria reentered the room carrying a large tray. On top was a large pitcher of beer and four glasses. She set it on the coffee table by leaning over with her legs stiff and allowing her short maid's skirt to ride high on her hips. Gothe smiled at the sight. Pacheco looked. Lima leered.

The scantily clad woman poured the beer carefully, making sure the sediment from the home-brewed concoction stayed at the bottom of the pitcher. She handed each man a glass, then left.

Gothe raised his beer in a toast. "To a successful venture," he said. Turning to Bolan he added, "Would you like to be a part of it?"

"Yes." Bolan answered.

The four men drank.

Bolan nodded his agreement to the other men's compliments on Gothe's brewing ability.

Then Gothe said, "All right. We must now talk business." He set his glass on a coaster next to the cigar humidor. "I am getting older," he said. "And to be frank, my hobbies—such as beer making—give me far more pleasure than my business. I am about to retire."

The soldier noted a quick worried look pass across Lima's face, but the man remained silent. "If you're ready to quit," he asked the man, "what are you doing hiring new men like me and Jaime?"

"Ah," Gothe answered. "A very legitimate question. And now, I must confess, your employment under me is to be only temporary."

Bolan feigned anger. "Are you telling me you got me all the way out here for just a short job?"

Gothe held up his hands. "Please, let me explain. I think you will be satisfied when you hear me out." When the soldier didn't respond he went on. "I have shared my wish to retire with a very old and dear friend," he said. "He is in a business...shall we say *similar* to mine? I have also informed him of my desire to conduct at least two very large deals prior to my retirement. When these are complete, I shall vanish from this life, and this country, forever."

Bolan watched the man's face. Gothe had the sincere look of an honest businessman, and his manner was that of a Latin American aristocrat. But there was nothing admirable about the man beneath the phony veneer. He drove his slave labor into the ground, stole millions of dollars annually from the country he called home and had proved he was capable of murder. Pacheco assured Bolan there were dead slaves buried all over the Osa Peninsula. Gothe had hired out the assassination of Costa Rica's superintendent of police. He had done his best to have Bolan murdered, and Bolan couldn't help but wonder how many other men had died at his orders.

"So let me get this straight," the soldier said. "You're just going to walk away from all this?" He glanced around at the elegance of the room.

Gothe leaned forward again. "No," he said. "That would indeed be a shame after I have worked all my life to build such a business and develop the contacts I have." He paused, then smiled. "What I intend to do after I have completed the next few shipments of antiquities, as well as the other business ventures in which we are about to engage with my friend, is to leave operation of this enterprise to you three men." His eyes went from Bolan to Pacheco to Lima, then back to Bolan again. "Julio, of course, has seniority and will be in charge."

Out of the corner of his eye, Bolan saw Lima's attention pick up. It seemed to be the first time he had heard this news. But it was obvious that he liked it.

"Jaime will be next in command, but you will be third, Mike," Gothe went on. "None of you will be on salary anymore. We will become partners. I will own fifty-one percent of the company in order to retain controlling interest, of course. I'll leave it up to the three of you to work out the details of how to divide the remaining forty-nine percent. I promise you, however that is done, you will still become rich. You'll make far more money than any of you have ever made in your lives."

He had been addressing the three as a whole, but now he turned to face Bolan directly. "Now, Mike, does that make your trip out here seem more worthwhile?"

"It's sounding more like it might be," Bolan responded.

Gothe laughed again. "I thought you would see it as such," he said. Now, both his face and tone turned serious, and even tired. "I want to retire. There are a few details still left to iron out, including one large shipment of...products...I wish to do with the friend I mentioned. It will be sort of a send-off for me, and will also introduce him to the three of you for future business dealings. And I assure you, he will be invaluable to you."

"Excuse me, Don Francisco," Pacheco said. "But this last deal of yours, it sounds, well, big. So exactly when does this new partnership begin? Before or after your grand finale?"

The antiquities smuggler laughed. "I don't blame you for asking. Officially it won't begin until afterward. But let me put it another way—I will share the profits of this final shipment with you. When it is over, you should each have a little more than one million dollars in U.S. currency stashed away in the bank of your choice."

Lima sat there stunned. Pacheco feigned surprise. Bolan remained deadpan. When Gothe looked directly back at him for reaction, he finally nodded. But like Pacheco, he was acting. And acting as well as the undercover specialist, he hoped, because he wasn't buying any of it for a minute.

Francisco Gothe had something up his sleeve. The soldier had yet to meet the man who was willing to just give away half of a multimillion-dollar smuggling business because he was tired and would rather go brew his own beer somewhere.

No, they weren't getting the straight story. Something else was in the works.

Gothe now turned to Lima. "Julio," he said, "come out of your trance. Did you think I had forgotten you? Did you think I wouldn't reward all the many years of service you have given me? When I leave, only you will know how to contact me. Until then, I would like you to take charge of all of the grave-site digs as well as shipping the antiquities. You already understand the production and enforcement aspects of our business. But now I want you to begin going over the books and acquaint yourself with management. I will be available to you for counsel, as well as to introduce you to my attorneys, accountants, the resort managers and others who run the front businesses."

Lima fairly beamed. "Thank you, sir!" he nearly shouted.

Bolan listened to the speech quietly, keeping a poker face. Lima was in seventh heaven and not smart enough to know he was being conned. The Executioner had known him for less than an hour, but he could tell the man probably didn't understand basic mathematics, let alone have the capabilities to go over the books of such an immense criminal enterprise as Gothe's.

Gothe turned to Bolan and Pacheco. "I will need the two of you in another area. I want you to represent me in this final deal, going along to look after my interests."

Bolan leaned slightly forward. "Why? Don't you trust this *friend* of yours?"

Gothe shrugged. "As you demonstrated when you refused to hand me your second knife before I had returned the first," he said, "one can never be too careful."

"I would like to ask two questions if I might," Pacheco said. "First, our partnership. Does this include the resorts and other legitimate real estate as well as the antiquities business?"

"A very good question," Gothe said, turning to the man. "And the answer is yes. In my retirement, I have no more desire to worry about whether one of my hotels has clean towels than I wish to worry about a ship full of pre-Columbian artifacts being seized by U.S. Customs."

Lima's eyes widened yet again. The pupils almost took the shape of dollar signs.

"Question two, Don Francisco," Pacheco said. "On the final deal before we leave, what exactly are Mike and I expected to do?"

Gothe held up a hand for a moment's pause. "I will explain that to you in a moment," he said, then glanced at his wristwatch. "But first, Julio, the day goes on. I believe it is time for you to organize the men for tonight's digging, is it not?"

Lima rose, still riding the high of thinking he would soon be the second largest shareholder in what might well be the world's biggest illegal antiquities-smuggling business. Not to mention millions of dollars worth of resort areas and real-estate holdings. "Yes, sir," he said, and looked as if he might have been tempted to salute.

As soon as he was gone, Gothe looked down at the floor and shook his head. "I have already spoken to your friend Pacheco," he said, obviously addressing the statement to Bolan. "He will fill you in later on what is really going on here. But I'm sure you already realize that Julio cannot possibly do as I told him he would do. On the other hand, as I told him myself, he has served me well within his limited capacities. So I saw no reason to upset him until it became necessary." He looked up and a smile now covered his face. "In fact, I have indeed rewarded him. For at least a little while, he is a happy man who thinks he will soon be king."

Bolan stared into the man's eyes, careful not to reveal the contempt he had for Gothe with his own eyes. The antiquities smuggler and murderer wasn't joking. In his egotistical, self-serving brain he really did believe he had done Lima a favor by giving the man false hope for a few hours rather than killing him immediately.

The soldier cleared his throat to change the subject. "This deal we're going on," he said. "Which is it? Drugs or guns?"

The antiquities smuggler chuckled slyly as he looked the Executioner in the eye. "This is Central America, Señor Belasko," he said. "We do both. But cocaine is king."

FRANCISCO GOTHE WATCHED his two new men leave, then lifted the silver bell and jiggled it in his hand. A moment later, Maria walked in shyly. "Yes, sir?"

Gothe didn't speak. He merely looked up at the ceiling. His bedroom was directly over the den, and the woman in the French maid's outfit knew what he wanted. Blood rushed to her cheeks as she curtsied. She kept her eyes down as she said, "Yes, sir. I shall go prepare myself." She didn't look at him when she left the room any more than she had when she'd spoken.

Gothe finished his beer and looked at the glass. A tiny amount of sediment had been poured from the pitcher into his glass. This meant Maria hadn't done her job properly. Perhaps a spanking would be in order prior to their lovemaking. He always liked that bit of foreplay anyway, and he suspected she secretly did as well.

Gothe thought of the young woman as he rose from his chair. He had had many mistresses during his years in Costa Rica, but she had always been his favorite. Perhaps it was because he had known her since her mother—one of his former lovers—had given birth to her. For a short period of time, he had even wondered if she might not be his daughter. Then a DNA laboratory in San José had been made available to those who could afford the tests, and he had taken her there himself. No, she was not his daughter. It pleased him in more than one way. It meant her mother hadn't been faithful to him, but she still deserved the death he had given her when she finally grew boring. And it made Maria available to him as a mistress herself.

Gothe laughed out loud as he remembered his relief at the results of the test. The guilty feelings that had accompanied his sexual attraction vanished far quicker than they had come. During his years, he had taken the lives of four men with his own hands. He had ordered the murder of more than he could remember. A half-dozen former mistresses were buried in the jungle along with several score of lazy slaves who couldn't learn to dig properly.

But sleep with his own daughter? No. Francisco Gothe would never do such a thing as that.

Rising from his chair, Gothe noticed the ache in his joints and took his time getting up the steps to the bedroom. Everything, it seemed, took more time now than it had only a few years before. Walking, eating, digesting what had been eaten. He stopped at the doorway and looked in to see Maria lying on the bed. She had removed her skirt and blouse and wore only a black garter belt, fishnet stockings and the little white maid's cap. The sight sent a jolt of electricity through his heart, which moved on to his loins.

"Sit up, Maria," Gothe commanded.

The dark-skinned beauty complied, her face blank.

"I noticed some sediment in my beer." He walked to the bed and cupped her chin in one hand, forcing her eyes up to his. "Were you as careless with the other men's glasses as well?"

"No, sir," Maria said. "I tried very hard to—"

Gothe smiled down at her. "Roll over onto your hands and knees, Maria. Face away from me."

Again, the young woman did as ordered.

Afterward Gothe laid back in bed and clasped his hands behind his head. He turned to look at the naked young woman sleeping next to him. She faced away from him and had curled into a fetal position. Her perfectly shaped buttocks still glowed a bright red, but she would recover. He hadn't been forced to punish her as severely as he'd thought he might have to in order to become aroused. The spots on her skin would fade completely in a few days.

Gothe rolled over and shook her gently by the shoulder. "Wake up, Maria," he said. "Go back to your other duties. I have work to do as well."

The beautiful young woman rose from the bed, dressed quickly and left the room. Again, she didn't look at him.

Gothe watched her go. Did he love her? He wasn't sure what love meant, actually. But he knew he at least *liked* her more than any of the others who had gone before her as his mistress. Rolling onto his side, he slid open the drawer in the stand next to the bed and pulled out a small address book. When he had found the number he wanted, he tapped it into the phone and held the receiver to his ear. It rang four times before a voice with a Nicaraguan accent said, "Hello?"

"This is Francisco Gothe calling," he told the woman who had answered.

A few moments later, a more familiar male voice said, "Francisco? How are you?"

"Business as usual, Ramon," Gothe answered. "And how are your wife and children?"

"Very well," Letona answered.

"And your mistress?" It was as proper a question between the two men as the other.

"Lola? Still as beautiful as a peacock, excitable as a rabbit and as sharp-tongued as a piranha," Letona said with a laugh. There was a pregnant pause in which he knew Letona was wondering who he should inquire about on Gothe's behalf. But Gothe had no wife or children. And Letona knew nothing about Maria. So the antiquities man saved his friend from further embarrassment by saying, "All are well here, too, my friend."

"Good," Letona responded. "Very good." Gothe heard a small hiccup on the other end. Perhaps Letona suffered from indigestion as he sometimes did. The Nicaraguan was no longer a young man, either.

After a few more pleasantries, Letona cleared his throat. "Francisco, we have done well together, you and I. And we could have done even better had you agreed to merge with me earlier." A small laugh came from the other end of the line. "We would have kept each other young—so young that you wouldn't even be considering retirement for many more years. But tell me, have you made your final decision?"

"Yes, my friend," Gothe answered. "I have made the arrangements here, and they have gone well. I'm ready to accept your offer."

"Very good!" Letona said. "You won't be disappointed. We will miss you around here, however."

"I will come visit."

"Yes, you must do that!" Letona replied. "Lola has a friend you would find most attractive. But for now, tell me, you were able to find the right men?"

"Yes," Gothe said. "But it wasn't easy, and it was only a few hours ago I became convinced they would do. The parameters for men who I needed was very narrow."

"Yes," Letona agreed. "They had to be smart. Lima and Mantara didn't fill that bill."

"No," Gothe said. He saw no reason to get off on a tangent about the fact that Mantara had been killed. Letona knew he planned to get rid of both men anyway. "Yes, the men I have now hired are smarter than Lima and Mantara."

"That alone shouldn't have been difficult to find," Letona said, and both men laughed. "It was the other problem with which have you trouble, eh?"

"Yes. They had to be smart. But not too smart. They couldn't have the insight to look through what I had told them and suspect it was a lie."

"You have always been an excellent liar," Letona joked.

Gothe laughed with him again. "Never to a friend," he said. "Then we are set?"

"Yes. I will contact you on the details for the shipment within the next twenty-four hours. It will bring you a very nice little piece of change to begin your retirement." He cleared his throat again. "And I understand our attorneys have met several times and are working out the final paperwork to transfer the resorts and other business into my name."

The statement brought a smile to Gothe's face. "Yes, my friend. And you are paying me a very generous price for them, I must say."

Letona laughed on the other end of the line. "Yes, far more than they are worth. But I am not buying a string of hotels, Francisco. I am buying the antiquities business."

"Then there is only one more item to discuss," Gothe said. "Actually, two items. Their names are Pacheco and Belasko."

"And they will accompany the shipment to New Orleans?" Letona asked.

"Yes. I've told them they are to look after my interests."

"Then there is nothing more to discuss," Letona said. "My men will take care of them." He paused, then added, "No charge."

Gothe and Letona said their goodbyes and hung up. The

antiquities smuggler sat where he was for a moment, thinking. The American had been smart when he refused to hand over his second knife before the first had been returned, and Gothe had used it as an example of why he wanted the two men to be on the ship to New Orleans. He had told them that they could never be too careful. And he had meant those words. What he hadn't told them was that as soon as they notified him that the cocaine had arrived safely, he intended to have them killed. He had no intention of entering into a partnership with a couple of gun-toting mercenaries. He was selling his business interests outright to Letona.

But what Letona didn't know was that Belasko and Pacheco would indeed be keeping an eye on the cocaine to make sure Letona didn't get any ideas of his own. Right up until the time they died, and by then his share of the money would have been wired to one of his banks and it would be too late for Letona to pull anything.

There was no honor among thieves, Gothe knew. And he knew equally well that he was no exception to that rule.

Slowly, his aging joints aching from the activity with Maria, Gothe sat on the edge of the bed and began to put his clothes back on. But even through the pain, he caught himself snickering as he struggled into his socks. Yes, as he had told Letona, his men were smart but not too smart. Smart enough to look after his interests with the cocaine far better than Lima or Mantara could have done. But their shortcoming came, as it did with so many men, in greed. They had let it blind them to the point where they actually believed he would hand them both a million dollars and make them partners. Greed. The downfall of many otherwise intelligent men.

Gothe struggled into his socks, then leaned down to grab his pants off the floor. The movement brought a sharp pain to his lower back, but he was used to it, and it didn't ruin his mood. Pulling himself to his feet, he zipped his pants and guided his arms into his shirt. As he began to button his shirt, he caught a scent of Maria's perfume in the material. He smiled again. Did he love the young woman? Perhaps. He really didn't know. And what a shame he would never find out.

Because as fond as he might be of her, before he could retire without worrying about his past catching up to him, she was going to have to die along with everyone else.

5

Jaime Pacheco followed Bolan down the steps of the winding stone staircase outside the front door. The two men stopped at the bottom. On the lawn, he saw the gardeners finishing their tasks for the day. Several of the rifle-toting men who had guarded the house earlier in the day were gone, and had been replaced with new faces.

As they'd left the den, Gothe had requested that Pacheco give his friend a tour of the grounds before showing the big American to his sleeping quarters. But as they turned the corner of the house, they met Lima on his way back from organizing the night's digging. The belief that he was about to take over Gothe's operation had to still have been on the man's mind because he was walking with a gait that would have made a peacock's strut look like a shuffle.

Pacheco couldn't resist. "Hey, Julio," he said pleasantly. "Gothe wanted me to show Mike around. Would you rather do it?"

Lima stopped a few feet in front of them. He came as close

to sneering as a man could and still speak at the same time. "He's your friend," he spit. "You do it." He paused as another thought worked its way slowly across his mind. "And I suggest you get used to doing what I say from now on," he added before swaggering past them.

Pacheco waited until the man was out of hearing distance, then laughed softly. "Somehow, I knew he was going to say no," he whispered to Bolan. He shook his head in amazement. "Poor bastard," he said, still watching Lima's back. "Doesn't even have enough sense to know he's already dead." He turned back around and motioned for Bolan to go with him.

The American fell in next to Pacheco, and they crossed the lawn toward the vast expanse of land cleared out of the jungle behind it. Pacheco had heard the story of the knife fight in the bar at the resort, and now he asked the man to tell him about it. He listened attentively as Bolan ran down the encounter, then laughed. "By the time it got here to us you had cut Jorge's entire arm off. Whether you'd cut it into one or two pieces was a subject of much debate." He shook his head, still laughing softly. "We are a romantic people, we Hispanics. And you've now become a local legend. It won't be long until we're writing songs about you."

"You know any of that bunch?" Bolan asked. "Montoya or Jorge or any of the other men? I didn't get the feeling there was any connection to Gothe."

Pacheco started to answer but stopped as they passed a man raking the newly mowed grass. When they were out of earshot again, he said, "Oh yeah," he said. "I know who Montoya is. But he and his bunch are nothing more than a bunch of low-life Osa trash. Don't get me wrong, they're evil souls who steal, rape and rob, and I imagine they have been behind a few unsolved murders. But there's no connection to Gothe there. He wouldn't give that sort the time of day." He tapped his forehead. "They don't even have as many brains as Lima." Ahead, they could see Gothe's private swimming pool. It was enclosed with a chain-link fence and had a pool house inside the enclosure. Pacheco steered them that way.

"How about a woman from that area?" Bolan asked. "Rocio?"

Pacheco's eyebrows lowered. "The name doesn't ring any bells. Do you have a last name?"

Bolan shook his head as they walked on.

"Was she with Montoya?"

"Not really, although I got the feeling they knew each other."

Pacheco shrugged as they walked on. "Everybody around that area knows each other," he said. "Want me to get in touch with my headquarters and see if they can find out who she is?"

The big American hesitated, then said, "No. Not for now anyway. Maybe later. She doesn't have anything to do with this."

Pacheco began to speak, then thought better of it. Whoever this Rocio was, it sounded more like a private matter than business, which meant it was none of *his* business. If the American wanted him to know more, he would tell him.

The two men walked on, with Jaime Pacheco glancing at the big man now and then out of the corner of his eye. He remembered him well from the period he had spent training at the secret installation. The man had been one of the instructors. So had the older Israeli who had driven the getaway vehicle when they faked Toledo's assassination. There had been other teachers there, too. Quite a few of them in fact. But he had sensed early on that there was something different about this man.

He was a leader of men.

They passed the swimming pool and Pacheco said, "Do you know what I wonder about each time I see another shameless display of Francisco Gothe's wealth?"

"What?"

"I wonder how many of the locals died to bring it about." He pointed at the chain-link fence. "How many lives did this swimming pool cost? How many men were whipped to death, or shot, because they couldn't keep up the pace set forth by that monster living back there in his castle." Pacheco shook his head in disgust as they passed. "And how many other men ruined their lives drinking cheap *guaro* because they had no hope? No future?" He fell silent for a few minutes. Then he turned to Bolan and stopped.

The big American stopped next to him.

"When I told my boss about the contract Gothe had given me to kill him, Toledo didn't know which of the other police he could still trust. So I suggested we request outside assistance from the secret place where I had been trained." He stared past Bolan as he went on. "I told him if we worked it right, we could send Gothe to prison for the rest of this life." He took a deep breath. "But that's not really what I wanted to do. And it's not what we're going to do, is it?" He didn't wait for a reply but went on. "Back in San José, when you suggested that you just fly down here, kill Gothe and get it over with, you weren't kidding, were you? You were serious." None of his words showed the voice inflection of a question. They were statements. But he turned to the American for affirmation anyway.

"No," Bolan said. "I wasn't kidding."

Walking on, Pacheco said, "I'm tempted to do it right now. Before the diggers go out again to be beaten and maybe killed. If we killed Gothe now, the whole operation would go straight down the tubes." He held out both hands, palms up, to indicate the grounds. "Even if we didn't kill Lima too—which I would—this operation would be ruined. No one else can run it. And we aren't going to take it over like he thinks we are." He stopped talking there because that part of Gothe's speech had been bothering him.

"Legitimate question," Bolan said. "But there's a very good reason why we don't take him out yet. You said it yourself. We're going after his friend, the drug runner. And we need Gothe alive until we find out who that man is. Not to mention the fact that this 'big final deal' we're supposed to go on has to be stopped, and it sounds like it's a go whether we're along or not." He paused a few seconds, and Pacheco knew it was the big man's way of giving him time to let it sink in. Then Bolan said, "Now, let me ask you a question. You aren't buying this story about us being offered a partnership, are you?"

Pacheco shook his head as they strolled on, passing another tall chain-link fence around the tennis courts. "This old friend he speaks of, the one who he's going in with on this last big shipment? My guess is the man's also buying him out."

Bolan nodded. "Right. That's the only way any of it makes sense. Gothe's just telling everyone what they want to hear. He tells us we'll be partners, and insinuates that either he, or one of us, will kill Lima. That's because he knows we'd never fall for that 'years of loyal' nonsense. But Lima's stupid. Gothe gives Lima the 'inherit the farm' routine." He paused and drew in a deep breath.

Pacheco felt himself frowning as an idea played around the fringes of his mind, trying to take shape. Most of what the American had said made sense. But some part of it was bothering him, and he couldn't quite get it to take shape. They walked on, and suddenly the thought crystalized. "Okay," he said. "But one thing bothers me. Gothe's not dumb, either. What if he suspects we've seen through his story? After all, we've got no proof except his word. He's got to wonder why we're playing along if that's the case."

"People look at others and believe everyone views the world the same way they do, Jaime. They think everyone has the same priorities as them, and the same strengths and weaknesses. Francisco Gothe thinks he's dangled enough dollar signs in front of our eyes to cloud our judgment." Bolan paused. "Or else he thinks we've got our own game going, and that if he doesn't follow through with his promise we'll try to take it from him anyway. But his actual thinking on that isn't important to us. What is important is that one way or another, he's planning to have us killed just as soon as we've finished guarding his investment in the coke run."

A cold chill fell over Pacheco's shoulders, then dripped down his spine. It made sense. And it was an angle he hadn't thought of himself, which scared him, too.

The two men reached the riding stables and the smell of horse manure, accompanied by an occasional neigh, drifted toward them. "Lima will also be a problem," the American went on. "Since he believes what Gothe said about turning things over to him, but with us being partners, he's going to want to kill us for his own reasons."

Pacheco nodded. That had occurred to him, too. "From his point of view, if we're out of the picture, he not only inherits the farm he's the only farmer on the land."

"Exactly."

The guest house stood a hundred yards or so upwind from the stables, and they headed that way. It was as elaborate, and of the same design as the castle.

"I saw the movie *Schindler's List* several years ago," Pacheco said. "Toward the end the hero, Schindler, feels guilty that he didn't sell everything he owned to save more Jews from the Nazis during World War II. 'My car,' he says. 'I could have saved ten more lives.' 'My suit. Two lives.' And so on." Pacheco stopped, rubbing a hand up and down the expensive stone wall of the guest house. "Sometimes I see Gothe as the negative image of Schindler. In my mind, I can picture him saying to his visitors, This guest house? A hundred dead slaves. But the big house, that cost several thousand." He turned to look at Bolan again. "Do you think I am crazy?"

"Probably," Bolan said. "But you aren't dangerous. At least not to the good guys."

Pacheco began the guided tour again, leading the man he respected so much past the edge of Gothe's nine-hole golf course. They made their way toward a large barracks-looking building in the distance. "The bunkhouse, Gothe calls it," he told Bolan. "The man heard the term in an old American western movie, I believe."

"Dormitory?" Bolan asked.

Pacheco nodded. "For the workers. But there are several private rooms for the overseers. Lima and I each have one. You will, too." He snorted. "They all have locks on the door so the diggers cannot cut our throats in our sleep."

They walked along in silence, then Bolan said, "It bothers you, doesn't it?"

"What?" Pacheco asked.

"Pretending to be scum like Lima and Gothe. Even though you know it's only a show, and that the outcome is for the good of the men you're overseeing, it bothers you."

Pacheco hesitated for a moment, then said, "Yes."

"Good," he said, and Pacheco could see him nodding his approval to the side. "If it didn't, there'd be something wrong with you. But keep it up. You're good at it and like I said, it's for a good cause."

The two men reached the dormitory and Pacheco led the way in. The huge common room for the diggers was on the other side of the building, but even through the wall they could smell the odor of sweat, decaying food and lingering death. The undercover man came to a door and tried the knob. Finding it unlocked, he pushed open the door. "You might as well take this one," he said. "It was Mantara's." He waved Bolan past him into the sparsely furnished room. "I'm next door. Lima is on the other side."

Bolan nodded as his eyes took in the bare bed, end table and lone chair.

"You'll want to keep it locked," the Costa Rican said. "You can get a key from Maria, the maid." He paused a second, then said, "You need any help carrying your stuff from the car?"

Bolan shook his head.

"Then I'll leave you for a little while. But first, can I ask you one more question?"

Bolan turned to face him.

"I assume you're going to orchestrate things so we find out who Gothe's friend is. What are we going to do then?"

The man met Jaime Pacheco's stare. In his eyes, Pacheco could see no emotion. What he saw was determination. And the soul of a man who had lived his life doing what he knew was right.

THE EXECUTIONER WAS traveling light, having stashed most of his equipment before coming to Gothe's headquarters. The antiquities smuggler and soon-to-be cocaine dealer still had to think Bolan was a merc for hire, a man who had been on the run from the law since the Toledo assassination. It wouldn't do to be hauling along all the space-age technology available from Stony Man Farm. The fact was, too much gear of any kind could get him burned. So he had brought his big knives, the Chinook, the Beretta, Desert Eagle and the little North American Arms. His weapons and a few changes of clothing were almost the only items he had brought. He had no doubt that his room would be searched the first time he left it. Gothe would have someone—probably Lima—go through his things just for security's sake. There would be no secrets in the room, and the soldier wanted nothing in it that might make Gothe suspect him of being anything other than what he was trying to appear to be.

Bolan still wore the double-knife shoulder rig under his open shirt as he dug through the soft-sided suitcase. The Szabowie and Crossada had served him well, not only in defense but as show pieces. They had been the perfect weapons for a man on the run—a man who might not want to risk getting caught with firearms but who couldn't afford to be left defenseless, either.

Now, however, it was time now for more serious weaponry.

Inside the suitcase Bolan found the pistols, and extra ammo for all three weapons. The guns themselves, and some of the magazines, he would carry on him. The 93-R's shoulder harness and the hip holster for the Desert Eagle were pushing his cover just a bit—few killers for hire wore such elaborate rigs, knowing they might have to ditch their weapons at any moment if police suddenly appeared. But there were exceptions to that rule, and he was now in an environment where Francisco Gothe *owned* the cops. So the need for such discretion had abated to a certain extent.

One other item in the suitcase, however, would give him away in a heart beat should he be found with it. It was definitely high tech, Stony Man Farm at its finest. The Executioner picked up the small black box, staring down at it. It was essential, and he had no choice but to risk being discovered with it. Luckily it was small enough to keep with him at all times.

AFTER A LONG AND elaborate dinner with Gothe and Pacheco Bolan returned to his room. The feast had consisted of *gallo pinto,* the national dish of the country, served by Maria. The soldier had been somewhat surprised when, after filling their plates, the woman in the French maid's uniform had taken a seat at the table next to Gothe. She was obviously more than just kitchen help, and Bolan suspected from the way Gothe glanced at her now and then that what he really kept her for took place in the bedroom. Her quiet, embarrassed demeanor and downcast eyes also suggested that she wasn't crazy about the relationship. But, for whatever reason, she had chosen to accept it.

Now, as he sat on the edge of his bed, he considered the most immediate problem at hand. He needed to learn the identity of Gothe's partner in this upcoming drug deal. That meant a soft probe of the house after the antiquities man went to sleep. Gothe had informed them at dinner that he'd spoken to his partner, and the deal was set to go down the next day. Bolan and Pacheco were given few details. All they knew was that the huge shipment of cocaine would be going by sea, and that they'd be expected to accompany it to its destination and then fly back to Costa Rica.

Bolan stopped digging through his suitcase long enough to consider the option of blowing off the drug deal, beating the information he needed out of Gothe and then eliminating the man before going after his partner. That battle plan sounded far more simple. The problem with it was that the cocaine would still go through, probably to the U.S., where it would wind up in the noses and arms of American citizens. No, he couldn't let that happen.

Returning to his original problem, the Executioner continued to dig through the suitcase. How was he going to cross the grounds without being seen by one of the many armed guards who patrolled the estate? He had brought no blacksuit—such an item found in his room would have been as telltale as a badge. But the clothing he had worn, and most of what he had brought as changes, were far too light for suitable night operations wear.

Bolan went through his suitcase again, finally pulling out a black T-shirt and dark blue jeans. He changed clothes quickly. Snores could already be heard through the thin walls inside Pacheco's room, but Lima's quarters, on the other side, were silent. The man was taking his new responsibilities seriously, and had gone off to supervise the night's dig. The workers' dorm was quiet, too. Even some of the offensive odor had left the building as the men moved out with the rising moon. Bolan knew that some of the other overseers had gone with Lima, but others now slept in their own rooms. That meant he couldn't afford to make any noise leaving the building. The Executioner wondered for a moment where the crew was digging this night. He didn't know. But wherever it was, men would be whipped, beaten, and perhaps worked to death or outright murdered. Such knowledge caused Bolan's jaw to set firm in determination for the mission at hand.

Moving quietly to the door, Bolan pulled it back slowly, pausing each time it creaked. When it was wide enough to slip through, he entered the hallway, then closed the door as carefully as he'd opened it. He heard the lock click into place, tested it with a twist, then moved away.

Once outside the building, the Executioner kept to the shadows, making his way slowly and quietly when behind concealment, but darting quickly when forced to cover open ground. The problem was that he hadn't been there long enough to study the estate guards' routine, and he didn't have time to do so now. He would have to take his chances, hoping his long years of training and abilities would see him through as they always had before.

Bolan reached the swimming pool and found the gate in the fence still open. Good. It not only made access easier, it bespoke a certain casual attitude on the part of the men assigned to oversee the grounds at night. Slipping through the opening, he slowly lowered himself into the shallow end of the pool, dunked his head under water, then pulled himself back out.

The grass at the front of the riding stables had been trampled away by thousands of hooves, and it was there the Executioner hurried now. Dropping to one knee, he scooped up handfuls of already damp earth and applied the makeshift cammo makeup to his face, neck and arms. He had no way to check his work unless he wanted to return to his room and the cracked mirror above the bureau. So, working by feel, he finished the job and moved on.

A carefully tended orchid garden sat ten yards from the house, and the Executioner dropped to his belly behind the plants. He had scouted out the alarm system both during his first meeting with Gothe that afternoon and even better that evening at dinner. It wasn't elaborate—a simple device with motion and auditory detectors. A low buzz would be triggered when a door was opened. But that buzz would turn into a loud siren and bells if a numeric code wasn't punched into the control box within a given amount of time, usually thirty seconds. The soldier had seen the control box just inside the front door when he'd first arrived. Now he had to hope he could find his way through the house from his chosen point of entry, determine the code and get it entered within the allotted time.

It would be close, and if Lady Luck didn't smile on him at least a little, the whole plan could blow up in his face.

Still hidden behind the orchids, the Executioner studied the side of the house. The front door would be closer to the control box and give him more time to decipher the code. But the front was no way to clandestinely enter the house by night. There would be permanent guards stationed in that area, and although he hadn't seen it since the sun had fallen, he suspected it would be well lit.

The Executioner was about to rise and sprint for the side door he'd chosen earlier when an undefined sound caught his ear. He froze on his belly, his arms beneath his chest, ready to push himself up to his feet. Still unidentifiable, but slightly louder, he heard the sound again.

The third time the noise came he recognized it as a drunken laugh in the distance. The muscles in his arms and legs still flexed and ready, he waited. More laughter. Then the indistinct sound of voices gradually becoming more clear. Peering through the orchids in front of him, the Executioner finally saw two men rounding the back of the house.

Both men staggered slightly as they walked, passing a bottle of some type back and forth. As they neared the house, the taller of the men cautioned the other. "Be quiet!" he commanded, pointing toward the castle's second story. "Do not awaken the dragon in the castle!"

The other man giggled drunkenly, then covered his mouth with his own hand. CAR-15 .223-caliber rifles swung from their shoulders on slings as the two guards staggered past in silence.

Bolan waited until they had headed down the gravel drive, probably to join up with the guards at the front of the house for another drink. As soon as he was sure there were no other men in the area, he bounded to his feet, hurdled the orchids and sprinted across the lawn to the doorway.

He had chosen this particular point of entry for three reasons. First, except for the front door itself, it appeared to be the closest to the alarm box. Second, it was slightly recessed from the rest of the castlelike house, causing the gray stones to cast black shadows over the area. With his dark clothing and mud-darkened face, he was counting on being able to take the time necessary to pick the lock silently. But picking it shouldn't take long, and that was the third reason the Executioner had chosen this spot to invade the house. The door was secured by nothing more than a simple snap lock.

Bolan slowed to half-speed a few feet from the door and caught himself with his hands against the stone. Ducking quickly into the recess, he pivoted back around, crouching as he looked out over the grounds. There was no indication that he'd been seen. Turning back to the doorway, he unclipped the Spyderco Chinook folder from his belt. He held the locking bar down as he opened it, making sure the blade locked into place silently, then worked it slowly between the door and frame.

A moment later the door snapped open. Bolan glanced down at the luminous hands of his wristwatch, noting the time.

Moving swiftly now, the Executioner did his best to walk the fine line between speed and silence. Closing the door behind him in case the guards came back, he moved quietly through the kitchen and into a hallway he didn't recognize. It had been impossible to do a decent recon of the house's interior without drawing suspicion, and a trip to the bathroom had told him only part of what he needed to know. He'd have liked to have had a set of blueprints to study, he thought as he hurried down the corridor. But there was an old saying about people in hell and ice water, too, and he wasted no time wishing for what he knew he didn't have.

Bolan hurried on. He thought he had thirty seconds after opening the door before the alarm sounded, but he couldn't be sure. Alarm systems such as he was used to dealing with were designed to give those entering legitimately enough time to enter the code before all hell broke loose. They could be set at any desired time from ten seconds to several minutes.

The Executioner moved quietly. The hallway took him past a semilit room with a billiards table and video games. He passed another darker room but smelled the distinct odor of yeast, and knew that had to be where Gothe brewed his beer. On a hunch, he cut into the next room he came to, walking blindly with one hand outstretched in front of him as he checked his watch again on the other.

He had twenty seconds left.

The door on the other side of the room was closed, and this forced him to slow his already maddeningly snaillike pace even further. He swung it back—thankful that it had been oiled recently—and stepped through the room into the conservatory. Finally oriented, he cut through the plants into the living room. But another look at his watch told him he had already been in the house twenty-two seconds. The Executioner drew a deep breath.

It was simple, really. He wasn't going to make it. At least not if the alarm was set to go off after the standard thirty-second interval.

Bolan hurried on. Insurmountable odds had never made him give up before, and he wasn't about to let them this time. Keeping calm, he pulled the small black box from his waistband as he crossed the last few feet of the foyer to the alarm system.

A short length of rubber-coated electrical wire was plugged into the bottom of the box, and a suction cup was hanging from the loose end. Bolan's hands were steady as he stuck the cup against the alarm box just below the luminous readout. The lighted display looked very much like the face of a telephone, he thought, as he waited for the bells to go off and the lights to flash. At the same time, he hoped against hope that the code detector—a joint invention by Gadgets Schwarz and Aaron Kurtzman at Stony Man Farm—would reveal the code before that happened.

The seconds ticked on. Bolan looked down at his watch and saw it had been thirty-five seconds since he'd entered the house. Was the alarm set to give Gothe forty-five seconds instead of thirty? Maybe. Gothe was getting older. He moved more slowly than a younger man. As a quiet ticking sound began in the code detector Bolan realized it made little difference. He wasn't going to have the code after forty-five seconds any more than he'd had it at thirty.

But as the second hand on his wristwatch told him forty-five seconds had passed, Bolan saw that the first two numbers of the four-digit code had been found. They were glowing brightly on the face of the code detector. Bolan held his wrist up next to the instrument and watched the fast-moving hand sweep on toward the fifty-second mark. Still, no alarm. The third number showed up on the screen. Bolan waited. Surely the system hadn't been set to activate any slower than a minute after being triggered. He had less than ten seconds left. It was still going to be close.

Finally another digit appeared on the screen, and the Executioner's finger jabbed the code into the face on the alarm box. He stood where he was, holding his breath, still not sure he had deactivated the system in time. But as his success began to sink in, his brain returned to the battle plan. He now had to creep through the house and locate Gothe's office, his center of operations, and find his computer. Somehow he had to learn in advance who the friend was who was going in with him on the drug deal and more than likely buying out the antiquities business. But he had seen no sign of an office or similar room in his two trips inside the house, and again he would be flying blind.

So far, he had been lucky. Maybe that luck would hold out.

Then he felt the hand on his shoulder.

BOLAN TURNED TO SEE Maria standing behind him, one of her index fingers pressed against her lips. The beautiful young woman no longer wore the French maid's uniform.

The fact was, she wore nothing at all.

She leaned up on her toes to whisper in his ear. "What are you doing here?"

Bolan wasn't quite sure what to say. If the young woman had known of his presence, why hadn't she alerted Gothe? How come the alarm hadn't already gone off, and why weren't a half dozen of the guards he'd seen around the house already aiming their CAR-15s his way?

When he didn't answer, Maria took his hand. "Come," she whispered.

The nude woman led Bolan back through the house. They passed a window through which streamed a few rays of light, and Bolan saw the welts and bruises on the woman's buttocks. His teeth clamped tight. He had suspected before, but now he knew why Maria always seemed so nervous. What he couldn't figure out was why she stayed with Gothe.

They entered the game room Bolan had passed earlier, and Maria closed the door softly behind them. She continued to whisper when she spoke. "He never comes here. We are as safe as we can be. But that is still not safe."

Bolan waited. He had no idea what the woman was up to.

Maria suddenly became aware of her nudity and tried to cover herself. Bolan grabbed the bottom of his T-shirt and pulled it over his head, handing it to her. "It's a little muddy," he said. "But it should work."

The statement seemed to break the ice between them. Maria giggled softly as she slid the shirt down her shoulders. The hem fell to her knees. "Why are you here?" she asked. "And why do you look like you are some commando?"

Rather than answer, he asked his own question. "Why are *you* here?" he asked. "If you knew I was in the house why didn't you tell your boss? Or did you?"

Maria glanced at the door as if it might have its own ears. "Señor Gothe is asleep," she said. "And no, I didn't tell him you were here."

"That's the answer to one of my questions," Bolan said. "The other was why are you here? I saw the marks." He glanced down at her hips, then back up to her eyes.

Maria looked down too, out of shame. But then she, too, looked up again. "I cannot leave. At least not yet." Most of the shyness she had exhibited before, when she'd been nude, was now gone. But now a portion of it came back and she looked at the floor the way he'd seen her do earlier at dinner. "There was something I sensed about you when you first came. I thought perhaps you were the man I had waited for for so long."

"Maria," Bolan said, "what are you talking about?"

"You are different," the beautiful young woman said. "You are not like Julio, or that dreadful Mantara who I am happy is dead. You seem...good. I cannot explain it. It is just a feeling. I get it about Señor Pacheco, as well." She took a deep breath and shivered, as if the T-shirt weren't warm enough. "I want to help you. Tell me what you need."

Bolan reached out and gently took her by the chin, tilting her eyes back up to his. His words might have been hard, but he said them in a soft voice. "You're risking your own life protecting me, Maria. And you aren't a psychic. Getting the feeling that I 'seem good' doesn't quite hack it. It isn't enough. Tell me the rest."

Maria's eyes flared with anger. "It is not enough that I want to help you? Not enough that I don't want Gothe to catch you here and have you murdered?"

The Executioner exhaled a slow breath. "Yes," he said. "That would be enough. If that was all there was to it. But it isn't. There's more, Maria."

For a few moments the only sound in the game room was the hum of the central air-conditioning unit kicking on. Then Maria took a deep breath and said, "He plans to kill you anyway. All of you. You, Señor Pacheco and Lima. You and Señor Pacheco must leave while you still can. Lima, I don't care about."

What he suspected was now confirmed. But there was a venom in Maria's voice when she spoke of Lima that didn't pass by the Executioner unnoticed, either. "What did Lima do to you?" he asked.

Even though she now wore the T-shirt that covered far more than the maid's uniform she had worn earlier in the day, Maria's arms returned to her body as if she were nude again. "I will let you guess," she said in a voice so low Bolan hardly heard the words.

"You didn't tell Gothe?"

Maria shook her head. "No. He would've blamed me. And then I would've been used goods to him. Perhaps he would have killed Lima, but he would have killed me, too."

"How do you know that?"

"Because that is what happens to his mistresses when he is finished with them."

"And you are—"

Maria looked irritated. "Of course I am. I am his current mistress, and will be until he loses interest. Or perhaps he will kill me when he kills you, when he moves away from here and retires."

"How do you know all this?" Bolan asked. "He tells you these things?" Somehow, it didn't fit the image he'd formed of Francisco Gothe.

"Of course not," Maria said scornfully. "He hardly speaks to me at all. I am nothing but a toy to him. A plaything for his perverted desires. But I overhear things. And this afternoon when...when he was through with me, he sent me away. But I stayed in the hall and listened to him make a phone call."

Bolan waited silently for her to go on. He was pleased to see her fear had turned to anger.

"He has sold his antiquities business to another man. The same man he is doing this drug deal with." She paused a moment and frowned.

Again, the Executioner's suspicions were confirmed. Slowly he nodded to himself. Gothe's scheme now made perfect sense. But he still wasn't satisfied that he'd gotten a good explanation as to Maria's motives. Why was the woman risking her own life for him? If she was actually loyal to Gothe—and even the red welts on her buttocks could have been placed there to gain Bolan's sympathy—this might be part of a setup. His instincts told him that wasn't the case. But his brain wanted concrete proof.

Bolan had dropped the gentle hold he'd had on the woman's chin. Now, he took it again. "There's more though, isn't there?" he said. "This still doesn't explain why you are here, why you sleep with him, and why you let him degrade you the way he does."

"I have my reasons."

Bolan nodded. "I know you do, but I don't know what they are. And I need to know."

Maria hesitated, and the indecision on her face was evident. Finally she either decided she could trust the Executioner or that it made no difference if he knew. "Because he killed my mother," she said.

"Your mother?"

"She was his mistress before me. There were others as I grew up."

"Wait a minute," Bolan said. "You grew up here? With him? Did he—"

Maria had anticipated the question. "No," she said. "Until I was sixteen, he thought I was his daughter. Other women filled his bed, and each disappeared when he tired of them as my mother had. But he...*looked* at me from the time I was old enough to remember." She shivered as if suddenly cold. "He is a monster," she said, and tears began to form in her eyes. "He has made me do—"

Bolan wrapped his arms around her and held her close. She cried against his chest for a few moments, then pushed him away again.

"I have stayed in order to get revenge," she said. "Revenge for both me and my mother. I knew that if I waited long enough, someday someone would come who would help me."

"You can call it revenge if you like, Maria," the Executioner said. "I'd just call it justice. And I'll help you get it." He looked down into the beautiful woman's eyes and saw tears streaming down her cheeks. "But in order to do that, you first have to help me." He watched the smile come over her face. The tears stopped.

"So, Maria," Bolan said. "What do you say you show me the quickest way to Gothe's office?"

"Why do you want to go to his office?" Maria asked.

"I need to find out who it is he's doing the coke deal with," Bolan replied. "That seems like the best place to start."

Maria shrugged, and then an impish smile curled her pretty lips. "I will take you there if you like," she said. "But if that is all you need to know, I can tell you that now. The man's name is Letona. Ramon Letona. He owns the shipping company that smuggles most of Gothe's antiquities out of the country."

6

A light froth of white capped the gentle waves as the *Evangelina* sailed through the water. An old-fashioned four-masted bark, the sheets were manned by a crew of eight men. Dressed in the uniforms of eighteenth-century British seamen, they roamed back and forth across the deck, adjusting the sails to get the most out of the moderate winds currently passing over the Gulf of Mexico.

To the naked eye, they looked exactly like what they were supposed to look like, sailors paid to dress up in reenactment garb to add to the ambience of a period-based pleasure cruise.

Close to twenty other hired hardmen, of all nationalities, wore shorts, polo shirts, baseball caps and other typical tourist attire. Although they looked more like they belonged in the century in which they lived, they, too, were playing parts. Their roles were to appear to be the clients of the cruise. The fact that there were no women onboard had led one port official to raise an eyebrow, assuming the charter had to be an "all gay" cruise.

The men onboard the ship were not gay. Or if any of them were, it had nothing to do with their decision to take the cruise. While the *Evangelina* was indeed masquerading as a pleasure ship, business was the true purpose of the voyage.

That business was drugs. Cocaine. Literally thousands of kilos of the deadly white powder were stored in the holds below. And someone within the Costa Rican government had to be getting his cut of the immense profit about to be made. Port officials had signed off on the ship without so much as even boarding her. And the captain in charge of the ship had been so confident that this would happen that there had been little attempt to even hide the coke belowdecks. It was stacked against the walls of the holds in clear plastic bags, covered only by tarps.

Bolan and Pacheco, wearing shorts and T-shirts and posing as clients on the cruise, stood by the railing on the port side of the ship. Several hours earlier, they had passed through the Yucatán Channel between Cuba and Mexico, staying close enough to the Mexican side to see the shores of the peninsula in the distance. The ship was operating under both power and sail and making excellent time. The soldier knew they could be only an hour or so out of New Orleans.

Bolan watched a giant sperm whale swim close enough to check them out, then nose dive below the surface with a flip of its tail. After Maria had told him about Ramon Letona, she had helped him slip past the bed where Gothe was sleeping. In the small study behind the bedroom he had found more information about the man on Gothe's computer.

Ramon Letona used Gothe's business interests to both create an image of legitimacy and to launder money. A quick Internet search by Bolan had shown that Letona, a Nicarauguan, owned the Central American Development Company. The CADC developed raw land, then built private houses, resorts, hotels and industrial buildings. The company owned two subsidiaries that were of even more interest to the Executioner— Costa Rica Import and Export which was based in San José, and Dolphin Cruises, Inc. The *Evangelina* was one of Dolphin's ships.

Bolan watched the whale resurface a hundred yards in the distance and float along the water. In short, Letona had the perfect business setup to smuggle drugs, illegal weapons, antiquities, or any other form of contraband. Bolan suspected Gothe contracted him to ship the artifacts along with Letona's own cocaine cargos. Gothe's profits then went through his resort hotels, and Letona's were lost back into CADC. In the meantime, Letona's development company continued to build, with their latest project being a large retirement community for elderly Americans. This meant he made frequent trips to the U.S., ostensibly to generate investors, but these trips would also offer an excellent opportunity to meet with their drug contacts.

The Executioner glanced down the rail to see one of the crewmen staring at him. As soon as they made eye contact, however, the man looked away. Bolan nodded to himself. He and Pacheco hadn't received the warmest of receptions onboard the ship. Most of these men were used to working together, and knew one another. And they all drew their pay from the same man—Ramon Letona. To have two new faces thrown at them at the last minute broke their routine. It was a dangerous business they were in, and it made them nervous.

In addition to the danger from both Costa Rica and the U.S. authorities, modern-day pirates still roamed the Gulf of Mexico and Caribbean. Usually drug smugglers themselves, these pirates would be more than happy to lift the cargo if word had leaked out as to what the *Evangelina* was hauling. So each man kept one eye on the horizon, looking for other ships.

Cannons were mounted on the deck, but they had been blocked—Bolan had checked them. Live guns, even on what looked like a rich eccentrics pleasure cruise, would invite the inspection of coastal authorities. But Gothe and Letona couldn't very well ask the men to go unarmed, either. So each of the drug guards, whether dressed as sailor or tourist, carried a pistol. Bolan had noticed the slight bulges in the wrong places beneath their shirts. Earlier, when he'd gone below, he had seen heavier arms stored in the fore hold of the ship. Automatic rifles, submachine guns and even a few shotguns. But these were all locked inside a steel cage. It was a time-honored tradition to keep heavy weapons out of the hands of men at sea. Close quarters for long periods of time could cause tempers to flare. And besides, at sea there was always some warning of potential attack. This meant sufficient time to get such weapons out and distributed.

The crewman down the rail fished a crumpled cigarette out of his pocket, lit it with a butane lighter that contrasted with his period costume, then turned and walked away. The whale disappeared again beneath the water, and Bolan glanced at his watch. His plan was simple. Within the next thirty minutes he intended to kill the vast majority of the drug runners. If things went well, he would leave a skeleton crew alive to sail the *Evangelina* toward New Orleans before eliminating them just before they hit port. If things didn't go well, he and Pacheco would have to trim the sails enough to allow the two of them to man the ship and limp on in on their own. Yes, a simple plan. At least in conception.

But hardly simple to carry out. Bolan and Pacheco were outnumbered fourteen to one. Not the kind of odds Las Vegas bookies would want. Which meant that success would require split-second timing, nerves of steel and maybe even a little luck. Bolan planned to use a time-honored strategy— divide and conquer.

But one other thing worried the Executioner as he continued to stare off across the blue waters of the gulf. Pacheco. Toledo had warned Bolan that while Pacheco was fearless, and the best undercover officer he'd ever known, the man was bad with a gun.

The Executioner knew he was as good with a gun as any man alive. Such knowledge was not conceit on his part, just fact. But along with the confidence bred from his skills came a realistic view of them. There were a total of twenty-eight men onboard, all of them armed. If he divided them down the middle, that meant fourteen for him and fourteen for Pacheco. But that wasn't the way it would go down. The vast majority of kills would be up to him. So strategy would have to come into play. Otherwise he and the Costa Rican undercover man would be feeding the fish while the *Evangelina* sailed into New Orleans to deliver its cargo of white death.

To his side, Bolan saw Pacheco glance at his own watch, then look up nervously.

The Executioner nodded. Pacheco already knew what to do, what part he was to play to get the game started.

The undercover cop nodded back, nervously licked his lips, then pushed away from the rail and walked across the deck. Just past the mainsail, he disappeared down the steps of the ladder to the underbelly of the ship.

Bolan waited, his hands still on the rail. Behind him, he sensed men passing back and forth. No other hired CADC gunmen stood at the rail around the ship as much as he did. Most were engaged in low-voiced conversations, and the Executioner guessed that he and Pacheco were the subject of more than one. The captain, a man who had introduced himself simply as Eagle Jack, was in his midforties with a brown-becoming-gray mustache. He had announced to the rest of the crew that the two newcomers were there to look after the interests of a new investor. That was all, and it was obvious that was all he had been told himself.

The men had to accept things as they were, but they didn't have to like it, and obviously didn't.

The two men closest to Bolan, however, weren't talking about him or Pacheco. The fact that the bureaucrat who had stamped their authorization papers had thought they were all gay had been the subject of much mirth among the men at first, gradually dying down as the voyage went on. But the couple just down the rail from the Executioner hadn't tired of the subject yet, and now a fat man, wearing a white tank top that stretched tightly across his large belly, reached over and patted the man next to him on the posterior. "Hey, Hector," he said. "The longer we sail, the better you look."

The man whose ass he had touched jumped, bringing about a chorus of laughter from several of the other men watching. He was in his early twenties, and not amused by the gesture. "In your dreams, old man," he said, brushing off the seat of his pants as if he'd just sat in a pile of mud.

Another set of chuckles broke out.

No sooner had the laughter died down than Pacheco's anxious face appeared at the top of the steps again. "Hey, Eagle Jack!" he yelled at the top of his voice. "Hey, Captain! Come quick!"

Bolan could see the man with the brownish-gray mustache all the way to the fore end of the ship. He turned, and the look on his face was more annoyed than alarmed.

Pacheco waved his arms violently to create more attention. "Captain, hurry! There's one hell of a leak below."

His words didn't seem to excite Eagle Jack in the least, and brought several snickers from the other men who heard them. The captain, an experienced old salt, knew that if the *Evangelina* had been taking on water he would have felt it. The ship would have ridden lower in the water and handled differently. What Bolan saw on Eagle Jack's face as he walked leisurely under the foresail was the look of a man tired of dealing with inexperienced sailors. Perhaps Eagle Jack was actually a seagoing man by trade rather than a full-time drug smuggler. Bolan considered the possibility. It was possible, and if so his infrequent jobs with this bunch of gunmen—most of whom he suspected knew little of ships—would indeed be annoying.

But whether the captain was a full- or part-time smuggler made no difference to the Executioner. Eagle Jack knew what he was doing. He knew what was stored in the holds below. So whether he had done it a thousand times or just this once, he was guilty.

And he would pay along with the rest.

Bolan pushed off from the rail and walked toward the steps. "Want me to go down and check it out with you?" he asked the captain as the man walked up.

Eagle Jack looked him up and down, then snorted. Another landlubber who'd just be in the way. Ignoring the soldier's question, he turned to the fat man in the tank top and the younger man standing next to him. "Quincy, Williams," he said. "Come with me. Just in case there's some truth to all this." He disappeared down the ladder.

Bolan stepped back to let the other two men go around him to the steps. They disappeared behind the captain.

Most of the other men were watching now, bored with the monotony of the waves and the steady wind. Bolan knew he had to give the men who had gone below enough time to get far enough away that they wouldn't hear him approach from behind. So he waited a good thirty seconds. Then he looked at the other men on deck who were still watching him, shrugged as if to say, "I've got nothing else better to do," and started down the steps.

As soon as he was below the line of vision of the men on deck, the Beretta 93-R, sound suppressor screwed tightly onto the barrel, came out from under his shirt.

JAIME PACHECO KNEW that undercover work was really nothing more than an acting job. There was no difference between playing a part onstage and playing the part of a criminal in an undercover police role. But there was a difference in the way audiences reacted to a bad performance. Onstage, if he didn't present himself convincingly, the people in the seats might throw tomatoes and cabbages at the stage.

If he didn't convince them when he was undercover, they used bullets.

Pacheco could hear Eagle Jack muttering under his breath as he led the man down the ladder, past one of the many canvas-covered stacks of cocaine stored in the first hold. As nervous as he was, he couldn't keep from marveling once again at the sheer audacity of the crew. The only thing they'd done to disguise the kilos was cover them with tarps. They were arrogant enough to think they wouldn't be searched by authorities before sailing out of San José. Somebody was being paid off, and as soon as this job with the American was over and Toledo was back in San José, he decided he'd see about going undercover with the port inspectors.

All of which, in turn, reminded Pacheco that he and Toledo had been wise to call in the big man from the United States. There was no telling who could be trusted in Costa Rican law-enforcement circles any more. From the special police units and investigators to patrolmen, from superintendents to inspectors, there was just too much money involved to keep very many of them one hundred percent honest.

Behind him, Pacheco heard the footsteps of the three other men. Eagle Jack, of course, Quincy and Williams. Eagle Jack looked Hispanic, but Pacheco hadn't been able to pick up on the accent. It sounded almost Brazilian, but not quite. The other two had to either be American or Canadian. Whatever they were, the three of them were whispering and laughing in soft voices, probably about him, and his fear that the boat was sinking.

Pacheco and the American had admitted to the captain early on that they were there to look after Gothe's interests and weren't sailors. Only a few of the hired guns on the *Evangelina* were actually seamen, mainly the ones dressed up in the little sailor suits with the knee britches, striped socks and buckle shoes. But none of the men had liked them since they'd come onboard, and they'd pretty much been ignored. The fact that they didn't know any more about ships than Pacheco, however, didn't stop them from wanting to have a good laugh at his expense. They just assumed he'd seen some normal spill in the holds and assumed the ship was going down.

That was fine with Pacheco. He wasn't after the respect of these drug-smuggling cutthroats. If their plan worked, the hardmen weren't going to live much longer anyway. But would the plan work? He just hoped so. And everything else the American had tried had worked out, even though it seemed impossible before he did it.

The footsteps behind him continued as Pacheco made his way toward the aft hold. Belasko planned to give them a few seconds lead, then follow. But if the big American got detained for any reason up top, Pacheco knew he was in trouble. Eagle Jack and other two men would soon see that there was nothing belowdecks that even a landlubber might think was a leak. Then the questions would start.

Jaime Pacheco could only hope to stall long enough for his partner to get below and trap the three between them. He'd have to hope he could think fast enough on his feet to answer the men's questions and to buy time. That was another big difference between stage acting and undercover work, he realized, as he stepped through the hatch into the aft hold. Onstage, he could memorize the lines. Undercover, it was all impromptu. And if his answers didn't convince these guys long enough for the big guy to arrive, he was likely to be lying dead in a pool of blood.

Pacheco stopped just inside the hold, turning, ostensibly to give the other men time to catch up. It bought him a couple of extra seconds.

They were hoping to take out as many men as they could before the rest figured out what was going on. So in addition to his Glock, which he didn't plan to use until later, he had a sound-suppressed .22-caliber Ruger semiauto handgun under his shirt. The Ruger was hardly the ideal weapon when it came to stopping power, especially for a man like him who wasn't the best shot in the world. He had never taken to guns very well. He just didn't have that innate feel for them some men seemed to have. Pacheco knew his own talents in that area were lacking, but he excelled at role-playing.

The other three men caught up to him and Pacheco turned away, at the same time pricking his ears, straining to hear a fourth set of footsteps. But he heard nothing. The silence didn't help his confidence.

Moving farther inside the hold, Pacheco saw one of the

ropes binding the tarps to the stack of cocaine had come un-knotted. He walked over to it and began slowly retying the knot. With the exception of one corner at the rear of the area, the stacked coke blocked the view of the walls of the hold.

"What the hell are you doing?" Eagle Jack demanded. "I thought you said there was a leak?"

"There is," Pacheco said, still fiddling with the knot. "But I thought I'd better retie this first."

"Shit, the way you acted a minute ago," Eagle Jack said, "I figured Moby Dick had chewed through the hull. Now you're stopping to tie knots? Jeez!"

Pacheco kept working the knot until the captain said, "Look, we'll take care of that later. Well, where the hell is this leak of yours?"

Pacheco turned to face the man, making a sheepish look come over his face. "I'll show you," he said slowly, as if sud-denly embarrassed. He turned as if to walk to the corner, then stopped again. "But I'm beginning to think maybe I overre-acted. You see...like I told you...I don't have much experience with boats." He was drawing his words out as much as he dared, stalling for time, hoping and praying that each extra fraction of a second he took with his words would add up to be the seconds he needed for his partner to arrive. "To be hon-est...the ocean has always made me nervous. I can't swim and—"

"Shut the hell up and show me the damn leak!" Eagle Jack yelled, his patience suddenly nonexistent. Pacheco saw his hand fall to his belt and work its way partially under his shirt-tail toward a bulge in the material. "I didn't like you guys being forced on me this morning, and I don't like you now. I don't trust you, either, and even if you're on the up-and-up and there really is some water down here, I ought to shoot your ass just for the peace of mind it'd give me."

Pacheco saw another opening, another chance to stall a few more precious seconds. "I'm sorry, Captain," he said. "I didn't mean to worry you. If I'd known—"

"Show me the fucking leak!" Eagle Jack's hand came out from beneath his shirt holding a bright nickel-plated .45-caliber Colt Commander. The barrel came up under Pacheco's nose to rest on his upper lip.

Jaime Pacheco knew he had pushed the man just about as far as he could go. He still didn't see any sign of Belasko. So he decided to give it one more shot and pray that what he was about to do purchased him a few more seconds instead of a bullet. He would never know whether that was the right decision, the best thing to do under the circumstances. Like so many other things he did undercover, he never really learned whether they had been valuable or not. Nodding swiftly, Pacheco turned and started toward the corner of the hold, headed to an open area behind another stack of packaged cocaine.

Where he knew there would be no water. No sign of any kind of leak.

Where he was very likely to get shot and draw his last breath.

Halfway there, he made his move, throwing the dice in the last gamble he had left up his undercover sleeve. With the skill of a vaudevillian, he suddenly tripped over an imaginary object on the deck and fell flat on his face.

"What the hell is wrong with you!" Eagle Jack's voice roared behind him. "What the hell are you trying to pull? If there was a leak back here, there'd be water all over the deck!"

On the floor, facedown, Pacheco heard the distinctive sound of the Colt's safety being flipped down. It sounded almost as loud as a steel drum in the confined chamber.

There would be no more stalling. No more hoping that his partner would arrive. He was on his own now, and he was about to die. Not only was it three against one, Eagle Jack—and probably Quincy and Williams by now—already had their guns drawn.

A sudden anger flooded Jaime Pacheco's veins. If he was to die, he would die like a man. He would go down swinging.

Reaching under his shirt, Pacheco found the Ruger's grip. He drew the pistol from his belt as he flipped over onto his back.

THE EXECUTIONER DESCENDED the steps as quietly as possible, knowing that sound belowdecks carried as easily as across water. As he had done when he'd crept through Gothe's house the night before, he had to find the happy medium between speed and stealth. Too fast would create noise that would tip off the men ahead of him to his presence. But too slow would leave Pacheco holding the bag, stammering around trying to explain why he thought there was a leak when there was no sign of water belowdecks.

Either one could get the Costa Rican undercover man killed.

Bolan crouched slightly, the Beretta gripped in his right fist as he shuffled past the canvas mountains of tarp-covered cocaine. The big sound suppressor—which could quiet the 9 mm bullet's roar to the point where all that was heard was a zip and the mechanical working of the steel slide—was pointed ahead of him, down at the ground at a forty-five-degree angle. The Beretta was equipped with luminous Trijicon sights that would glow in the dim lighting below. But they would be of little value. The Executioner had survived too many close-range battles to think he'd have time to look for his sights. He would point the Beretta at his target and pull the trigger.

Keeping close to the wall, Bolan moved on. As he neared the hatch to the aft hold, he heard voices. The words were unclear. But there were no footsteps; the men had stopped.

Picking up his pace as much as he dared, the Executioner hurried on. Every plan had its strong and weak areas, and this had been the weak area of this one. The timing left little margin for error. He had to get there before Eagle Jack and the other two men smelled the trick. And he, and Pacheco, had to kill all three of them before they got off a shot. If even one bullet was fired from their guns, it would sound the alarm.

Reaching the hatch, Bolan heard Eagle Jack say, "What the hell are you trying to pull? If there was a leak..."

With those words, the Executioner knew he was out of time.

Lunging through the hatch, Bolan no longer worried about the sound of his footsteps carrying into the other hold. In fact, he hoped the men would hear them and be distracted from Pacheco. It might give the undercover man a split second more to get into action.

As soon as he'd entered the hold, Bolan saw all four men. Pacheco was on the floor, facedown, in the process of rolling over. Eagle Jack, Quincy and Williams stood over him, all holding pistols.

As they heard him enter, all three men turned toward the Executioner.

Bolan had already thumbed the selector switch to single shot. The Beretta rose at the end of his arm. He pointed the barrel squarely between Eagle Jack's eyes and simultaneously pulled back on the trigger. The 93-R coughed once, and a hole appeared in the center of the captain's forehead.

Riding the light recoil of the machine pistol as the empty brass was ejected, the Executioner swung his weapon slightly to the right. Williams was holding a huge Taurus Raging Bull revolver. The Beretta came to a halt, and Bolan squeezed again. This time his round struck the chest, drilling through Williams's tight white tank top, through the mounds of curly black hair and layers of fat, then into the heart. A splat sounded above the metallic workings of the 93-R's slide.

Neither Eagle Jack nor Williams had yet hit the deck as again, without hesitation, the Executioner swung the Beretta slightly on. Quincy was trying to aim the Browning High-Power clenched in both his hands at the Executioner.

Bolan's third 9 mm round sailed under the young man's chin before penetrating his throat. A geyser of crimson shot forth from the severed jugular vein as Quincy's knees buckled. Almost like bowling pins now, the men went down. First the captain, then Williams and finally Quincy hit the deck, all within the space of a half second.

The Executioner turned his attention to Pacheco. The undercover man now lay on his back, leaning forward, with his sound-suppressed Ruger held in both hands. His eyes were wide with astonishment as he stared at Bolan.

"Are you okay?" the Executioner asked. He whispered the words, for they were far from done, and he didn't want anything to alert the men still on deck that things were amiss.

Pacheco took a second to respond, but finally he nodded. "Yeah," he said. "I'm fine."

"Then why are you on the floor?"

"It was a pratfall. To stall for time. I—"

Bolan waved off the rest of the explanation. It didn't matter. He waited for Pacheco to get up. When the undercover man stayed where he was, he said, "What's wrong?"

Slowly Pacheco shook his head. "Nothing," he said. "I've just never seen anything like that before. You took those guys out faster than I could have pulled the trigger even once." He finally rose to his knees. "Tell me," he went on, a grin of amazement still on his face, "are you going to do that to the rest of them, or do you plan to let me have one or two?"

Bolan reached out and hauled the undercover specialist to his feet. "What I'm going to do is let you go up top and bring down some more men. Tell them Eagle Jack said he needs more help."

"I can do that." Pacheco nodded. "How many you want me to ask for?"

Bolan frowned, thinking. Now that they were already in place, they not only had the element of surprise but could set the stage as well. "Tell them we need five more men to help below," he said.

Pacheco visibly gulped. "Did you say five?"

"Five," Bolan repeated.

Pacheco shrugged. "I guess you know what you're doing," he said. "You have so far." He glanced over his shoulder toward the fore hold. "Say, maybe we should get the rifles first. Or shotguns, maybe?"

Bolan just looked at him. "You have the key to the lock?" he asked.

"Uh...no. But we could shoot it off with the Beretta. It's quiet."

The Executioner nodded. "Yes," he said, "we could. But how do you plan to silence the rifles and shotguns when we shoot them?"

Pacheco shook his head. "I see your point," he responded. "Sorry. Dumb idea."

"Not completely," he said. "We may be able to put them to use later. I'll take care of the lock while you're topside."

Pacheco smiled, obviously happy that his idea hadn't been as foolish as he'd thought. "Tell me," he said. "How long are we going to keep playing this game of me bringing them down and you shooting them?"

"Until it quits working," Bolan answered. He pointed toward the ladder. "Now go."

As Pacheco moved out of the aft hold, Bolan began dragging the bodies on the floor to the side of the room. There was no place to hide them, but there didn't need to be. All he needed was to have them out of first sight when the new men came through the door. The fact was, the sight of their fellow gunners dead on the floor might even give them pause and buy him and Pacheco another second or so.

As soon as he'd finished with the bodies, Bolan hurried past the ladder to the fore hold. Through the screen, he could see the various long guns lined up in a wooden rack. The cage door was secured by a simple padlock, and one quiet round from the Beretta sent it flying in pieces from its mount. The Executioner opened the door and stepped inside.

The automatic rifles—roughly two dozen of them, all Colt M-16 A-1s—were obviously there in case of pirate attack. The submachine guns could be used if an attacking ship got close enough. Both were for shooting *away* from the ship, and neither was ideal for a gunfight onboard—too much penetration could destroy vital equipment. The Executioner looked to the end of the rack where several shotguns stood. For the battle he was about to take part in, they made a lot more sense.

Walking quickly to the end of the gun rack, the Executioner grabbed two Remington pump 12-gauge shotguns. Both magazines were loaded, but the chambers were empty. In a large wooden crate next to the gun rack he found extra boxes of ammo and several bandoleers filled with shotgun shells. With the pump guns and extra shells in his arms, he left the cage, closed the door behind him and hurried back through the center hold.

The tarp covering the cocaine next to the ladder had been tied down with rope, but it was loose. He stuffed the shotguns and bandoliers on top of the stack and pulled the canvas back down over it.

Bolan hurried back to the aft hold, taking up a position in the left-hand corner of the room. He pulled a fresh magazine from his pocket and traded it for the partially spent box in the Beretta. He hesitated for a moment, looking at the selector switch on the side of the weapon. Should he use a 3-round burst? No. He would stick with single shot. One pull of the trigger, one round. If he went to burst mode, the Beretta would be too difficult to control as he repeatedly switched targets. Rounds could be wasted between men. More important, fractions of time could be lost. And even with Pacheco on his feet this time, the Executioner suspected that he'd have to take out at least three of the five men himself.

Perhaps two minutes had gone by when Bolan heard voices and footsteps coming his way again. He hadn't told Pacheco to be sure to lead the way through the door upon his return, and he could only pray that the undercover man was smart enough to figure that out on his own. Given the layout of the hold, it was the only sound strategy they could utilize. Again, they would have only split seconds before the gunmen realized something was amiss, and if Pacheco brought up the rear those few seconds would be lost. True, they could catch the men in a cross fire that way but, in these cramped quarters, they stood just as much chance of shooting each other as the bad guys.

Bolan drew a deep breath as he waited. He was leaning against one of the stacks of cocaine on the right side of the hold, facing the hatch. If Pacheco came first, his body would block the other men's view through the small opening. When he saw the Executioner against the wall, the undercover man would naturally take up a position to the right, stepping out of the way to allow the other men to enter. He could then partially block the view of the bodies on the floor, and if the men entered at a normal pace, it would take one or two seconds for the situation to take shape in their minds. They would see Bolan as they came in, of course, but if he kept the Beretta hidden that shouldn't tip them off either.

The Executioner waited. If all went well, he and Pacheco should be able to pull it off. But, again, it would be a game of seconds. Bolan's timing would have to be perfect.

As the footsteps neared, he turned slightly and let the Beretta fall to arm's length behind his leg. With his other hand, he reached up as if adjusting the tarp covering the cocaine. Out of the corner of his eye he saw Pacheco duck his head as he came through the hatch. Just as Bolan had hoped, the undercover man stepped to the right.

A second later a hulking man wearing a black T-shirt and white tennis shorts wedged his thick body through the hatch. He groaned as he straightened again, both hands going to his lower back. Right behind him came one of the crewmen in his British sailor's outfit. He didn't appear to suffer from any such lower back problems, and as soon as he was in the hold his eyes shot directly to the bodies only partially hidden behind Pacheco.

"What the fu—?"

The Beretta came around behind the Executioner's back in one swift smooth move. Shooting from the hip at such close quarters, Bolan hammered two quick rounds through the British sailor's chest. Before the crewman could fall Bolan had turned the 93-R on the thick man in the white tennis shorts. Another duo of 9 mm slugs pounded through the black T-shirt, the holes invisible against the dark material, but a volcanic eruption of red shot out the man's back where the exit wounds appeared.

The other three men Pacheco was to have brought with him hadn't yet entered the hold. As he moved to the center of the room to look through the hatch, the Executioner saw the undercover man draw his sound-suppressed Ruger and aim through the aperture with both hands. The small-bore pistol barely jumped in his hands as he pumped his own twin rounds into the chest and face of a gunner wearing a faded madras shirt. The man was in the midst of trying to draw a SIG-Sauer pistol from his belt, and Pacheco's third bullet hit the gun itself with a loud clank before ricocheting off. But the first two had done their job.

The man sank to the deck, and Bolan saw that while Pacheco might not be the most lethal gunfighter around, he wasn't the worst, either.

Bolan took careful aim over Pacheco's shoulder at a middle-aged man with a white beard and matching flattop haircut. A lone 9 mm hollowpoint slug flew past Pacheco's ear into the man's nose. Pacheco flinched as he realized Bolan's round had narrowly missed him.

The fifth and final man had drawn a Glock from under his shirt. But as he looked through the hatch at the Ruger and Beretta pointed his way, he lost his nerve to use it. Dropping the weapon, he opened his mouth to scream, beginning to turn at the same time.

Simultaneous .22-caliber and 9 mm rounds chugged out of the sound-suppressed weapons. Bolan's bullet struck the man in the temple, taking off half his face. Pacheco's smaller caliber round caught the man in the side, disappearing through his shirt in the rib area. Yet another man hit the deck.

And was dead before he got there.

Pacheco turned to face the Executioner. The undercover man was breathing hard from the adrenaline surging through his body. His eyes were wide. "Well," he said through the half-slap-happy grin curling his lips, "at least you let me help this time."

Bolan was worried about the undercover man. Pacheco had just seen more violence in fifteen seconds than most cops saw in a lifetime. His eyes were not only wide, they had a distant look to them. It wasn't over yet, there was no time for therapy and the Executioner didn't need him losing it right now.

Bolan patted him on the shoulder. "Good job," he said. "And the odds are getting better. We've already gotten eight out of twenty-eight."

Pacheco chuckled softly. "Yeah, now we're only down ten to one." His voice sounded strained when he said, "I assume I need to go up and get a few more men?"

Bolan nodded. "We've got no other choice," he said. "Besides, when you're on a roll that's no time to give up the dice."

Pacheco looked down at the bodies littering the deck, his eyes still wide. He shook his head in amazement. "You do this sort of thing every day?" he asked.

Hoping to relieve some of the tension he still felt emanating from the other man, he said, "I never took to golf or fishing. Now go get us a few more, and let's get this over with."

The undercover man looked up. "How many you want this time?" he asked, his voice cracking slightly. Before Bolan could answer he said, "Another five? Maybe ten? Hell, why don't I just go up there and bring them all back down here with me?" Now he broke into a semi-hysterical laughter. "Better yet, I'll just tell them that I've got an expert marksman down here. Maybe then they'll just jump overboard." He started laughing uncontrollably again.

Bolan had as good a sense of humor as anyone. But what

he was hearing and seeing now was a man on the verge of a breakdown. The stress of being undercover for so long was finally taking its toll.

The Executioner jammed the Beretta into his waistband and stepped forward, grabbing both of Pacheco's shoulders and shaking them roughly. "We'll laugh about this all you want to later," he said. "But not now. Get control of yourself." He paused, then in a more gentle voice, added, "You've got to get a grip on things, and you've got to do it now. Do you understand me?"

Slowly the thousand-yard stare began to fade from Pacheco's eyes. He nodded his head.

"Good." Bolan dropped his hands from the man's shoulders and drew the Beretta again. "Now, I want you to go get five more men," he said. "Act excited, and tell them the leak is spreading and the captain called for them. My guess is we may be able to pull this off one more time. After that, the guys left up top are going to wonder what's going on."

Pacheco was coming around again. "Okay," he said. "And...I'm sorry."

The soldier waved a hand, dismissing the comment. "Don't sweat it," he said. "And keep in mind it'll all be over within a few more minutes."

Pacheco turned and ascended the steps once more.

Working fast, Bolan dragged the bodies still in the first hold through the hatch and stacked them against the wall with the others. But there would be no hiding them now—there were just too many. If he stood where he'd been before, as soon as the men from up top came down the steps they'd be able to see the corpses through the opening.

It was time for a change of strategy.

Bolan moved back into the first hold and turned to face the steps, his body blocking the opening to the rear room. He put his hands on his hips as if impatiently waiting, the Beretta still in his fist but hidden behind his back. He waited as the seconds ticked away, hoping Pacheco hadn't encountered any trouble up top. The man seemed to have regained control of himself, and he was a fine actor.

A few minutes later Bolan heard movement at the top of the ladder and then a pair of shoes appeared on the top steps. A moment later, Pacheco's face came into view. He saw Bolan and frowned.

Before the men following the Costa Rican could descend far enough to see, Bolan quickly waved the man toward him. Pacheco hurried forward. The undercover man even began to whistle softly as he walked forward in the narrow passageway.

Behind him, other men were descending the ladder, and Bolan heard low grumbling voices. As Pacheco neared Bolan, he lifted his T-shirt with his left hand. He drew the Ruger with his right but kept the pistol in front of him, blocking it from the view of the men behind him.

The first man down into the hold wore oil-stained khaki pants and an equally stained, formerly white, canvas bucket hat. He frowned when he saw Bolan facing him and Pacheco turned the other way, both men blocking the hatch. "What's going on?" he demanded.

Bolan looked over Pacheco's shoulder and said, "Wait until everybody gets down here. I don't want to have to repeat myself five times."

The answer seemed to satisfy the man. At least for the time being.

The next man to descend the ladder was balding, in his fifties, and had a cigarette hanging from his lips. He asked a similar question, but the man in the dirty bucket hat said, "Shut the fuck up and wait."

The next two men looked like brothers. The first to descend was slightly older with a few strands of gray streaking through his hair at the temples. Both had dark olive skin and identical heart tattoos on their biceps. Inside the hearts was the word Mama.

Bolan watched the last man come below. In his early twenties, he had closely cropped hair and the stubble of a goatee on his chin. He wore a skintight ribbed tank top.

"Okay," the man in the bucket hat said, "where the hell is the captain?" He jerked his head suddenly back slightly, his eyes shooting past Bolan and through some small uncovered space that led into the rear hold. The Executioner could tell he'd seen the bodies—or at least some part of what was obviously a dead body—by the expression on his face.

And the man was no rookie. His face went from confusion to fear in the space of few seconds. His hand went to his belt.

The Executioner's hand was already coming around from his back to the front. And with it came the Beretta. He had to push Pacheco to the side with his free hand, and that slowed him a fraction of a second. But he had still pumped two 9 mm rounds into the chest of the man in the greasy hat by the time the Russian Makarov pistol was halfway out of his belt. The hardman slammed back against the wall of the hold at the same time Pacheco rebounded off the same wall closer to Bolan. The Costa Rican turned to face the other men, and as he did the Ruger fired.

The lone rimfire round caught the man with the cigarette dangling in his mouth in the shoulder, spinning him into the guy in the ribbed tank top. Pacheco fired again, catching the same man squarely in the back and splitting his spine.

Bolan took a half step to the side in the close confines and aimed the 93-R at the older of the two brothers. A double tap of the trigger sent two near-silent Parabellum hollowpoint slugs into the man's head. The first caught his chin at a slight angle, twisting his head to the side. The follow-up shot drilled into the gray streaks just above the man's ear, turning all of his hair a dark wet black.

The young man in the ribbed tank top was still behind the middle-aged man Pacheco had shot, holding up the corpse in front of him like a shield. A girlish squeal came from his lips as Bolan and Pacheco both turned their attention to the younger of the brothers at the same time. Another 9 mm round was fired from the Beretta, another tiny .22 slug from the Ruger. The larger round caught the younger brother in the chest while the .22 caliber round drilled through his lower abdomen. He was dead before he hit the ground.

So far, Bolan and Pacheco had been successful through both skill and luck. The skill had been Bolan's. The luck, Pacheco's. But now, that luck finally ran out.

A hand emerged from behind the human shield, holding a Smith & Wesson 469 semiauto pistol. A second later three rounds exploded.

Bolan raised the Beretta aiming just over the shoulder of the dead man in the kid's arms. A single round rushed through the air and caught the man with the S&W in the right eye, exiting to send a storm of blood and brains blowing backward over the steps behind him. The kid dropped his human shield and fell to the ground on top of the other dead man.

The young gunman had fired wildly, in panic, and he had hit no one. Still, he had done a tremendous amount of damage. Damage that the Executioner might, or might not, be able to repair. The S&W rounds had not been sound suppressed like Bolan's and Pacheco's. They had sounded like nuclear explosions against the walls of the hold, and while they wouldn't have had the same deafening quality by the time they reached the main deck, Bolan had no doubt that they'd been loud and clear.

Now, the rest of the crew on deck knew something was going on below. They knew two strange faces were down there, and that shots had been fired.

The real battle was about to begin. Bolan and Pacheco were still outnumbered over seven to one, and the enemy had the high ground.

7

"Watch the ladder!" Bolan ordered Pacheco as he turned toward the canvas-covered cocaine along the wall of the hold.

"What?"

"Just do it!" the Executioner stated. He ripped the tarp back to expose the shotguns.

"Oh," Pacheco said, his question answered for him. He kept the Ruger aimed toward the top of the steps.

Bolan grabbed one of the shotguns. "Here." The gun went sailing through the air, and Pacheco shifted the Ruger to his right hand and caught the shotgun with his left.

"Mag full, chamber empty," the Executioner said as he tossed two bandoliers after the scattergun. Pacheco caught them too, and slid them over his head and across his chest. "I feel like Che Guevara," he said, stuffing the Ruger into his pants.

"Just hope you don't die like him," Bolan said as he slid into another pair of bandoliers, then lifted the other 12-gauge shotgun. He racked the slide, chambering a round, and the sound echoed off the walls of the hold. Flipping on the safety, he moved to a position next to Pacheco at the foot of the ladder, keeping his finger on the button, ready to disengage the blocking device at a moment's notice.

That moment came almost immediately.

A burly man with three-days' growth of beard, wearing Bermuda shorts and a white shirt suddenly appeared against the blue sky in the opening above them. He held an old, well-worn Spanish-made 9 mm Star in his hand. Almost all the coloring had been worn away, and the gun looked a dull gray in the sunlight coming down on the Gulf of Mexico. The gun was old and ugly. But like someone had once said, "They weren't made to look pretty. They were made to kill people." And that's exactly what the man intended to do with his.

Bolan fired a split second before Pacheco, the 12-gauge buckshot having little time to open up at the short range. All of the small lead balls hit the man in a pattern the size of a silver dollar, which drove his shirt back against his chest like the wind blowing the sails on the deck behind him. Pacheco's blast did the same one-tenth of a second later, and not more than an inch away from the Executioner's hit. Suddenly the clean white shirt was a torn, burned, ragged red and the man was sent tumbling down the steps.

Both Bolan and Pacheco stepped back to avoid being hit by the falling corpse. But they kept their shotguns trained at the aperture above. With his left hand, the Executioner jerked two shells from his bandolier and topped off his mag, replacing the round he'd just fired as well as taking advantage of the extra space he'd created when he'd pumped the first round into the chamber.

Pacheco did the same, then said, "What do we do now?"

Bolan didn't answer. He was asking himself the same question. Nothing ever went as planned—that was a given—and he hadn't counted on being trapped below. But he was thankful for the brief respite in the firing during which he could reevaluate the situation as it now stood. The men above, he had to suppose, were confused at this point. They didn't know what was going on. From their point of view they had heard shots, then the man in the white shirt had come to investigate, gun drawn, and then another shot had toppled him down the steps out of their sight. That's all they knew.

That was enough to know they were in danger. And enough to know that they needed to shoot anyone who showed his head above the deck.

No, Bolan suddenly realized, that wasn't all they knew. They knew that he and Pacheco—the two new guys—were both below. So they would just naturally presume that *they* were behind the problem, whatever the problem actually was. And it was the Executioner's guess that they'd soon come to the conclusion that the two new faces were "plants", members of another group of drug-smuggling pirates put on board to assist in a hijacking.

Unless he missed his guess, there were men climbing the masts right now to scout the horizon for whatever vessel was about to come kill them and steal their cargo.

"Hey!" a voice called down the ladder into the hold.

Bolan could tell the man was standing just to the side of the opening. "What?" he yelled up.

"What the hell's going on?" the same voice asked.

The Executioner looked to Pacheco and the Costa Rican read his mind. "Little problem down here," Pacheco called back up. "The two new guys. They pulled guns. But we got 'em."

There was a long pause up top. Then the voice said, "I don't think so. I think *you're* one of the new guys."

Pacheco turned back to the Executioner and shrugged as if to say, "Not every performance gets a curtain call."

Bolan considered the situation. For the time being, they were safe. None of the men seemed inclined to come down after them now that they'd seen what had happened to the man in the white shirt. But he and Pacheco weren't going anywhere, either. And before long they'd arrive in New Orleans. Then the coke's buyers would arrive, and they'd have even more men to face. The odds against them were bad enough now. They'd be even worse then.

His shotgun still aimed upward, the soldier glanced toward Pacheco. "I'm going up and take a look," he said.

"Are you crazy?" Pacheco asked.

"Probably. But I don't see any other way out of this. Do you?"

"No. But getting your damn head blown off doesn't sound like a viable way around it to me, either."

Bolan shrugged his shoulders. "You have a better idea, I'm willing to listen to it."

But Pacheco didn't.

The Executioner looked back to the ladder. The shotgun was going to be more trouble than it was worth—clumsy and hard to maneuver as he made his way up the steps. He laid it on the deck next to the ladder and drew the Desert Eagle from beneath his shirt. He checked the magazine and chamber, then double-checked to see that the Beretta, still in his waistband, was also full. Satisfied, he lifted the hand cannon and started slowly up the steps.

Above him, Bolan could see a tiny patch of white against the blue. One lone white cloud against an otherwise clear blue sky. Now and then, as the wind gusted, a corner of the mizzen sail flapped into view. Otherwise, the soldier could see nothing. But he knew the man who had called down into the hold was still there. He could sense his presence.

One step at a time, the Executioner ascended. With each step, he wondered if it would be his last. If it was, then so be it. He had resigned himself to dying a violent death long ago when he'd vowed to dedicate his life to fighting evil in every shape in which he found it. Over the years he had faced criminals, terrorists, enemy soldiers and spies. Many times, he had come close to dying, but each time he had cheated the grim reaper. He was long overdue, and he knew it. Each day his first thought was that he would live that day to fight again, not for himself but for those who couldn't fight for themselves. He asked the universe for one more sunrise, one more sunset, during which he could rid the world of a few more of the wicked predators who preyed on those weaker than themselves.

Someday, it would be over. Then, the Executioner would sleep. Sleep, knowing he had done his best, and that his war had finally ended. Until then, he'd continue to fight hard.

With each step, Bolan could see a little more of the deck, and each time a larger part came into view, he paused. Suddenly his ears picked up the man next to the ladder.

The sailor had moved from the port side of the opening to the rear. He would be directly behind the Executioner if Bolan walked up the steps the normal way. The soldier could hear his breathing—it was the low, labored breathing of a man whose body screamed for oxygen while his brain commanded his lungs to remain shallow. Sooner or later, the body always won, and the tension this man was under was causing that victory over willpower to come sooner rather than later.

With his head still below the deck, Bolan turned slowly to face where he knew the man hid. He was close, otherwise the breathing would have been inaudible. And at the angle at which the Executioner now stood, the man had to be lying down to remain unseen. Bolan guessed he would be on his side, just beyond the opening, with his gun in his hand and aimed at the hole he knew someone had to eventually come out.

Quietly the Executioner depressed the magazine release on the Desert Eagle. With almost painful slowness, he removed the box and dropped it into his pocket. From another pocket he produced an identical .44 Magnum magazine. But there was one small difference.

The box mag that went into the Desert Eagle now held .44 Magnum armor-piercing rounds rather than hollowpoint rounds.

Bolan pressed the magazine home, hoping the small click as it locked into place went unheard, or at least unrecognized. Then, with much quicker movements, he raised the weapon and aimed the barrel at a spot above which he knew his target had to be. Without delay, he pulled the trigger and the hand cannon roared. The thick wood of the deck splintered as the powerful hollowpoint slug hit it. It was likely that it penetrated the deck.

But the second, third and fourth armor-piercing rounds did without a doubt.

Bolan didn't know what part of the man he'd hit, but it had to be painful. The howl like that of a coyote whose leg had just been slammed by the jaws of a trap issued forth from above him. Bolan followed the first four shots with three more, and the howl suddenly evaporated into thin air.

Quickly the Executioner dropped the armor-piercing magazine and stuck the hollowpoint rounds back in. Taking advantage of the shock he suspected the other men would be experiencing, he quickly snapped his head up and out of the hole. In the brief second he was exposed, he saw men diving for masts, lifeboats, davits and any other cover they could find. Doing a quick 360-degree spin, he saw that there were men both in front and behind him. Then, just before he jerked his head back down he saw the man he had just shot through the deck with the armor-piercing ammo.

One round had taken off the gunman's left foot. Another seemed to have severed his spine, and he lay in death at an awkward, almost unhuman, angle. At least one of the other rounds had found his face and had destroyed it.

"How's it look?" Pacheco asked as the Executioner descended the steps once more, stuck the Desert Eagle back in his waistband holster and picked up the shotgun.

Bolan looked up at the opening above again. The same white cloud still stood alone in the sky. He thought of the men on deck above, each of them armed, and each determined to get the cocaine to New Orleans and collect their wages.

"What are we facing?" Pacheco asked.

Bolan turned to look at him. "Death," he said simply, then turned back to aim his shotgun at the opening once more.

THE SHIP FELL SILENT, the steady swish of the waves breaking against the *Evangelina*'s hull the only sound as they sailed on through the Gulf of Mexico. It was a peaceful sound, a white noise that might well have, under other circumstances, lulled the men aboard the ship into sleepiness. As it was, however, everyone on and below the main deck was wide awake.

This quiet, they all knew, was more like the eye of a hurricane. It was the quiet before the storm.

Bolan knew they were at a standoff. At least a dozen men, all armed with pistols, remained topside. He and Pacheco were fairly safe where they were. The Executioner doubted any more of the gunmen would risk coming to the ladder after he'd killed the last two who tried. But that safety would evaporate soon. Bolan glanced at his watch. They couldn't be more than another half hour out of New Orleans, and as soon as they docked the drug buyers would come on board to join the smugglers. The buyers might even come out onto the water to meet them if they had their own boat and radio contact.

Bolan felt the skin on his forehead tighten in concentration. He dropped one hand from the shotgun and scratched his chin. No, they couldn't wait any longer. One way or another help was coming for the drug dealers, but not for them. If he allowed these men to sail on, the best he and Pacheco could hope for would be that U.S. Customs or the Coast Guard would board the ship to inspect it, and the chances of that were remote. Organized drug smugglers like those aboard the *Evangelina* weren't stupid. They made careful arrangements ahead of time—either paying off crooked officials or sailing into remote areas where authorities weren't likely to patrol.

The Executioner felt himself shaking his head. No, he wasn't going to let that happen. He couldn't allow these men to control the ship any longer.

He had to do something.

Bolan turned to Pacheco. "I'm going topside."

Pacheco looked at him with the expression of a man who'd

just seen a Martian. "Again? Are you completely out of your mind?"

The Executioner ignored the remark. "We can't stay down here for the rest of our lives," he said. "And we'll be hitting New Orleans soon."

"Good," Pacheco said. "Then these guys will get arrested and—"

"That'll never happen," he said, cutting him off. "But even if they did get arrested, they'd bond out and head straight out of the country. Even if they stayed to face trial, they'd plea-bargain for a light sentence, and be back in business the day after they were released." He paused to let it sink in, then added, "It's not an option, Jaime."

The undercover man understood. But he didn't like it. "Suicide's an option though, huh?"

"You don't have to go with me," the Executioner said. "Stay here. Keep your shotgun trained on the hole and shoot anyone that comes into view."

Pacheco shook his head. "No," he said. "If you go, I go."

The Executioner started to argue then stopped, studying the face of the Costa Rican cop. Pacheco's eyes were sharp and clear again. His voice was steady, and he wasn't showing any of the other signs of a breakdown that he had earlier. Still, the Executioner hesitated. Pacheco was indeed a good undercover operative, and the man had courage. But his abilities as a gunman were still limited, and a gunman was what was called for at the moment. Pacheco stood a good chance of getting killed within the first ten seconds after he stuck his head up out of the hold.

On the other hand, Bolan realized, Pacheco was a policeman. And he was intelligent enough to recognize his own limitations. He had a right to make his own decisions, and if he wanted to risk it, he deserved the chance.

Still, Bolan hoped to discourage him. Pacheco wasn't likely to be of much help, and there was no point in throwing his life away. So the Executioner was blunt. "I don't need you," he said.

"I know you don't need me," Pacheco came back. "I've seen you do things I've never seen any other man do in my life do. Things I didn't think any man *could* do." He paused, looking up into Bolan's eyes with determination. "But whether you need me or not, you've got me. If you're going topside, I'm coming, too. You can't stop me, either. You can't go up there and keep me down here at the same time." He chuckled softly. "Not even you can be in two places at the same time."

Slowly the Executioner nodded. "Okay then," he said. "I'll go first. I'm going to cut to the aft end of the ship as soon as I'm on deck and work my way around clockwise. Give me a five-second head start, then go forward. Counterclockwise. If things go well, we'll meet up somewhere on deck and have a lot of dead bodies behind both of us. You shoot anyone who moves."

Pacheco's smile was tinged with stress. "Except you, I'm assuming?" he said.

"Except me," he agreed. He topped off the Remington's magazine again, then shrugged out of the two bandoliers he'd strung across his chest. He'd take the scattergun along with him and use it until he ran out of shells. But there would be no time to reload during the gunfight ahead, and as soon as the Remington clicked empty, he'd have to go with his pistols. That didn't bother him. The Desert Eagle and Beretta had seen him through more tight scrapes than he could remember.

Taking a deep breath, the Executioner checked the chamber of the shotgun once more, then turned and started up the steps.

IN COMBAT, the Executioner knew, nothing could ever be counted on. He had seen men kicked in the groin fall backward instead of curling forward into the natural, standing fetal position. He had seen men take multiple high-velocity rounds to the body, some of which had hit the heart, continue to fight. Once, he had even watched a man who'd had the entire top of his head blown away by a rifle round keep firing his own weapon for almost a full minute before collapsing. No, nothing could ever be counted on to go exactly the way the soldier planned or hoped it would.

So Bolan was slightly surprised when he emerged from the hold to find that the men on deck had taken up almost relaxed postures around the boat. Many were not even behind cover or concealment of any kind. Perhaps they assumed no one in the Executioner's position would be crazy enough to show himself up top knowing how outnumbered he was.

Whatever the reason for their casual attitude, it cost two of them their lives as soon as the Executioner's feet hit the deck.

Bolan had depressed the shotgun's safety a second before rushing up out of the hold. He triggered the scattergun as soon as he saw the closest gunman. Standing not ten feet from the ladder, the man wore blue jeans and what appeared to be an old Soviet Spetsnaz T-shirt. The Executioner wondered for a moment if the gunman—who had a Stechkin Soviet pistol hanging at the end of his arm—might once have actually been with the Soviet special forces. Some had taken the wrong road once the Soviet Union had fallen, finding employment with drug and gun runners the world over. But his mind quickly moved to other subjects as soon as a 12-gauge blast of double-aught buckshot turned the blue and white stripes a dark black-red.

Taking a quick step to the side as he pumped the Remington, Bolan swung it toward a shocked man with a Springfield 1911 in his fist. A cigarette dangled from the man's lips, seemingly frozen in place. With another squeeze of the trigger, the Executioner dropped the drug smuggler.

By now, the shock had worn off and the rest of the crew dived for cover behind various fixtures on the *Evangelina*'s deck. A lone return round flew past the Executioner—hurried and wild—as he sprinted to the side of the ship and ducked under the billowing mizzen sail. The sail offered concealment but no cover, and several more rounds punctured the canvas as the trauma of Bolan's sudden and unexpected appearance wore off.

Continuing on, the Executioner racked the slide on the shotgun again, then sent another 12-gauge pattern of shot into the chest of a man who had just stepped out from behind a lifeboat. The blast caught the man high on the left side of the chest, throwing him back where the top of his thighs hit the rail. With a scream of both surprise and horror, he flipped over the rail and into the sea.

Bolan slowed as he reached the lifeboat, pumping the shotgun once more and turning a full 360 degrees. He saw no more targets and dropped his pace to a walk, crouching slightly as his eyes scanned between the sheets flying overhead. He ducked under the jigger topmast sail and moved toward the aft of the ship. As he reached the aftermast, he caught a glimpse of red suddenly dart between the gaff boom and the rail. He triggered the scattergun once more.

The blast caught a gunman in the side, spinning him like a top as it soaked the shirt a darker hue. A rush of air came out of a destroyed lung, froths of crimson floating on the man's breath. A Swedish M/07 pistol fell to the deck, the man on top of it.

Rounds from an unseen hand now forced the Executioner to backtrack, diving to the deck and rolling partially under the lifeboat. In this cramped position the shotgun became cumbersome. Partially empty anyway, he abandoned it, drawing the mammoth Desert Eagle. For a moment, as the roar of gunfire died down, silence fell over the ship. Bolan's eyes narrowed as he scanned the deck, searching for a new target.

He found it midship. Visible below the main lower topsail, he could see the bottom hemline of a pair of white shorts, hairy calves, white socks and running shoes. Without hesitation, the Executioner pumped a quick .44 Magnum slug into both knees. The first round out of the Desert Eagle was the armor-piercing load that had been fed into the chamber before he'd switched back to the other magazine. The second round was a hollow-point. But on small bony targets like the knees, not even a forensic expert could have guessed which round had done the damage to which leg. Both of the man's knees were utterly destroyed.

A scream came from behind the sail as the kneecapped gunner collapsed. He rolled to his side, a French-made 9 mm MAB PA-15 still clutched in one hand. A grimace of agony covered his face.

Bolan ended his pain with the next .44 magnum round. It shot from the barrel of the Desert Eagle at over 1200 feet per second, catching the man in the side of the face, just above the jaw. The gunner forgot his knee—and everything else. His head exploded as if a fragmentation grenade had detonated in his mouth. The almost headless corpse rolled to its back beneath the mainsail.

The Executioner was about to climb out from under the lifeboat when he saw Pacheco on the deck. The Costa Rican cop held his shotgun in both hands, the wooden stock pressed against his shoulder. He ran forward, away from where Bolan lay, sprinting toward the halyards at the foresail. Suffering from tunnel vision, he ignored a gunman in a flowered shirt who suddenly appeared from behind a sail and took aim at him with a Walther PPK.

Bolan jerked the Desert Eagle across the deck, let it come to rest and pulled the trigger. Another mammoth Magnum round exploded from the Eagle, striking the man in the flowered shirt in the upper arm. The PPK went flying from his fist and he doubled over, his other hand grabbing the massive wound.

The Executioner took more time now, using the sights and lining them up on the man's nose. But the wounded gunman started to rise just as he squeezed the trigger and the round caught him in the throat rather than the face.

The result was just as devastating, and there was one less drug smuggler to stand against them.

Now Bolan rolled out from under the boat and leaped to his feet. The shotgun still lay on deck where he'd dropped it. He kicked it back under the lifeboat—out of sight of any of the men who might pass by and decide to add it to their own arsenal. Making his way across the deck through the halyards of the mizzenmast, he reached the port side in time to see one of the crewmen raising an Argentine-made copy of the Colt 1911. The man got off a hurried shot that sailed over the Executioner's shoulder.

It was his last act of life. Bolan double tapped the Desert Eagle's trigger, sending a duo of hollowpoint slugs into the front of the man's shirt. The rounds passed through the man's chest and out his back, taking blood, tissue and part of his spine in their wake. Residual blood fizzed out the entry holes in a thick mist, splattering the sails before drizzling down to the deck.

On the starboard side of the ship, the Executioner heard more gunfire. Most of it sounded like 9 mm, and could well have been from Pacheco's Glock. On the other hand, many of the weapons he had already encountered were 9 mms, and it might mean that the Costa Rican undercover man had gone down.

A tall lanky figure suddenly appeared from behind the foresail, a stainless-steel Colt Anaconda gripped in his hands. The big revolver used the same devastating ammunition as Bolan's Desert Eagle, so it was as equally deadly.

Bolan snapped off a quick round that skimmed across the barrel of the Anaconda before hitting the tall man in the pit of the stomach. The Colt went flying from his fist as he fell into a sitting position. Gut shot, his face contorted in torture. But only for a second.

The Executioner's next round struck just above the bridge of the lanky man's nose, taking off the top of his head as if he'd been scalped.

More gunfire came from the front of the ship as Bolan dropped the near-empty magazine and replaced it with a full load. He pocketed the partial—just in case. He had been limited in the amount of extra ammo, and while he still had the Beretta and one extra mag for it, he was running low on .44 Magnums. Two partials—one the hollowpoint he had just dropped, the other the armor-piercing he had used earlier to shoot through the deck—were all that were left.

And the Executioner still had work to do.

A rapid succession of rounds echoed across the deck from where Bolan guessed Pacheco had to be. Again, he hoped the semiskilled gunman would hold his own. His knees bent slightly, the soldier moved cautiously forward, his eyes again scanning back and forth for any sign of the enemy. He drew even with the forward lifeboat on the other side of the deck, and a flash of movement behind it caught his eye.

The Executioner hit the deck as three fast rounds sailed over his head. He had seen only an extending arm, and a pistol of some sort behind the small boat. Now, both gun and arm had disappeared again. On his belly now, he swiveled to face the starboard side of the ship, extended the Desert Eagle in both hands and propped his elbows on the deck. The hand cannon leaped upward twice in his hands as the recoil shot through his forearms. Two huge holes appeared in the lifeboat and a groan issued forth. But still, Bolan could see no target.

Aiming slightly to the left of the two holes already in the boat, Bolan added another pair. Then, before he had time to check their effect, he swung the Desert Eagle to the right. Another pair of slugs blasted from the muzzle and as their roar died down the sounds of a body falling to the deck drifted across the ship. Beneath the boat, Bolan saw a pair of legs.

They were drenched in blood from ankle to knee.

The Executioner kept the Eagle at the ready as he cautiously shuffled back across the ship. When he reached the lifeboat, his eyes flickered fore and aft along the ship. He saw no one, and wondered again if Pacheco had survived. The other gunfire had died out now, too.

Moving behind the lifeboat, Bolan looked down at the deck. A man—or the shell of what had once been a man—lay on his back, open but lifeless eyes staring at the deep blue sky above the Gulf of Mexico. The body was untouched from the waist up, but the entire lower half of the man was soaked in blood. The Executioner squinted in the bright sun. One of his rounds—he had no way of knowing which—had struck the femoral artery in the man's inner thigh. He had bled out.

Footsteps sounded to the Executioner's side and he whirled that way, the Desert Eagle in front of him, his finger taking up the slack in the trigger. The footsteps suddenly halted.

"Hey," Jaime Pacheco said nervously, the Glock in his hand falling to his side, "I promised not to shoot *you*. Doesn't that work both ways?"

Bolan couldn't suppress the grin that spread across his face. Pacheco might not be the best fighter he had ever worked with, but he was still a warrior. He had guts, and those guts— and maybe God, too—had seen him through. He had splatters of blood all over his shirt and shorts, but it wasn't his own. He'd made it.

"A tacit agreement," the Executioner said, lowering the Desert Eagle. "And this is no time for either of us to start breaking promises."

ACCORDING TO PACHECO, he had killed five men. He was wrong, Bolan discovered, as he made his way to the fore of the ship checking bodies. One man—dressed in the British sailor costume—was dying. But he wasn't dead yet.

A dangerous mistake on Pacheco's part. More than one supposedly dead man had "risen from the grave" to kill again before succumbing to a bullet, and the Costa Rican's oversight could have cost him, Bolan, or both of them their own lives. But the Executioner saw no reason to admonish the man now. It would accomplish nothing, and the look on Pacheco's face told him that the undercover man had already recognized the severity of his mistake. Besides, Bolan could take advantage of it. The dying man could still be put to good use.

Bolan leaned down over the man who lay sprawled on his side near the railing. "What's your name?" he demanded.

While the crew seemed to be made up of international hired guns, this man was obviously Hispanic. "Arturo..." he breathed, as his lifeblood continued to drain from the wound in his chest.

"Costa Rican?" Bolan asked.

Slowly Arturo shook his head. "Peru...vian..." he whispered. "I am...dying?"

Bolan saw no reason to lie to the man. "Yes," he said.

"There is...nothing...you can do?"

The Executioner studied the huge gaping wound in Arturo's chest. "No," he said. "It may take a while, but you're going to die."

"Good God," gasped the man on the deck. Tears filled his eyes, and a weakened hand went to his neck, sliding down a gold chain.

The Executioner looked down at the gold cross the man had clutched in his fingers. The emblem of Christianity was soaked in blood. Arturo's eyes filled with terror.

Bolan leaned in closer. "Arturo," he said, "this is your one chance to do something good. You can leave this world with your last act being a sin, or you can leave it with your last act being something good." He paused, letting the gravity of his words sink in. "I know which way I'd rather go out. But only you can make that decision for yourself." He paused to let the man think about it. "So tell me, which will it be?"

Arturo's head tilted forward so he could stare down at the blood-soaked cross in his hand. The movement brought a grimace of pain to his face. "I will...help you," he groaned.

"Then tell us exactly where the ship's supposed to go, and who you're supposed to meet."

Arturo's eyes had glazed over but now they cleared momentarily. "I don't know...the men...." he said. "But we are not sailing...into port...not in New Orleans."

"Where's the ship supposed to go?" Bolan asked.

A thin smile curled at the corners of Arturo's lips. "Barataria," he breathed.

The Executioner turned to Pacheco who stood just to their side. "Find the ship's first-aid kit and see if you can slow the bleeding," he said. "The longer we can keep him alive, the better chance we have of getting information out of him."

Pacheco turned and hurried away.

Bolan stood, walked to the bow and gazed across the water.

The ship's wheel had been tied down and the *Evangelina* continued to sail toward the New Orleans area.

But not New Orleans herself. They would be taking a slight detour. To a place called Barataria.

The Executioner's jaw tightened as he checked the compass to make sure they were still on course. Barataria.

It wouldn't be the first time that site had been used for smuggling.

LOOSELY TRANSLATED, Barataria meant "a place where seagoing dishonesty takes place."

The section of Louisiana known as Barataria was a sea marsh extending from the banks of the Mississippi River southward to the Gulf of Mexico. Locals referred to it as the "trembling prairie" because it was sometimes hard to tell whether one was on land or water. Over the centuries since Europeans came to the New Orleans area, thousands of boatmen had found that they were not as skilled at finding their way through these labyrinths as they believed themselves to be. And they became lost forever.

Because of these confusing paths, almost as soon as it was discovered Barataria became a favorite hideout of pirates, smugglers and other ne'er-do-wells. The name, in fact, appeared on the earliest territorial maps. Exactly who christened the region with such a dubious designation is lost to history.

While the natives of the early nineteenth century turned a blind eye toward the unpopular law prohibiting the importation of new slaves from Africa, their grandsons felt the same contempt for a government that outlawed alcohol during Prohibition. For a while, the illegal traffic slowed. There was always the occasional vessel spiriting taxable items past customs authorities, and now and then a shipment of marijuana came to shore. But it was not until the 1960s, when America's new "drug culture" was born, that the Barataria area of southern Louisiana returned to its previous days of infamy. Once again the winding lagoons came alive with secret cargo. First, the marijuana and heroin trade boomed. Then, as the numbers of those who embraced the new "consciousness" grew, cocaine became king.

So the Executioner was simply following a tradition several centuries old as he, Pacheco, and the dying Arturo sailed the *Evangelina* toward Barataria.

Bolan took another look at the wheel, checked the instruments to reassure himself they were still on course, then returned once more to the man on the deck. Pacheco had done a good job of patching Arturo's chest wound, but the man was still going to die. It wouldn't have mattered if they'd had a helicopter to take him on into New Orleans. His life's blood was draining away too quickly.

Pacheco was kneeling next to the man when Bolan approached. He stood, and in a low voice whispered, "He's dying."

"I know," Bolan said.

"He keeps asking for a priest."

The Executioner stared at the undercover man. "Well, do you have one?"

Pacheco recognized it as a rhetorical question and didn't answer. "It's just that, well...just that..."

"That he doesn't seem to be all bad?" Bolan asked.

"Yeah," Pacheco said. He reached down to his belt and nervously adjusted the Glock in his waistband. "I guess that's it."

"Few men are," the Executioner said. "Nor are they all good. But they chose the paths they take in life, Jaime, and those paths are either good or bad."

The Costa Rican nodded. "I get your point. Even the worst of people do some good things. If only by accident."

Bolan nodded. "Or because it helps them, too. In the same sense, even good men can do bad things. Maybe this guy needed to feed his family. Maybe he grew up in a family of drug smugglers and was told there was nothing wrong with what he did. I don't know. But I do know that if his family needed food there were other ways he could have gotten it for them. And if he was taught this from childhood, he's a grown man now and somewhere along the line he had to figure out for himself that he was taught wrong." The Executioner paused to take a deep breath. "No, I agree with you. It's too bad. But he made his decision, and it got him killed. It'd be nice if things were different, but they aren't. That's life."

Pacheco gulped visibly, then nodded.

Bolan knelt next to the man on the deck. Arturo's face had taken on the sickly gray common to men of his skin tone when in ill health. His eyes were half closed. The Executioner reached out, gently shaking him by the shoulder. "Arturo," he said, "wake up. I need you."

The man on the deck of the ship opened his eyes. "Yes?" he said.

Pacheco had found a topographical map of the region south of New Orleans when he'd gone to get the first-aid kit. A confusing route through the swampland had been traced with a yellow highlighter. It ended near several islands in a large lake. Now Bolan shoved the map under Arturo's nose. "Where are you meeting the buyers?" the Executioner demanded.

Kneeling behind Arturo, Pacheco reached under the man's neck and gently lifted his head so he could see better.

"Show me," Bolan said. "Point."

A dying hand struggled up. A bloody finger left a spot on the map. Right where the yellow route ended.

Bolan pulled the map back. "This route that's traced in yellow," he said. "What is it? I can see a dozen easier ways to get through the swamps than this one." He turned the map around and looked at it again. "Besides, it's down the bayous and the ship draws too much water. We'd never make it."

Arturo shook his head back and forth, his eyes closed. Then he opened them again and stared across the deck at the nearest lifeboat.

"You...someone takes a smaller boat to the spot?" Bolan asked. "They meet you and come back?"

Arturo tried to nod, but he was too weak. "Yes..." He was barely able to exhale.

"Is the map accurate?" Bolan asked. The bayous could be tricky, changing course within hours. They often varied greatly from year to year due to rainfall.

"We...used it last...week," Arturo said. His eyes were glazing over again. "Father?" he said. "Father, forgive me...."

"But why the long route to that spot?" Bolan asked. "Why not take a shorter way?"

"Father!" Arturo moaned.

Pacheco looked at the Executioner. "He wants a priest."

Bolan looked back at him. "We don't have one onboard. Unless you're ordained."

Pacheco was about to reply again when Arturo suddenly screamed, "Priest! Bring me a priest!"

The Executioner looked down at the man. "Arturo, tell me one more thing."

"A priest!" Arturo said. "I must have a priest!"

"We'll get you one," Bolan said. "You take a small boat to this spot on the map. The buyers meet you there?"

"Yes, then they return with us to the ship with their own boat to off-load the cargo." Arturo was breathing hard now that the end was near. The adrenaline pump as he fought for life during his final few moments gave him the wind to scream again. Suddenly he sat up with the strength of a healthy man. With wild eyes staring at Jaime Pacheco, he screamed, "Father! I knew you would come! I ask forgiveness for my sins!"

The Executioner looked to Pacheco.

The undercover man shrugged and said, "What could it hurt?"

Bolan stood. As he turned and walked back to check the course of the ship again, he heard Pacheco say, "Take my hand, my son."

8

"Wouldn't it be easier just to sink the damn ship, then go get Gothe and Letona and be done with it?" Pacheco said as he slid the oars through the oarlocks in the lifeboat. "I mean, we've already killed everybody on the ship."

They began to cross the waves toward the swampland ahead. Bolan had grown to like Jaime Pacheco over the past few days. And one of the man's most likable qualities was the almost childlike innocence that stayed with him in spite of the kind of work he did and the miscreants with whom he came in daily contact. "Just be happy you're alive."

Pacheco leaned back slightly in the boat, hooking his feet under Bolan's seat for balance. "Yeah, I guess you're right."

"Besides," said the Executioner as he continued to row, "you're good at undercover work."

Pacheco laughed. "You think I made a convincing priest?"

"If I needed one, I'd want your number."

"With the life you live, you better," Pacheco said. "No, seriously, I felt sort of strange doing that, you know?"

The Executioner nodded as he rowed on. "Yeah, but you made a dying man happy."

Pacheco sat forward again, crossing his arms across his knees. "Now it's between him and God."

"It always was," the Executioner replied. "Get the map out."

Pacheco reached into his back pocket and pulled out the crumpled topographical map. He had folded it to show the entrance to the marshland, and he held it up now for Bolan to see. The soldier looked at it, turned briefly in his seat to get his bearings, then rowed on.

The lifeboat rose and dipped on the gentle waves as they neared the entrance to the bayou marked in yellow on the map. It still looked to Bolan as if there were faster ways to Barataria Bay. But the route had been traced for a reason. Maybe the rains had changed the terrain since the map was printed. Or maybe the buyers picked them up somewhere along the way. Or taking it could be a simple precaution in case the DEA, U.S. Customs or Coast Guard agents seized the *Evangelina* and then tried to pose as the smugglers to nab the buyers. No one would take such a circuitous route unless they knew they were supposed to, and if anyone showed up at Barataria from another direction the buyers could quickly lose themselves in the swamps.

Bolan rowed on. He had asked Arturo about it. But he had been too late. By then, the man had been out of his mind. All he could think of was a priest. The Executioner supposed he should count himself lucky that the man had lived long enough to give them the information he had. But whatever the answer to the question might be, Bolan's gut instinct told him to follow the route on the map.

"You never answered my question," Pacheco said as they left the Gulf and entered a broad bayou.

"What question was that?"

"I asked why we didn't just sink the ship and go back after Gothe and Letona. The buyers aren't going to get the dope now."

The muscles in Bolan's arms, shoulders and back were warmed up well now and starting to pump as if he'd been lifting weights. "They won't get *this* dope," he said, "but they'll get other shipments. Even if they lose their whole connection over this, they'll find another. And another. And another." The Executioner stopped rowing long enough to wipe the sweat off his forehead, then began rhythmically stroking the oars again. "We're going to make sure that doesn't happen."

Pacheco looked down at the map again as they passed a high mound of seashells topped by live oak trees. They had seen several such small islands in the marshland since leaving the Gulf. *Cheniers,* they were called, if Bolan remembered correctly. Regardless of what their name might be, they were important landmarks in terrain such as this.

"Turn here," Pacheco said, pointing to his right. "I think."

"You think?" the Executioner asked.

"Yes," the Costa Rican said. "This country is confusing. It is worse than the jungle. What is it you call it again?"

"Swamp," Bolan said. "Or marshlands." He raised one oar out of the water, turning in the direction Pacheco had indicated.

"Yes, swamp," Pacheco responded. "Marshland. Well, I hate the swamp and marshland." He sighed, then pointed out at the flat plain of high wet grass that seemed to have no end. "Look at it," he said. "It doesn't know if it's land or sea."

Bolan rowed on, taking the twists and turns that Pacheco indicated, sometimes stopping to look at the map himself. Often it was difficult deciding which way to go, even for a veteran navigator such as Bolan. The irregular shoreline was cut by too many bayous and rivers to count, as the waterways made their way toward the Gulf. Each decision was made with no more than eighty percent certainty, and Bolan was reminded that it was rarely the wilderness itself—desert, jungle, swamp, or whatever—that killed a man. Rather it was the cumulative effect of having to come to too many life-or-death conclusions of which he couldn't be certain. The stress from that uncertainty mounted up after a while, playing on the nerves and gradually killing the spirit. Sometimes it even killed the will to survive.

Bolan glanced at the deck of the boat as he continued to work the oars. They had loaded two of the M-16s, a pair of Heckler & Koch MP-5s and extra magazines for both weapons before leaving the *Evangelina* anchored in the Gulf. The cocaine had all been dumped over the side of the ship during the last few miles as they sailed in. The Executioner smiled to himself, remembering what Pacheco had said as they poured the last of the white powder over the rails.

"These fish will be very happy," the cop had quipped.

The bayous widened into large lakes, then narrowed again into more bayous. Suddenly they emerged from the reeds into what could only be Barataria Bay. The sky above became a golden blue, and an archipelago of small, low-lying islands topped by forests of emerald trees and bands of glowing white sand.

Bolan stopped rowing and let the boat drift out of the bayou into the bay. Again, he wondered why the route had been marked as it had. They had taken a tremendously oblique route and returned, he was certain, to a point not all that far from where they'd started. He stared out across the bay, beyond the islands, and what he saw convinced him even more. Yes, they had circled back on themselves. Beyond the bay he could see the deeper waters of the Gulf of Mexico. The waters of Barataria Bay were calm, but if he listened closely he could even hear the pounding surf in the distance. Although he couldn't see it for the swampland surrounding the entrance to the bay, unless he missed his guess, the *Evangelina* was anchored less than a mile from where they sat at this moment.

The soldier didn't need to question the route further, for the answer suddenly appeared behind them. As he and Pacheco sat staring out at the islands that pirates like Jean and Pierre LaFitte, Dominque You, and the Italian buccaneers Gambi and Nez Coupe had once called home, the sudden sound of an outboard engine caused them to look back down the bayou they had just left.

The men who appeared in the fishing boat behind them looked like modern-day pirates. But unlike the buccaneers who had once flown the Jolly Roger, carried flintlock pistols and cutlasses, and sailed clipper ships, the men in the modern boat flew no flag. And they bore assault rifles and submachine guns.

THE BOAT THAT HAD come up behind them was a simple fiberglass bass boat with an outboard engine clamped to the stern. Five men were perched on the high fishing seats. They wore a combination of camouflage fatigues and casual clothes, boonie hats and one Atlanta Braves baseball cap. The weapons in their hands were just as eclectic. Two AK-47s, one AK-74, one Uzi and a small Czech-made Skorpion submachine gun with a folding stock.

The boat racing across the bay toward them, which had suddenly appeared out of nowhere from the side of one of the islands, was very different—an A U.S. LCAC—Landing-Craft Air Cushion Vehicle—with a weight of 150 tons and a speed capability of over forty knots. The Executioner was vaguely familiar with the surface-effect ship. It was basically a flatbed transport vehicle but had two side surfaces that stretched along the hull. An open well ran down the center of the payload. Other than that, the deck could be pretty much fitted out as desired. Heavy weapons, like fixed M-60s or other machine guns, were rarely mounted to the craft. It was primarily for transportation of soldiers and their equipment from ship to shore.

This LCAC, however, had been customized to fit other specific needs. Several semipermanent storage sheds had been bolted to the top—four at each of the corners and four more spaced evenly across the deck. They were all painted white, and appeared to have been constructed of plywood.

Two of the structures in the center of the boat matched their corner counterparts. But the other two looked like pickup camper shells that had been cut flat with a blowtorch, then bolted to the boat. The job had been neatly done, and the small rectangular windows in the sides were still intact. The storage sheds cut down on the number of men who could ride the vehicle but increased the security of the boat's cargo.

Which in the case of this LCAC, the Executioner knew, was expensive enough to make extra precaution cost effective. Cocaine prices rose and fell like any other commodity. But it was never cheap.

Bolan scratched his chin as the vessel-vehicle skimmed across the water their way, remembering that several LCACs had gone missing a few years ago when the last presidential administration had all but ignored the U.S. armed forces. Rumor had it they had been "sailed out the back door" on to the black market. Now the Executioner knew where at least one of them had ended up.

The LCAC drifted closer, and Bolan saw that roughly a dozen armed men stood onboard between the short storage sheds. They were dressed similarly to the men in the fishing boat behind them on the bayou. One man, standing at the bow with his arms across his chest, seemed to be taking the "pirate thing" a little too seriously. As the LCAC drew closer, Bolan could see that in addition to black paratrooper boots, cammo pants, and a khaki T-shirt, he wore a black bandanna tied over his head and had a small gold earring in his left ear.

The only thing missing was an eye patch and a parrot on his shoulder.

The LCAC cut its engines and drifted up in the water. One of the men came forward carrying a coiled line. Twirling it around his head like a cowboy winding up with a lasso, he tossed it over the side toward the lifeboat. The line uncoiled as it flew through the air, the last few loops landing on the deck between Bolan and Pacheco. What the men wanted was obvious, and Bolan uncoiled the rope and handed the end to Pacheco who turned and tied it off to the lifeboat's bow.

A moment later they were being towed across the bay toward the nearest island. The bass boat behind them followed.

Not a word had been spoken between the two groups when the LCAC slid up onto the sandy beach of the island. Several of the men jumped out and pulled the lifeboat in by hand. By now, the reason for the labyrinthine path that had been marked on the map was obvious to the Executioner. As he'd suspected they might be, they'd been spotted somewhere along the way and followed. This ensured that they were indeed the party from the *Evangelina*. And it also gave the buyers a chance to make sure the lifeboat wasn't being followed. The men in the fishing craft would have walkie-talkie contact with the LCAC, and such contact meant that had there been any sign of problems the surface-effect ship would have plenty of time to disappear.

When the lifeboat reached shallow water, Bolan and Pacheco got out, wading to shore. The man with the black bandanna stood on the beach, his feet wide apart, hands on his hips. He didn't carry a rifle like the others. But a gold-plated Colt Government Model Combat Commander glistened under the sun on his hip. "I don't recognize your faces," he said, squinting, as the men from the lifeboat reached shore. He had a thick Southern accent, maybe Alabama, maybe Georgia. But it sounded nothing like the Cajun dialect common in that region of Louisiana.

Bolan started to speak but Pacheco beat him to it. "Don't know how you could," the undercover cop said, "since we've never met before."

"How come Ricardo and José didn't come as usual?" the man with the bandanna wanted to know.

The question had all the earmarks of a trap, and Pacheco recognized it as such as easily as the Executioner. "I don't know why they didn't come because I don't know any Ricardo or José," the Costa Rican said. "At least none who were onboard our ship."

"And the name of your ship would be...." The man let his words trail off to form a question.

Pacheco had taken the lead in the dialogue and was doing a good job. Bolan decided to let him keep talking. It gave the soldier a chance to shift part of his attention to the rest of the men who were now dropping onto the sand from the LCAC.

"The *Evangelina*," Pacheco said. "I'm Pacheco. He's Belasko. What do we call you?"

"You can call me whatever you want, as long as you've got what we're here to buy." He eyed them both up and down, obviously still not completely convinced there was nothing questionable going on.

The men from both boats were not aiming their weapons at Bolan and Pacheco. In fact, most of the rifles and subguns hung at the ends of ballistic nylon slings around their necks and shoulders. But they were casually spreading out to encircle the soldier and his partner, and Bolan had no doubt this was an important interview they were now undergoing. If they didn't answer this man's questions in a way that satisfied him, they'd fall to a hailstorm of automatic rounds and die right there on the sand.

"We've got it," Pacheco said. "You got the money?"

"I wasn't planning on trading chickens and livestock," the man with the Colt came back. "You'll see it when I see the coke. Who's your captain?"

Pacheco sighed as if bored with the obvious interrogation. "Eagle Jack," he said. "Want to know my favorite color, too? Take my fingerprints? Maybe a DNA sample?"

The drug runner didn't find any humor in the gibes. "How come Jack didn't come out himself? He usually does."

Again, a red flag went up in the Executioner's brain. But it obviously did in the mind of the Costa Rican undercover cop, too. "Like hell he does," Pacheco said. "I told you we've never met before, but I've known Jack long enough to know that lazy bastard isn't going to row across his bathtub, let alone take this silly-ass route through the swamp you put us through. Besides," he added, suddenly breaking into laughter, "the bastard's got a case of the shits."

Bolan laughed to support Pacheco's undercover act. The Costa Rican was using one of the time-honored strategies of role camouflage: When in doubt, divert the subject. And one of the best ways of diversion, according to Leo Turrin, Stony Man Farm's own undercover expert, was to get on to a subject that embarrassed someone. It quickly sent minds on "rabbit chases."

"What the old fart's probably got is a case of the clap," the man with the bandanna said, joining in the laughter. Bolan watched his eyes and saw that there was still no humor in them. What the Executioner saw was a cold and calculating mind that hadn't taken Pacheco's bait. He wasn't finished with his testing.

"You unload the shipment yet?" the modern-day pirate captain asked.

"Unload it?" Pacheco said incredulously. "Where? We supposed to strap it to the backs of a herd of sea turtles and have them haul it in for you?"

"Jack always unloads it."

Pacheco waved a hand in front of his face. "Oh, bullshit," he said. "Look, how long is this crap going to go on? I mean, I can understand a reasonable amount of security. You've got U.S. Customs, Coast Guard, DEA, and probably half a dozen other narc outfits to look out for. But you've run us through that rat maze of yours, and now you've asked a half-dozen trick questions. Why don't we just go do the deal and then we can all go our separate ways? It's in the ship where it always is and where it's supposed to be." He paused a moment, sighed in exasperation the way Bolan had seen him do before, then pointed to the LCAC. "Isn't that why you've got this fancy-ass pontoon boat?"

The answer seemed to satisfy the pirate. He turned to the men around him. "Haul ass," he said. "Let's get this over and done with."

Turning back to Bolan and Pacheco, he said, "Hop onboard. You can ride with us. We'll tow your lifeboat back after we bring the stuff back here."

"We still don't know what to call you," Pacheco said.

"Late for dinner, for all I care," the man replied.

"Then I'll call you Bandanna," Pacheco stated. "Makes for more clarity in my mind."

"Whatever," the newly christened man said. "Now get onboard."

Bolan moved to the lifeboat and reached down, lifting one of the rifles.

"You won't need that," he called out. "We've got plenty of firepower, and we're all on the same team, right?"

The Executioner looked up. For the first time since they'd met, the hardman had opened his mouth in a wide smile. Bolan saw a gold tooth gleam in the sunlight. It matched the finish on the dope buyer's Colt. The man's hand had fallen to the golden gun's grips. Several of the other men had stopped on their way to the LCAC and were now facing the Executioner. None of them had aimed their weapons his way, but they now had their hands on them rather than letting them swing freely from the slings.

The inference was clear, and Bolan dropped the rifle back into the boat. He and Pacheco climbed up onto the deck of the LCAC and both took up positions on the port side. Looking over the rail, straight down, the Executioner could see that these modern-day pirates had not even bothered to remove the markings from the stolen transport vehicle. Reading upside down, he could see U.S. Navy clearly stenciled on the side structure.

The craft backed off the beach into the water. A moment later they were motoring across the bay toward the Gulf.

The Executioner began a head count out of the corner of his eye. In addition to the man Pacheco had dubbed Bandanna, there had been fourteen other men onboard the LCAC when they'd first encountered it at the mouth of the bayou. Now the five from the fishing boat had joined them as well. That made it an even twenty.

The odds were now only ten to one. Or, more likely if

Pacheco remained true to form in the gunfighting department, about fifteen to one for the Executioner, leaving the remaining five for the undercover specialist. Bolan glanced to the man at his side.

Jaime Pacheco looked at him and grinned. No worry showed in his eyes. But the Costa Rican had to know as well as the Executioner that they'd have to make their play soon. Once the LCAC got close enough to the *Evangelina* to see that there were no men on deck—at least no standing men—they would know something was wrong. Even if they didn't care about the lives of the ship's crew, they would care a lot about the fact that the cargo holds were now empty.

The LCAC breached the mouth of the bay and turned to the left. Bolan saw that he had been right—the *Evangelina* was still anchored a few hundred yards out from shore, roughly a quarter mile down the coastline. Had they rowed the direct route from the ship, they'd have reached the bay in less than an hour.

In the LCAC, the trip back would take under ten minutes. The Executioner knew he needed a plan.

"So," Pacheco whispered as the LCAC skipped across the waves and salty sea air blasted their faces. "What do we do?"

Still at the side structure, holding on to the rail, Bolan glanced his way. "Wait until I start shooting," he whispered out of the corner or his mouth. "Then take cover behind there." He indicated what appeared to be some sort of housing with a slight nod of his head. It wasn't good cover or even particularly good concealment, but it was the best the boat offered, and if Pacheco kept between the housing and the side of the boat, he'd have a relatively small area to defend. In the full-blown firefight that was about to erupt onboard the LCAC he'd be as safe as possible.

It was the best Bolan could do for the undercover cop.

Pacheco still didn't look concerned, and that worried the Executioner. He had seen it happen before to men with whom he'd teamed up. They would witness his skills a few times, then unconsciously take a giant leap of faith after which they believed Bolan to be unbeatable. He wasn't, he knew it, and he had the scars on his body to prove it. The problem came when the men he worked with began to think of themselves as indestructible, too. They took wild chances and endangered both of their lives. When things got to that point, the men became more hindrance than help. It was worse than working alone because the Executioner not only had to look after his own safety but that of the man who accompanied him. At those times, when he could, he got rid of the partner as soon as possible. Short of throwing Pacheco over the side of the LCAC, he didn't really see how that could be done.

"Listen to me, and listen very carefully," Bolan whispered, at the same time keeping his eyes on the leader of the men on the LCAC. The man Pacheco called Bandanna had retaken his place at the bow, and was talking to a clean-shaved man with a long ponytail. He wore a black T-shirt, thick leather medieval-looking gauntlets on both wrists, and seemed to be the second in command.

The Executioner leaned slightly closer to Pacheco. "I want you to do what I said. Exactly. Stay between that housing and the rail. Don't move out away from it no matter what happens. And don't start shooting until you hear my first round." Bolan stopped abruptly as the germ of the strategy he would employ suddenly entered his mind. "Or until you *know* the fight is on."

Pacheco looked confused. "What's *that* mean?"

"It means I'm going to work quietly as long as I can get away with it."

It was enough for Pacheco. "Okay."

"Just stay there and shoot whoever you see," Bolan reminded him.

"Except you." Pacheco beamed.

The joke had grown stale, but Bolan forced a smile anyway. "Except me."

The LCAC moved on in the water, and the Executioner began to formulate his moves. Again, he couldn't afford to set his plan in stone. He would have to make up most of it as he went, relying on his instincts, reflexes and the element of surprise. Once more, he hoped the men onboard the vessel wouldn't think anyone would be crazy enough to take them all on at once, in such a small and enclosed area that offered no chance of escape. Their astonishment wouldn't last long— they all looked like seasoned hardmen—but the more he could take down during the one- or two-second edge his sudden attack gave him, the better.

Twenty men. One Executioner.

And one good man who just didn't happen to be particularly good with a gun. Pacheco would try—he had the heart and the soul of a warrior. But whether he would be of assistance or yet another barrier Bolan would have to hurdle remained to be seen.

The Executioner looked across the boat to the leader again. The drug dealer was still talking to the ponytailed man who thought he was one of King Arthur's finest. It would be best if Bolan could take out those two first—killing the chiefs of any tribe usually put at least some damper on the enthusiasm of the warriors. But as long as they were together, there was too much chance of a commotion that would alert the other men. And besides, they were at the front of the boat where everyone's eyes tended to go. No, he would be better off starting at the back. He'd have to work his way up the chain of command rather than down.

Making sure there were no curious eyes, Bolan reached under his shirt. Both the Beretta and Desert Eagle rode their holsters in his waistband. While the leader hadn't allowed them to bring their rifles or subguns, they hadn't been checked for other weapons. Evidently the leader assumed that men so outnumbered and outgunned wouldn't be foolish enough to start anything. But it was neither of the pistols the Executioner wanted at the moment, and his fingers slid along his belt until they found the Spyderco Chinook knife clipped between the guns. He couldn't think of a better weapon for what he had in mind. The Chinook had plenty of cutting power, and its small blade could be hidden behind his arm as he went about his business, which was killing as many of these coke dealers as possible before they figured out what was going on.

Drawing the Chinook, the Executioner opened it slowly, holding the locking bar down with his thumb. The blade locked into place silently.

All of the men in this modern-day pirate crew appeared to be American—he had heard them all speak by now. The Executioner turned toward the aft of the LCAC where a man stood alone at the side structure smoking a cigarette. His almond-shaped eyes and the auburn tint to his skin told Bolan he had at least some Asian heritage in his blood. He also had an AK-47 slung around his neck.

The Executioner held the Chinook in a contoured ice-pick grip, hiding the blade behind his forearm as he walked casually toward the man. He kept his eyes peeled as he moved, scanning to see if anyone had turned his way. All of the men onboard seemed preoccupied with other matters.

When he was close enough to catch the man's attention, Bolan said in a low voice, "Hey, you got an extra cigarette?"

The gunner scowled at the inconvenience. But both hands went to the bulge in the left breast pocket of his camouflage fatigue shirt. As he began to unbutton the flap, Bolan's hand shot up and out.

The curved edge of the Chinook caught the man in the side of the neck, sliced through his carotid artery and came out the other side of his throat. That gave the man five seconds to remain conscious and twelve before he died—at least according to the close-quarters combat training charts. But Bolan had never been a big believer in charts, or in leaving things to chance. So, raising the knife slightly higher, he plunged the tip down and through the subclavian artery just behind the collarbone.

Now the charts gave the man an estimated length of consciousness of two seconds, and another two and a half after that before going to atone for his sins. The Executioner didn't time it. He just knew the man was dead even before he fell forward into Bolan's arms.

Twisting the hardman's body to face the sea, Bolan draped him over the railing. He listened carefully as he turned back from the rail, his eyes scanning the deck for any sight or sound that what he'd just done had been noticed. He got no such indication.

The Executioner held the fighting folder behind his forearm again as he moved along the rail toward the rear of the boat. Two men stood in front of the massive turbine engines that powered the craft. One was of medium height and weight with a carefully tended handlebar mustache. The other was thin and had a shaved head. The man with the mustache looked up from their conversation as the Executioner approached. He frowned, seeing the blood soaking the front of Bolan's shirt. But before the frown could turn into a conscious thought the Chinook had passed across his throat, then Bolan moved on to burrow it into the heart of the bald man next to him.

The bald man was thin, and the Executioner was thankful for that. The blade of the Chinook was three and three-quarters inches long and the average man's heart was a little over three and one-half inches below the surface of his chest. That meant only a quarter inch, at best, could enter the organ to do its damage. But it appeared to be enough. The bald man opened his mouth in shock but no words came out. Bolan pumped the blade twice to be sure, then withdrew it and glanced back across the LCAC.

Again, it appeared he'd gone unobserved.

The boat still chugged through the water as Bolan lifted both men over the rail, dropping them into its wake for an unceremonious burial at sea.

Three down. Seventeen to go.

By now, the Executioner was soaked from head to waist in the blood of the drug dealers. He caught a reflection of himself in a piece of chrome on a fan housing as he moved on. It was so much blood it appeared he'd been painted. But it also gave him an "unreal" look. It should have a startling effect on the next men he encountered as they tried to figure out just what they were seeing.

Those next men stood along the rail on the starboard side of the boat, leaning against a storage area used to secure their drugs. As he moved in, he could see that the man closest to him was one who had been in the fishing boat that had followed them. He wore a faded OD boonie hat and had an Uzi slung around his neck. The other man was in the process of growing a Fu Manchu mustache and imperial beneath his bottom lip. Spiky black and red hairs stood out from his face at odd angles.

The two died as quickly as the others had, and Bolan dropped them over the side.

The Executioner took a second to rethink his position. He had been lucky so far, and had eliminated five of the enemy without yet being discovered. But that luck couldn't hold out forever. And he was now having to move forward to seek his prey, meaning visibility among the men would be better. His hand moved under his shirt and found the Beretta. Drawing it with his left hand, he thumbed the selector switch to single shot. He would continue with the Chinook until it was time to switch over. Then, if his luck still held to some degree, perhaps the sound-suppressed 93-R could account for a few more dead drug dealers before all hell broke loose.

A trio of men were next in line, all facing the front of the boat as the LCAC drew near to the *Evangelina*. The man in the middle was the one who had worn the Atlanta Braves baseball cap. The one to his left Bolan remembered as having a face pitted with acne scars. Next to the rail was a man with a flattop haircut. All three had M-16s slung over their shoulders. Smoke drifted up from in front of the men as they passed something back and forth. Bolan couldn't see what it was any more than he could see their faces. But the sweet smell of marijuana coming back to him on the wind was un-mistakable.

Bolan moved in behind them silently, flipping the Chinook around into a front-saber grip. He started on the right of the three, thrusting the wickedly sharp tip of the blade into the side of the neck, then ripping it out the front of the throat. A gurgling sound issued forth from the man's lips as Bolan jerked the knife back around and thrust it into the kidney of the Braves fan. At the same time, he grabbed a handful of the hair beneath the cap, using it for support. The Executioner pumped the short thick blade of the Chinook up and down in the man's lower back, then withdrew it once more as the acne-scarred drug guard, holding the joint in his hand, spun in surprise.

The Chinook was chambered low after the kidney shot, and now Bolan drove it out and up at a forty-five-degree angle. The curved tip entered just above the man's Adam's apple and penetrated through the soft palate into the brain.

The three men hit the deck almost simultaneously.

At the same time the Executioner's luck finally ran out.

Bolan dropped the Chinook and lifted the Beretta to shoulder level as one of the men, wearing the strange combination of OD fatigues, an embroidered Mexican peasant shirt and a desert cammo U.S. Marine drill instructor's vest, raised the Uzi in his hands and tried to sight down the barrel. But the Executioner's reflexes were a split-second faster, and a sound-suppressed 9 mm subsonic round drilled him dead between the eyes.

The man collapsed on the deck, and Bolan shifted the Beretta to his right hand, turning it toward the man from the fishing boat who had carried the Skorpion. This man was faster than his friend had been. But he sacrificed accuracy for that speed, and his quick burst of 7.65 mm rounds flew wide.

Bolan's hollowpoint slug caught the man with the Skorpion squarely in the chest. The small subgun flew up into the air as the man jerked spasmodically in his death throes, hitting the top of the side structure and bouncing into the sea. The man who had wielded it closed his eyes as he slid down the side of the ship to a sitting position, and died.

One shot, one kill.

Ten down. Ten to go.

But the burst of 7.65 mm rounds that had escaped the Skorpion had changed the rules of the game. The entire crew had been alerted to the fact that they were under attack. Bolan knew he might have a few more seconds during which confusion reigned as the drug runners tried to figure out exactly what was going on and who their enemy was. But for all practical purposes, the element of surprise was over.

Gunfire broke out on the other side of the deck, from the area where Bolan had told Pacheco to take cover once the gunplay began. He hoped the undercover cop would have the good sense to follow his orders and stay put. But he couldn't worry about that right now.

Right now it was the Executioner against the world.

As always.

9

Return fire suddenly fell around Bolan like a hailstorm of lead. Two rounds sailed past his head—one on each side—and missed cutting off his ears by the width of a hair. Another bullet skinned across his kneecap, burning as if he'd just fallen on his knees and skidded across concrete. He felt blood running down his calf. But his legs still functioned, so he knew no permanent injury had been done.

The Executioner dived forward to his belly. As he did, his shirt billowed out behind him and yet another bullet passed through the material, entering near the back of the neck and exiting close to the tail. As he hit the deck, he felt the warm spots where the supersonic rifle rounds had scorched the material around the holes in his shirt.

Crawling behind the nearest storage shed, Bolan swung his Beretta both ways. The only men he could see were the ones he'd already killed. He nodded to himself, thankful that he'd started this campaign at the back of the ship and worked his way forward. He had taken out half the men now. And the rest were all in front of him. At least he didn't have to watch his back as well as his front.

Shifting the Beretta back to his left hand, the Executioner flipped the selector switch to 3-round-burst mode. He drew the Desert Eagle from under his shirt with his right hand.

The big hand cannon could stop a man almost as fast as a .308-caliber pistol. And it made at least as much noise. But the time for silence was over. Now, the more noise he could make, the more confusion he was likely to create among the enemy. And the more confusion he created, the more likely he and Pacheco were to survive what would appear to be in-surmountable odds.

He recognized these men for what they were—drug runners, not highly trained Special Forces soldiers. Oh, they were as bloodthirsty as men came, and they couldn't be underestimated. Their game was more back-shooting and ambushing. Stand-up warfare, fair fights, man-to-man combat was something they did their best to avoid.

They still outnumbered Bolan ten to one.

Round after round pelted the camper shell where Bolan hid. He stayed low, for two reasons. First, men who were only semitrained soldiers tended to shoot high when excited. The second reason was there was no place else to go.

The LCAC had still been moving through the water when the firefight began, but now the engines were suddenly cut and it slowed, drifting through the waves as whoever had been guiding the ship stopped to take part in the battle. Rifle and submachine gun rounds continued to rip out the sides of the camper shell, leaving large exit holes with sharp ragged edges in the metal. Sooner or later Bolan knew one or more of the rounds would find him. He was lucky that hadn't happened already. Something had to be done.

The Executioner took a deep breath. Crazy and unexpected had worked before. Would it work again? He didn't know. But he saw no other way out. Not only were the bullets zipping through the camper shell all around him, they were beginning to open up large enough holes that the men would soon be able to see him. The shell had never been cover. Soon it wouldn't even be concealment.

Bolan rose suddenly, a gun in each hand. He began depressing the Beretta's trigger a fraction of a second before his head ascended the camper shell, and by the time he had brought the machine pistol around in front of him, the first round of his initial 3-round assault was already starting out the barrel. A quick flash-sight of the deck registered in his mind, and what his eyes saw his mind defined in a thousandth of a second.

Men. Sheds. Most men hidden. Several not.

The bullets from the burst struck around the deck, doing no harm. But they had worked as cover fire, momentarily freezing the men who were visible.

Bolan pressed the trigger of the Beretta again, sending more rounds across the deck with his left hand. With the Desert Eagle in his right, he took more careful aim, dropping the sights on the face of a drug runner wearing purple-tinted sunglasses. The Eagle fired in his hand and a .44 Magnum hollowpoint slug blasted from its barrel. The sunglasses on the man's face exploded into pieces of black plastic frame and shattered violet lens.

The Executioner had noted earlier that two of the drug dealers had been black, and one of those men showed himself again now. Tall and muscular, he wore an OD fatigue shirt. The sleeves had been ripped off at the shoulders and huge deltoids, biceps and triceps gleamed with sweat as he swung his AK-74 toward Bolan.

Still creating his own cover fire with the Beretta, Bolan moved the barrel of the Desert Eagle over and pulled the trigger. Another of the big Magnum bullets roared from his fist, drilling into the black man's chest. The hardman slammed back against the side of the other camper shell. With a scream of rage rather than pain or fear, the gunner tried to aim the Russian rifle again, using his dying breath to try to settle with his killer.

Another round kept him from evening the score.

Bolan fired another 3-round burst from the 93-R, hitting none of the men but not expecting to. His 9 mm rounds were simply meant to keep them at bay. Essentially he was playing the part of two warriors—one with each hand. His left, with the Beretta, was the machine gunner laying down cover fire. His right hand had become a sniper, using the machine gunner's cover fire as protection while he took aim with the Eagle.

But it was time to move, and he knew it when new return fire flew his way. He couldn't tell exactly from which direction it came, so again he did the unexpected.

Rather than drop back behind the camper shell, or charge around one of the sides, the Executioner dived forward over the short building, directly toward the enemy. With his pistols outstretched in front of him as he flew through the air, he continued to fire with both hands. Two rounds from the Beretta struck the other black man more by accident than intent as he suddenly appeared at the side of one of the corner sheds. One round took off the tip of his chin. The other skidded across his throat at an angle. But it was deep enough to cut into the jugular vein, and he died of a throat cut by a bullet rather than a blade. And a freak shot at that.

Which was okay with the Executioner. Unless Pacheco was doing better than he expected the Costa Rican to do, he still faced seven more of the gunmen. He would happily take all the luck and freak shots he could get.

Once more, the seemingly foolhardy tactic had taken the drug runners by surprise. Bolan hit the deck on his belly and took advantage of one man's shock to drill him between the eyes with another big Magnum round. The drug runner—of either Hispanic or middle Eastern descent, it was impossible to tell—had leaned around the side of another of the storage sheds. The back of his head blew out and he fell facedown on the deck.

Bolan rolled across the deck, pushing the man's body out of the way and squatting against the shed. He had no sooner

taken up position than the familiar sound of a Heckler &
Koch MP-5 met his ears. The plywood next to him began to
splinter. Turning slightly, the Executioner saw a head above
the German submachine gun. It was topped by dry, strawlike
hair. One of the eyes sighting down the barrel had two blue
teardrops tattooed beneath it.

Aiming the Beretta, Bolan lifted his hand, pointed at the
teardrops and squeezed the trigger. The trio of 9 mm slugs
flew over the jumping MP-5 and the straw-colored hair
whipped backward. The subgun fell forward onto the deck,
hit a pool of blood on the surface and slid almost into the Executioner's hands.

Bolan was tempted to look heavenward in thanks, but
there'd be time for that later.

The Executioner jammed both pistols back into their holsters as the H&K slipped toward him. Across the ship, he
could still hear sporadic gunfire. It didn't appear to be coming his way, so he had to figure it was either aimed at Pacheco
or fired by the Costa Rican himself. Either way, it meant the
man was still alive.

Bolan lifted the slippery subgun and turned it around,
quickly hitting the magazine release and dropping the 30-
round box. The steel mag had no indicator holes, and he
quickly turned it parallel to the ground, found the point of balance, then slammed it back into the weapon. The balance
point wasn't the ideal way to estimate the remaining rounds
in the MP-5 or any other gun, but this hardly seemed the time
to stop, thumb out all the cartridges and count them by hand.
His best guess was that he had around ten to fifteen rounds
still waiting. One was already chambered.

The gunfire on the other side of the boat had stopped while
he was checking his ammo, and now Bolan realized he hadn't
heard any more fire from the bow of the boat in several seconds, either. By his count, fifteen of the twenty men were
down. Five remained, and they included the leader and his
buddy with the ponytail. One or more of the remaining coke

buyers might still be on the side of the boat—it depended on whether they'd killed Pacheco or he'd killed them. The five men had to be ahead of the Executioner. Shots had still been coming from that direction a few moments before.

Bolan dropped below the last row of storage sheds. Somewhere, just on the other side of the short building, was at least one man. Maybe more. The shed was a plywood structure with no windows. That was a mixed blessing—he couldn't see through it to locate the enemy but the enemy couldn't see him, either.

Now a strange quiet fell over the LCAC as it drifted calmly along the Gulf with the waves. The ship gently rose and fell, rose and fell. Overhead, a seagull squawked and flew by.

With the patience of the seasoned warrior, Bolan waited. He knew the sudden discontinuity would eat away at the drug dealers' nerves far more than it would his.

The man with the ponytail was the first to crack under the pressure. Bolan didn't know it was him at the time, but he heard the movement directly on the other side of the shed. Slow. Deliberate. Someone was rising from the deck.

The Executioner heard the slight squeak of wood. Whoever it was had just climbed on top of the shed between them. It was a tactic the Executioner might have used himself in order to avoid the danger that might lurk at the corner of each building. The sheds were short, easily climbed, and sometimes over the top was the safest way to go.

But this didn't prove to be one of those times for the man with the ponytail.

Bolan saw his shadow when the drug runner was still two feet from the edge of the shed. The dark silhouette was inching forward, a pistol gripped in both hands. The long, tied hair bounced behind him, and it was then that Bolan realized who it was.

The Executioner stayed low. He braced his elbow against his ribs and aimed the Desert Eagle straight up. He continued to wait.

The shadow moved forward, then stopped as if some premonition of death had warned of something lurking directly below. Bolan remained motionless, hoping the man would eventually give into the urge to see what was below. When that happened he'd peer over the side. And when he did that Bolan would shoot him.

Some primal instinct or perhaps just fear itself caused the shadow to reverse its course. Slowly the hardman began to move back across the shed the way he'd come.

Bolan made his decision in a heartbeat. He had to wait a few more seconds to put it into action. And as he waited, he considered the possibilities. Something deep inside told him there was more to this than just met the eye. The gunner hadn't decided to cross over the shed, then lost his nerve at the last second. He had *never intended* to go all the way. His plan all along had been to let his shadow be seen, then retreat.

It was a trap.

Bolan watched the shadow move out of sight and then rose, hoping he could catch the long-haired man just as he crawled off the roof. That would be the time when he'd be most vulnerable. He would have to take out the ponytail man first because he was part of the trap. But the faster he could do that the better. It would leave him more time to take out the other man, or men, who were hiding on the other side, ready to spring the trap.

When he rose, he did so quickly and without hesitation. The Desert Eagle led the way as the Executioner struggled to take in the new scene that met his eyes. His brain barely had time to register that the ponytailed gunner was indeed descending the side of the shed as Bolan pulled the trigger, then immediately scanned across the deck for other threats.

He found only one—a man wearing a black bandanna, and holding a gold-plated Colt in his hand. The man was aiming the fancy pistol directly at him, and grinning ear to ear. The gold tooth in his smiling mouth shone as brightly under the sun as the 1911 Government Model in his hand.

Bolan acted out of instinct, and again it was over before

he really knew what had happened. The Desert Eagle fired twice more. Suddenly, the drug leader was lying on the deck along with the bodies of the rest of the men who had come to buy Gothe and Letona's cocaine. He lay on his back, staring upward as the Executioner walked forward, the big Magnum pistol aimed down at his head. His lips moved as he tried to speak, but no words came out. He looked at Bolan, his eyes fixing on the Desert Eagle. Then slowly, although the lids stayed open, the light faded in his eyes.

There were still two of the twenty men unaccounted for.

A movement behind him caused the Executioner to spin around. It was like a rerun of the final battle on the *Evangelina* as Pacheco stepped forward, grinning ear to ear.

"The others are dead," the Costa Rican undercover man told the Executioner.

BLACK NIGHT. Black sky.

And blacksuits.

Bolan and Pacheco checked their own jump gear, then each other's as the plane neared the drop zone. "You remember how to do this kind of jump?" the Executioner asked. "Low altitude, low opening?"

"Yes," Pacheco said, feigning affront. "I've done it a million times." He reached down to pinch the stretchy black material covering his thigh, then let it snap back into place. "I always liked these suits," he said. "They make a lot more sense than those baggy fatigues that get caught on everything you walk past."

"You may get caught up in something anyway," Bolan said. "We're cutting it awfully close to the tree line. So make sure you've got a knife handy in case you wind up hanging from a limb. We're set to touch down at the very edge of the jungle, just inside Gothe's estate. Any closer to the house and his guards are bound to see us." He looked the undercover man in the eyes. "There's a good chance they may see us anyway. So keep your guns as ready as your knife."

"Okay," Pacheco assured him.

Bolan turned to face him. "You sure you still want to come?"

Pacheco frowned at the Executioner. "That wouldn't be a comment on my shooting abilities, would it?" he asked.

"No. Just giving you a chance to back out if you want to."

"Have I backed out of anything yet?"

The question was rhetorical, and Bolan didn't answer. At least not out loud. Inside his head, however, he said "no." It was the truth. The Costa Rican undercover man might not be the best man with a gun, but he had other talents that made him a good warrior. And he was willing to stick his neck out, take a chance. That was more than some of the finest target shooters in the world could say.

The Executioner moved to the front of the plane where Jack Grimaldi sat at the controls, with Ricardo Toledo at his side. Costa Rica's top cop was about to come back from the grave and resume his responsibilities as superintendent of national police. Behind Toledo, with a beer in one hand, a notepad in the other and bottle of *guaro* in the same staple-mended jacket pocket he'd had on a few nights earlier, sat Jeronimo Gomez. Bolan had promised the journalist an exclusive on the story and stayed true to his word. After picking up the Executioner in Louisiana, the plane had stopped in San José.

Grimaldi saw Bolan in the reflection from the windshield and glanced at his control panel, then his watch. "About a minute," he said without being asked. "Better head back and get the door open."

Toledo extended his hand. "I don't know how to thank you."

Bolan shook it. "There's no need to."

"Yes," Toledo replied. "There is. My country and I are very grateful."

"I know how to thank you," Jeronimo Gomez said. He reached inside his jacket, pulled out the bottle of *guaro,* and said, "Want one for the road?"

"No thanks," he said. "I'm the designated driver on this jump."

Gomez was half drunk, and his skin glowed a bright red.

But he hadn't lost his sense of humor. "Don't take my offer too lightly," the newsman said. "It's a rare occasion when I don't keep every drop for myself."

Pacheco already had the door open and the wind was whipping into the cabin when Bolan returned. The undercover man had his Glock and the sound-suppressed Ruger strapped to the waist of his blacksuit. Bolan carried his usual Desert Eagle in a ballistic nylon hip holster on the belt that also bore extra magazines and other equipment. The Beretta 93-R was in its shoulder rig. Both men wore light tactical vests that had six pockets for extra 9 mm magazines. But the mags in those pockets wouldn't fit either Bolan's Beretta or Pacheco's Glock.

The magazines had a 30-round capacity and were meant for use in the Heckler & Koch MP-5 submachine guns slung over Bolan's and Pacheco's shoulders. Both of the submachine guns had been carefully fitted with sound suppressors.

"Ten...nine...eight," Grimaldi called out and Bolan turned toward the blackness outside the plane. When the pilot got to one, the Executioner jumped. As he fell through the night, he looked up and saw Pacheco exit the plane a few seconds behind him. A moment after that, he tugged the rip cord and his black nylon night chute blossomed above him to disappear against the sky.

The landing couldn't have gone better. Bolan hit the ground, rolled to his side and popped back up on his feet. Quickly he slipped out of the harness and gathered in the chute as Pacheco landed no more than thirty yards away. When both parachutes had been secured, they took a few steps into the jungle and stuffed them beneath a termite-infested tree trunk that had fallen to its side.

"You ready?" the Executioner asked.

"Let's do it," Pacheco answered.

Bolan led the way out of the jungle toward the barracks. He could see none of the guards this far from the house, but that didn't surprise him. He had watched them patrol the night before, when Maria had led him to Gothe's study, and they seemed to stick closer to the house and other buildings.

Sprinting across the estate toward the barracks, the Executioner thought back on the events of the past few hours. When he had contacted Stony Man Farm after the gunfight at Barataria Bay, he had asked Aaron Kurtzman to hack into Gothe's personal files. The Stony Man computer wizard had come across a very interesting new document that hadn't been there when Maria took Bolan into Gothe's office.

Evidently Gothe's and Letona's attorneys had finalized the contract of sale for Gothe's legitimate business holdings. The document was stored on Gothe's hard drive, the only thing missing being the two men's signatures. Kurtzman had then conducted a search of the airline passenger lists and learned that Ramon Letona was onboard a flight to San José, with a connecting flight to the landing strip at the southern tip of the Osa Peninsula.

It didn't take a Ph.D. to put that two and two together. Letona was on his way to Gothe's to sign the papers and close the deal.

Next, Bolan had taken Pacheco up on an offer the Costa Rican had made earlier. He'd had the undercover expert contact police headquarters in San José, and they'd learned that Rocio's last name was Sanchez. The request had confused Pacheco at first—he'd even asked Bolan if he'd fallen in love with the woman at the resort where he'd stayed. But he'd laughed in delight after Bolan explained the real reason he was interested in Rocio.

"That's great!" Pacheco had said. "Now *that* is justice."

Armed now with all the information he needed, Kurtzman had gone to work with both computers and printer. When Grimaldi arrived in southern Louisiana he brought with him the fruit of Kurtzman's labors in a large white envelope.

Bolan could feel the thick envelope in the breast pocket of his blacksuit as he ran the last few yards to the dormitory. He had seen no signs of life around it, and he assumed the diggers were all at work. He wished there was some way he could tell them this would be their last night as slaves.

A quick look through the door assured the Executioner that the dorm was empty. He motioned Pacheco to follow, then circled the building to the entrance on the other side. Quietly opening the door to the hallway, he went door to door, checking the rooms of the overseers. The doors that were locked he kicked open, the MP-5 sweeping the rooms. But all of the overseers were out, too, and he wondered if Julio Lima was with them.

Neither the diggers nor their overseers would know what was going on until the morning when they returned. But that was okay. When they learned what had happened, he suspected the men who had been driven like animals would decide how best to take care of the overseers who had whipped, beaten and sometimes murdered them.

Leaving the dormitory, Bolan and Pacheco jogged across the grounds to the stables. Two guards were sitting in front of the structure. Both were drunk, and laughing.

"I am next!" a red-faced man with a full black beard announced.

"Like hell," the man next to him, younger and clean-shaved said. "You are too old anyway."

Their laughter and banter faded into the night as the two men in black finally entered their blurry vision. They reached awkwardly for their M-16s on the ground.

The rifles stayed in the trampled dirt outside the stable. Both Bolan's and Pacheco's sound-suppressed MP-5s spit full-auto lead into the men. The guards wiggled on the ground for a moment, then lay still. A voice inside the stable called out in Spanish, "Jésus! Antonio! What's going on?"

A second later a bare-chested man carrying a rifle in one hand and zipping up his pants with the other came out of the stable. Bolan noticed that he had several shallow slashes across his face as Bolan let the MP-5 cut a Z-pattern from the man's chin down to his groin. The guard toppled to the ground and the Executioner drew an ASP flashlight from his blacksuit and trained the bright beam on his face. The slashes were fresh and had been made by fingernails.

Bolan moved carefully into the stable. The stench of manure was strong as one horse whinnied and another snorted. Then a whimpering sound came from one of the far stalls. The Executioner moved toward the noise, keeping the flashlight aligned with the barrel of the SMG to use as a point of aim. Bolan and Pacheco both dropped low, checking the strewed hay around the hooves of the horses in the stalls they passed. They found no men.

But when they reached the corner stall, they found a woman. Or rather a girl.

The Executioner's jaw tightened in anger as he looked down at the young woman on the filthy floor of the stable. She couldn't have been more than fifteen. Her blouse had been ripped away and her skirt rode over her waist. Her underwear had been ripped off one leg but still hung on the other. She hadn't given in without a fight.

The bright ASP laser-flash showed fresh blood under the fingernails on both of her hands.

Bolan knelt next to her. "Are you all right?" he asked in Spanish. "Did he hurt you?"

The girl nodded, then shook it. "He tried," she said. "I am all right. He hurt me some. But he didn't do what he wanted to do. You arrived before he could."

"Do you live close by?" Bolan asked.

The girl nodded.

"Then go home. Fast. And don't look back."

The Executioner and Pacheco escorted her out the stable door and watched her flee down a path into the jungle. They moved toward the tennis courts, where another pair of guards were strolling along the fence, smoking cigarettes. They, too, looked as if they'd been drinking, and they didn't notice the two men in black until Bolan and Pacheco were less than twenty feet away.

"Take the one on the left," the Executioner said as he raised his MP-5. He tapped the trigger and a burst of 9 mm rounds zipped out of the subgun's short barrel and into the head of the man on the right. A second later, Pacheco's weapon spit with equal silence. But his rounds hit his target in the chest.

The Executioner took off again, hearing Pacheco at his heels. As they neared the swimming pool, they saw four of the guards inside the fence. Two were seated on the diving board, the other two standing nearby talking to them. These men were more alert, and turned their weapons toward the intruders as Bolan and Pacheco sprinted through the gate.

Coming to a halt ten feet away from the group, the Executioner cut a figure eight back and forth through the group. Many of the muffled rounds penetrated the men to continue into the pool behind them. The splash they made when they hit the water was louder than the MP-5 itself. To his side, Bolan saw Pacheco open up on full-auto, too. All four men were killed quickly.

A noise from the pool house caused the Executioner to pivot and he saw yet a fifth guard coming out of the dressing room. His M-16 was slung over his shoulder. His eyes were cast down and, like the man at the stable, he was in the process of zipping up his pants.

Both Bolan and Pacheco stitched him head to foot. He never looked up, and fell not knowing what had killed him.

The Executioner stepped over the body and moved carefully into the pool house. It was empty. This man's pants had been unzipped for another reason. But whether he was a rapist made little difference to Bolan at the moment. He was part of an ongoing criminal enterprise that shipped stolen artifacts and drugs, and murdered people.

He deserved what he'd gotten just like the rest.

A quick circle of the pool showed no more of Gothe's guards in the area, and the two men in blacksuits moved toward the guest house. Bolan suspected that Letona would be staying there, and he might as well get the man out of the way immediately. When they reached the gray stone building, the Executioner tried the knob and found it locked. Lifting a boot, he kicked hard, just under the lock, and the door swung inward.

Two men sat in the living room as Bolan led Pacheco inside. Neither of them looked like a successful Central American businessman to Bolan, and he suspected they were Letona's personal bodyguards. A heavyset man, wearing a white shirt with a brown leather shoulder holster over it, looked up from the porno magazine he was leering at. When he saw the men in the blacksuits, he dropped the magazine and reached for his holstered weapon.

Shooting from the hip, Bolan laced the man's chest with four 9 mm rounds. To the side he heard a door open and turned to see a taller, more slender man come out of a room in the back carrying what looked like a freshly mixed drink. Pacheco's first round of the next burst shattered the glass in his hand. The second two caught him in the lower and upper chest, respectively.

Bolan turned to the last of the three bodyguards. The third man had been sitting in a chair watching television, and so far the undercover specialist had hit him in the shoulder. The bodyguard was howling like a wolf, his face a mask of pain as he tried to reach the pistol on the table next to him.

The Executioner tapped the trigger once more and all three rounds hit the heart. The man flopped back against the chair, the gun now forgotten forever.

Dropping the near-empty magazine from the H&K, Bolan shoved a fresh one into the well. Pacheco saw him and did the same. Two doors led from the living room to separate parts of the guest house, and Bolan pointed at Pacheco, then to the door on the right. Pacheco nodded and started that way, his MP-5 at the ready.

Bolan took the door to the left—the one through which the man with the drink had come. He entered a kitchen but found it empty. The closets were equally deserted, as was the small utility room at the rear of the dwelling.

Returning to the living room, the Executioner hurried

through the other door after Pacheco. The cop had just finished searching the two bedrooms and had no more luck than Bolan. They returned to the living room and stopped.

"You ready for it to get interesting?" the Executioner asked.

"I'm not exactly bored right now," Pacheco said.

"It looks like Letona is up at the main house with Gothe. There'll be more guards around there, and we'll have to take them out before we go in. You up for it?"

Pacheco nodded. "Sure. Then, if I'm still alive, I may take Toledo up on his offer."

"What offer?" Bolan had seen Pacheco and Toledo talking privately for a few minutes during the flight.

"He offered me a full-time position teaching at the police academy," Pacheco said. "Think I should take it?"

"Sure. For about a week. Then the boredom would either drive you back undercover or you'd eat your own gun."

"You're right," Pacheco sighed. "I wouldn't be able to stand the day-to-day grind." His eyes flickered for a second, then he said, "But there is one major change I'm going to make when this is all over."

"What's that?" the Executioner asked.

"I'm going to start spending a lot more time on the firing range."

Bolan had the decency not to verbalize what a tremendous idea he thought that was. "Let's get this over with," he said, and started out the door.

THE SWEET SMELL of marijuana smoke drifted through the night air as Bolan and Pacheco crept around the side of the house. They stopped at the corner, and the Executioner peered into the front yard. Three men stood near the steps leading up to the front porch, taking turns on both a bottle and a joint. Bolan flipped the MP-5's selector to semiauto, and fired three quick, but precise, rounds.

The first 9 mm bullet drilled into the temple of an overweight guard as he was reaching for the joint. As his head splattered like an egg, the hand-rolled cigarette fell to the ground. The other two men were so stoned they didn't seem to notice all the blood. Instead they both dropped to all fours looking for the roach.

The Executioner's next round caught the man nearest him at an angle, entering through the lower rib cage and traveling on to the heart. That caught the eye of the other man on the ground, and his glazed eyes turned toward where Bolan stood at the corner of the house. He had just enough time to open his mouth, but not quite enough to scream, when the third 9 mm hollowpoint slug entered his left eye socket.

Bolan led way up the stone staircase to the front door. It was locked as he'd expected it to be. A pair of sound-suppressed 9 mm rounds took care of that problem. Swinging the door back, he heard the alarm buzzer go off. Turning to the box, he punched in the same code he'd discovered the night before and the soft buzzing ceased.

But the buzzing had been heard, and Gothe's voice came from the back of the house. "Is someone there?" he asked.

The Executioner knew he had to be in the den, where he conducted so much of his business. Leading Pacheco again, he hurried through the living room, then the conservatory, and finally dropped the two steps into the den.

Gothe sat in his favorite chair. Lima was in his usual spot on the couch. A small man in his late fifties with thick black hair streaked with white occupied another chair across from Gothe. Maria, dressed in her French maid's uniform, had just set a tray on the table between the men. The tray held another pitcher of Gothe's home brew and three glasses.

On the table next to the tray was an official looking document and a gold ballpoint pen.

All eyes in the room jerked toward them as Bolan and Pacheco entered. Only one of the faces, however, smiled. Maria. The men looked as if they'd all just seen ghosts.

But Gothe was nothing if not able to roll with the punches. "Ah, Belasko. Pacheco," he said, his tone sounding as if he had expected them all along. "I take it everything went as planned?" He glanced at his watch. "You made good time." Turning his head, he said, "Maria, bring more glasses for—"

"Forget it, Maria," Bolan said. He raised the barrel of the MP-5 and trained it on Gothe. "We won't be staying."

Maria nodded, quickly shuffling away from the men to the far side of the room.

Gothe smiled pleasantly. "All right," he said. "I can understand that you gentlemen are disappointed. And I admit, I lied to you." He sighed wearily. "Perhaps that was wrong of me."

"Everything you've done in your life has been wrong, Gothe," Bolan stated.

"Perhaps," Gothe replied. "But be that as it may, I'm willing to make it up to you now. What do you say to a large cash settlement? You just take it, and go away."

"No," the Executioner said. "I don't think that's going to be enough."

Gothe sighed as if he were dealing with an unreasonable child. "Gentlemen, be realistic. I don't wish to be insulting, but you both know that neither of you could possibly have operated this business. You are hired guns. Very good hired guns I must say. But that's what you are. Everyone has different talents, and business is not one of yours. You could no more have run my operation for me than Lima could."

To the side, Julio Lima's head jerked. Bolan could tell it was the first inkling he'd had that he, too, had been double-crossed.

"Ramon is a businessman," Gothe went on. "So it is to him I must sell. Now, back to your cash settlement. How does one million U.S. dollars for each of you sound?"

Bolan didn't answer. Instead, he stepped forward and lifted the papers off the table. As he'd suspected, they were the contract of sale for Gothe's real-estate holdings. The purchaser was Ramon Letona. And both signatures had already been inscribed. The Executioner looked through the pages, then rolled them up and dropped them into the pitcher of beer where they were immediately soaked.

Gothe laughed out loud. "What good do you think that will do?" he asked, waving a hand in front of his face. "We will just draw them up again. A million is not enough? Tell me, how much do you want?"

"We're not here for money," the Executioner said. "And there's no need to draw up the papers again. I've already done that for you." Reaching into his blacksuit, he pulled out the envelope, took out the papers and set them on the table. Picking up the pen, he handed it to Gothe. "Sign," he ordered.

Gothe squinted as he studied the document. It was almost identical to the one Bolan had just dropped into the pitcher of beer. But there were a couple of major differences. And Ramon Letona was no longer even mentioned. When Gothe noticed the changes, he said, "What? This is preposterous!"

"It might be," Bolan answered. "But if you expect to leave this room alive you're going to sign it." He took another step in and raised the MP-5 until it was a foot from Gothe's face. "You've got ten seconds."

Letona had sat frozen throughout the encounter, and Bolan suspected he was waiting for his men to come from the guest house to save him. But as they waited, Bolan watched his mind work behind his eyes, and saw the exact moment he decided that wasn't likely to happen.

Like Gothe, Letona was used to having other men do his dirty work for him. He was used to paying others to fight his fights, and protect him. But now, the entrepreneur and drug financier suddenly realized he was on his own. And he panicked.

The nickel-plated pistol that came out of Letona's jacket pocket was a .25-caliber Beretta. His trembling hand tried to raise it toward Bolan, but it never got all the way up.

Barely twisting at the waist, Bolan pumped a sound-suppressed hollowpoint slug into the man's forehead. The back of Letona's head blew out, and he fell back to a sitting position in his armchair.

The Executioner turned back to Gothe. "Five seconds left," he said. "Then the same thing happens to you."

Gothe picked up the pen. He started to sign his name, then looked up. "And if I sign, you won't kill me?"

Bolan shook his head. "No, Gothe, as much as I'd like to, I won't kill you. Not if you sign your name."

The antiquities smuggler scribbled his signature across the paper and then set the pen down. Bolan held the H&K in his right hand as he picked up the document and checked it. Satisfied, he walked across the room and handed it to Maria. "Congratulations," he said. "You now own a substantial part of the Osa Peninsula. Of course you need to sign it too when you get around to it."

The woman looked at him quizzically. Then it dawned on her. She looked down at the paper in awe. Her mouth fell open, and she covered it with one hand.

"The fact is," Bolan went on, "you own all of Gothe's real estate and other businesses except the antiquity smuggling and one of the resorts. The antiquities business just went bellyup. And the Santuario de Agua resort is going to a lady named Rocio Sanchez."

Maria just stared at the paper.

Gothe stood.

"Stay where you are," Bolan ordered.

"Look," the antiquities smuggler said. "You got what you wanted. And you promised you wouldn't kill me if I signed." His face was a mask of pure hatred.

"And I won't kill you," Bolan said, laying the SMG on the table beside him. He turned around. "Pacheco?"

The undercover man stepped forward and took aim at Francisco Gothe.

Suddenly Maria grabbed Bolan's discarded weapon and aimed it at Francisco Gothe. She pulled the trigger and a burst of fire struck the man who had abused her for so long squarely in the chest.

Lima jumped to his feet and started for the door.

As if she had shot submachine guns all her life, Maria turned the H&K on the man who had raped her and cut him to shreds with the rest of the magazine, before collapsing, sobbing, to the floor.

Jaime Pacheco stepped forward, shaking his head. "I guess we're finished here."

· "Justice has been served," Bolan stated. "It's time to go home."

James Axler
Outlanders®

SEA OF PLAGUE

The loyalties that united the Cerberus warriors have become undone, as a bizarre messenger from the future provides a look into encroaching horror and death. Kane and his band have one option: fix two fatal fault lines in the time continuum—and rewrite history before it happens. But first they must restore power to the barons who dare to defy the greater evil: the mysterious new Imperator. Then they must wage war in the jungles of India, where the deadly, beautiful Scorpia Prime and her horrifying bio-weapon are about to drown the world in a sea of plague....

In the Outlands, the shocking truth is humanity's last hope.